For my d[ear] Nessie &

Thank you ever so much for your generous hospitality & kindness. May the Lord continue to richly bless your ministry.

~Andrew Case

ANDREW CASE BOOKS
www.hismagnificence.com
www.facebook.com/andrewcasebooks

Andrew Case, *Little Woman*

© 2015 by Andrew Case

All rights reserved. Any part of this publication may be shared, provided that you do not charge for or alter the content in any way.

For more information please visit
www.HisMagnificence.com

ISBN 978-1508778813

for
my best frog

Little Woman

ANDREW CASE

Girlhood is the opening flower of womanhood. It has charms all its own. The wonderful change from the child to the woman, the marvelous blossoming of young, healthy girlhood, will ever be God's great miracle in life's garden. Like a half-open rose is girlhood. We are charmed, both by the beauty of the bud and by the wonderful coloring of the rose. We behold the familiar traits of childhood that have always charmed us and held our affections, but blended with these in ever-changing variety are the graces and powers of womanhood.
–Mabel Hale

Chapter 1

Sunshine Lane, in Will's mind, did not live up to its name. In fact, he was sure it must be the darkest street in all of Dallas. After six long years of living there, he had seen enough of the city to know.

If a street bore the name *Sunshine* there ought to be some semblance of light. One ought to see happy oak trees soaking up warm rays, spangling the street with leafy shadows, Will thought. There should be tidy yards and clusters of flowers. Instead, Will's second story window looked down on cracked pavement, and not a tree in sight for miles. The high apartments all around kept Sunshine Lane in perpetual shadow and every building seemed to stand in defiance to beauty. Flaking paint, yards overgrown with brown weeds, and dilapidated buildings were commonplace in Will's neighborhood.

125 Sunshine Ln., where Will lived, was a large house. The family who built it had a penchant for Victorian architecture. A hundred years ago it had been a mansion in its own right, proudly welcoming all with four large pillars in front. They had spared no expense on beautiful stone and woodwork, large bay windows, and two chimneys—giving the house four considerable fireplaces. Once the rooms had been expansive, with high ceilings and shining wood floors, and a garden in the backyard had opened up into a lovely field with a pond. But 125 Sunshine Ln. had changed since then. Long gone was the family joy that once warmed the place. The walls and floors were beginning to sag with age, the stone pillars had been painted brown, and the paint was now cracked and peeling. The fireplaces were boarded up, and ugly brown carpet covered squeaky, uneven floors.

The owner of 125 Sunshine Ln. was Mr. Perry, a man who seemed at least three times Will's twenty nine years of age. In times past generous offers had poured in from individuals and developers to buy the property. But Mr. Perry stubbornly refused even though he had not lived in the house for years. While most everything around transformed into more and more brick and concrete (including the field and pond), Mr. Perry's house only grew older and more derelict every year.

One particular day Will was writing at his desk by the window and overheard two men talking about his house.

"Did you ever see such an eyesore?" said the older man. "Looks like it's been abandoned for ages—dead as death."

"That house died a long time ago when the family who built it finally left," said the younger man. "Before that I hear it was a lively place. I can imagine what its glory days must've been like. Shame it's been left to decay like this."

"Oh I remember some of them glory days. This here street used to be one of the finest, most genteel places to live. And now look at it. I used to come here as a child and play in the field out back. There were trees and squirrels and we had ourselves more fun than a dog in a meat market. I reckon it was the best place in the neighborhood for sport."

"You thinkin' they'll be tearin' it down soon? It's about that time, I'll say."

"Well, they tell me old Mr. Perry still's a hangin' on to the place. He keeps rentin' it to every sorta bachelor folk. I think only one's there right now. A queer fellow, they say, sorta lonely like. He ain't much for what usually goes on in this neighborhood. Keeps to himself mostly, they say. A bit old fashioned like the house itself. But I can't be sayin' much but that he's a good man for all that. Kind as ever you seen. Good Christian charity in that fellow. But queer as horse feathers."

Will smiled. That wasn't the first time someone had thought him strange. As for the house, he agreed that it was time to tear it down. He had wasted too many hours of his life fixing things that Mr. Perry took too long to get around to. First there had been the infestation of flies that kept coming in through vents from the attic. Something had died up there and the kitchen had kept filling up with the pests even though the windows were closed. Then there were the plumbing and electrical problems. 125 Sunshine Ln. had not been built with such modern things in mind. Therefore all that had been added was something of a patchwork. Will had lost count of the times he had had to fix a leaky toilet, a clogged drain, a short in rat-gnawed wires, or a blown fuse. None of his housemates had ever lifted a finger to help. He was lucky if they washed their own dishes or paid their part of the bills on time. Indeed, with termite-weakened boards, slanting, creaking floors, caved-in chimneys, and countless layers of paint, this house was ready to say goodbye to the world.

The two men were still talking.

"I still don't understand why nobody's found it if what they say's true. *I* say it's nothing but a lot of malarkey that somebody made up for a good yarn," said the younger one.

"It" was something Will had also heard about before. Treasure. A house as old as 125 Sunshine Ln. was bound to have its share of legends, and this was the one that everyone in the neighborhood knew. According to what "they" said, the original proprietor of the mansion had kept some of his fortune in a secret place within the property. And, as the story went, he had died suddenly without telling a soul where it lay. No one had ever found it. Some said it was in the yard at the bottom of the old well. Others said that it was probably under the floor boards of the cellar or in the walls. Most took it to be nothing more than a fable. Will thought that if there were any truth to the story, someone would have discovered it and taken it long ago. Or if it was still there it likely wasn't worth much.

In spite of his skepticism, Will did enjoy the thought of hidden treasure. Ever since his boyhood the idea of buried treasure had captivated him, as it tends to with most boys. He had even gone so far as to make treasure maps for fun. His process for making them had eventually grown into something elaborate. First, a sheet of paper needed to be soaked in tea to make it look old and brown. After drying, it would need to be wrinkled a bit, and then Will would carefully burn some of the edges with a candle. Next came the task of creating an imaginary island, drawing it with bold, black ink, marking all the typical places on it, such as "Dead Man's Cove." The final touch had been to take a little chicken's blood (whenever the house cook was cleaning a bird for frying) to splatter on it. This produced a dramatic effect of authenticity, as though a pirate had been stabbed or shot in a struggle over the map.

After the map had been made ready, Will would fold and place it in an old, musty volume in his father's library. Then he would casually suggest to one of his playmates that they take a look at that book. When they discovered the map he would feign as much surprise as they, and he would see how long he could keep them believing that it was a bona fide pirate map. But Mother or Indiana, his sister, would usually spoil the joke before any plans were made to set sail.

Will's mother never had had patience for his games. She had wanted him to be a businessman ever since he was young. To Will that had sounded like the most boring thing in the world. Businessmen never frolicked and laughed their way through life. They wore boring brown suits and carried boring briefcases with still more boring papers inside. When had a businessman ever fired a canon or ridden a horse in the wind and made the earth thunder beneath him? When had a businessman ever played with a chameleon or stored away pieces of eight in his briefcase? Will had never been impressed with the idea.

His father, on the other hand, had wanted him to follow in his footsteps and become a lawyer. The Millhouses had always been greedy for money, and lawyers made plenty of it. But to Will there had been nothing appealing in such employment. Rarely does a young boy dream of being a lawyer, and Will never changed from his aversion to it. After all, when had a lawyer ever walked halfway across Iceland just for an adventure? Will's grandfather on his mother's side had when he was twenty, and the thought of becoming a lawyer had never crossed *his* mind. That streak of daredevilry seemed to have completely skipped Will's mother who had fallen in love with a swish lifestyle and a husband who could afford it. Now they lived their lives for money and for the next vacation to the Continent.

From before Will was born his parents had been aloof and distant. Mother, like her own mother before her, had let their paid nursemaid take care of most of his raising. He had learned not to expect to see her for most of the day while she visited wealthy friends, walked in the gardens, or read alone in her study. When the nursemaid had become a little too expensive (due to poor management of the estate), Will had been taken to spend most days at his grandparents' home. They had cared for this shy little introvert for some of the most formative years of his life. Grandfather's stories had captivated Will's heart and mind, while Grandmother's cooking beguiled his appetite. Both were proud Jews, but hardly devout in their practice. They rejected Jesus Christ as the messiah, but Grandfather never flagged or faltered in his enthusiasm over the Tanakh, what Christians call the Old Testament. He had made the ancient poetry, wisdom, and stories come alive for Will. "The best literature in the world," he would say. "'As a slave eagerly longeth for the shadow'…that's poetry, Will! The greatest poetry in the world—the book of Job."

Will believed him.

"'Where is the way to the dwelling of light?' Tell me if you know, Will."

Will didn't know. He thought about that question for years. It was one of those memories that never leave you and you can't quite explain why.

Once ten-year-old Will had asked his mother that question. It had been a rare moment when she had come into his room to say goodnight. She had been drawing his curtains closed when he asked. He had been deeply in earnest, but Mother said, "How should I know? Is that some silly nonsense Grandfather has been putting into your head?"

After that Will had never asked Mother any more meaningful questions. But he kept thinking about how to find the dwelling of the light.

Chapter 2

"Mother," said Will as he sipped a glass of cold juice she had served him, "why do you think Father doesn't love you?"

This was the first time in nineteen years that Will had asked his mother such a question. She started a little.

"Darling, it isn't like that."

But Will knew it *was* like that. He observed how Father never showed affection to her in public, and how he eagerly took long weekends away from the house with his friends. He noticed when Father seemed always to be at another dinner party while his wife sat alone at home and tried to forget her loneliness with wine. (Although Indiana still lived at home, she often stayed out late with her friends.) It was hard for Will to see his mother trying to hide her hopelessness. She and Father had been drifting apart for years already. Will had never figured out exactly why, but he knew it was happening. Once when Mother had had too much to drink she told Will that she was going to leave Father and that she couldn't take the pain anymore. Will had only been fifteen at the time and it had frightened him. She had never gone through with it, but Will had lived in a constant worry that she might at any moment.

Father had always been an extroverted charmer with everyone…except Mother. He was courteous towards her, but even that often lacked sincerity. At home he was mostly silent. Everywhere he went there was someone he knew and everyone spoke highly of him. "You're one lucky woman to be married to this fellow," they'd say, expecting her to agree heartily. She would play along convincingly enough, but Will could always see that it was forced. Father would even treat their pet dog, Oscar, better than her. Oscar was the one who snuggled with Father on the couch by the fire in the winter, and it was more often Oscar who nestled into Father's side for the night rather than Mother. Oscar got special treats, while Mother got curt replies.

Will decided to drop the subject for now. It was the night of Indiana's twenty-third birthday, and Mother was busy making preparations. The guests would be arriving soon. Will watched his mother expertly order maids around the kitchen. For all of her disappointment in life and addiction to leisure, she was a stupendous household manager. No one could say anything to the contrary. Will admired and appreciated that about her, and she was generous with her guests, always offering them her very best. Will helped set the table and arrange the living room for the party, even though he knew his mother disapproved of him stooping to "servant's work." He glanced at himself in the mirror above the mantle. Green eyes peered back at him framed by an olive skinned face and yellow hair. There was nothing particularly exceptional about his appearance. Some people over the years had mentioned that he had remarkable eyes, but he didn't understand why. He had let his beard grow out recently and his sister liked how it made his jaw line look more defined. He straightened his tie and went to welcome the first guests who had just arrived.

It was his grandparents.

"Shalom! Where's the birthday girl?"

Indiana was still "getting painted" as Father always said. Was Indiana a natural beauty? Far from it. When she worked hard to make herself look dazzling, she did seem very pretty. But without primping it was almost as though one were looking at another person...and not a comely one. Some thought her looks lacked stability. Even her figure could seem lithe one minute and a bit dumpy the next.

The next guests were Indiana's friends Molly, Jeremiah, and Jed. Will knew that the two boys were gone on his sister. She relished the attention, toying with them shamelessly. No one knew where she had gotten her coquettishness from, but Molly was a prime suspect. Molly had been a poor influence on her since their teenage years, and they had a penchant for egging each other on in their flirtations. Jeremiah and Jed were decent enough, but Will couldn't help greeting them a little stiffly. Jed was a top athlete at his university and had recently broken the school record in the quarter mile. Both boys came from affluent families and took it for granted.

Before long a few aunts and uncles arrived with a cousin or two. Everyone brought ornately wrapped gifts that Will surmised contained more than a few pricey items. After all, his family preferred to hobnob only with the "best" of society, which to them was limited to those with the largest bank accounts. Champagne was served, the cake was cut, and some of the presents were already being unwrapped when Will heard a knock at the door. When he opened it he was not surprised. Blaze Thunder was always late.

"Will! It's been far too long! C'mon, give me a hug."

Once upon a time Blaze Thunder had been Will's housemate. He and Will had met during their university studies and ended up living together after they graduated. One of their first conversations had been about his name.

"Is that really your *real* name?" asked Will.

"Isn't it a gas? I love it. Yeah, it's real," said Blaze. "My parents were gypsies, so they changed their surname to Thunder because they worshipped Thor, the god of thunder. Then they named me Blaze because they were always a little…odd. Rebellious too."

Blaze had had one simple aspiration for most of his life. As a handsome and stylish young man, he wanted to become a moving picture star. If that didn't work out, he planned to dabble in the world of fashion design. Blaze was the kind of person who possessed an illusive charm that no one could exactly define, but that they distinctly knew was present. This gave him much trouble with women, some of which he loved and others of which were a nuisance.

Although Blaze and Will couldn't have been more different, and in spite of them secretly pitying one another, they got along swimmingly. Will pitied Blaze's vain, worldly aspirations, and Blaze felt sorry for Will who, in his eyes, seemed to live a rather mundane life. If Blaze had been a book worm like Will he might have waxed eloquent and described his former housemate's life as "hebetudinous", but he only collected books for decoration and never read them. More often than not Blaze was out all evening at some questionable establishment or at the house of some person who fanned the flame of his emptiness. Part of Blaze's charm lay in his ability to talk for hours about both serious and inconsequential things, and make it all sound intriguing. In truth, he usually knew little about which he spoke. But he had a talent for marinating his speech in the sauce of affection and garnishing it with momentousness.

Blaze loved to eat expensive meals at the finest restaurants, but sometimes he could not find someone to go with him. And Blaze did not prefer to eat alone. This led to more than a few outings with Will, where Will got to eat like a king and Blaze paid the bill. Being an only child, Blaze had received a massive inheritance when his rich grandfather died. Now he spent more money on food and clothes every year than most average men earned in two.

Indiana had been in love with Blaze for a long time. She dallied with many men like Jed and Jerry, but Blaze was different. Blaze at least was aware of Indiana's attraction to him but it mattered little in his mind. He laughed it off as a schoolgirl's crush. No matter how hard she tried to capture his attention she always failed. She became nervous around him and usually did or said something clumsily. Will was glad Blaze hadn't brought her a gift. No false hopes would be raised tonight.

"You'll never guess who I saw yesterday," said Blaze.

"Who?"

"Matthew Stevens! He just got back in town from his time in Paris."

Matthew had been another person on Will's lengthy list of past housemates. In all he could count about thirty he had lived with over the years. Matthew had been Will's first roommate at university. After the first semester he had moved to a different room because he'd thought Will a bit strange, but later on they had become good friends. Blaze had lived on the same dormitory floor, and the three of them had shared late nights together engaged in all sorts of mischief.

Will's next roommate had been Gary, who soon had got the nickname Hairy Gary because of his large furry body. He had always been out with his girlfriend and had a gift for wasting time with all sorts of trifling entertainments. Then came Bowen, whom Will had met in choir. He had been a master's student studying conducting. Most of his spare time had been spent putting together puzzles by himself and then framing them. Short and thin, Bowen had one of the highest voices of any man Will had ever known. He could sing alto in the choir with ease.

Then there had been Nick the law student who had ended up as a chef, Frank, the weightlifter who had had a tendency to eat strange things, Bobby who had played football but had wanted to be an eye doctor, Hal who had bought a canoe with money he didn't have, and Carmen whom everyone thought was a girl from his name when Will talked about him.

There had been Tim who hated to be touched and had become a pastor, Roy who was fat and balding and had become the sorority beau for Sigma Alpha, Paul who hadn't known that one could use a towel more than once before washing it or that chicken was protein, Ricky who had never missed a class and had fallen in love with a cellist who broke his heart, Shawn who had walked around the dorm naked for fun and married the university queen, and Patrick who had plagiarized one of Will's papers and almost got expelled. Some washed their dishes and kept their rooms clean; most of them didn't. All of them were married by now and had children…except Blaze. Blaze couldn't make up his mind about women.

As the birthday party continued, Indiana opened her gifts and exclaimed over some of them, but Will grimaced every time she didn't say thank you. Her lack of gratitude was embarrassing, but no one seemed to notice. Will had experienced ingratitude several times before, and it had stung him to the heart. The first time had been when he was in middle school. He had admired one of his teachers so much that he decided to give her a special gift for her birthday. He had spent long hours writing a short story for her and even made it into a makeshift booklet. He had been proud of his creation and his friends had to admit that it was lovely and thoughtful. He had shyly and unceremoniously given it to her when class was over, and the next day she had nothing to say. He waited a week, and although she was as sweet and polite as ever, she never so much as acknowledged it. Even after a month he still waited, expecting something—anything. But silence and indifference only remained on her part and his young heart was stricken with disappointment.

Then there was the instance with his mother. Will's parents had gone to Italy on holiday and had asked Will to take care of the house for them. He decided to surprise Mother by leaving the house even cleaner and more organized than the maids could have done. Mother had always been fastidious when it came to her home and Indiana never bothered to keep the maids occupied. Will had given the maids a holiday and scrubbed and sweated to the point of exhaustion, but it was all made light in his heart by love. Every last detail was perfect and polished. But the night when they arrived Mother had walked in the door, scarcely greeted Will, and with one glance had said, "This place is a mess. Those worthless maids ought to be fired. How is a woman to sleep in a house like this?" It hadn't been true, and Will went back to his house with a cold pain in his soul.

Will's gift to Indiana this year was a stylish leather hand bag and a book he hoped she would read. One was not important and the other was eternally so—a book that spoke beautiful truths about God. But Will suspected that it would never be opened. It would join the ranks of other volumes he had given her which only sat unread, accumulating dust. She would love and use the handbag, of course. But she would go on living as if life were not more than food nor the body more than clothing. Father and Mother were the same way, only they sometimes attempted more politeness in ignoring the God whom Will held to be more precious than anyone or anything they could imagine. He wanted them to know Him and they wanted him to know that they just weren't interested. They were comfortable, they were rich; why change anything?

The time came for cake to be served. Everyone sat around the living room sipping wine and trying to think of something to say.

"Aren't the new styles of shoes from Europe simply fabulous?" said Molly. "My father brought me these from France last week." She lifted up her feet and turned them for everyone to see. The women made sounds of approval. All the men but Blaze feigned interest.

"Blaze, when are you finally going to enroll in the fashion school at Milan? You've talked about it for years," said Indiana.

Blaze was notorious for talking on and on about dreams and ideas and never doing them.

"I'm going to see what L.A. has for me first. If I can't make it in Hollywood, then I'll be headed to Milan."

"Hollywood" sparked a conversation about one of the latest pictures. The film had a political agenda, which led to a discussion of the current mayor.

"He's such a worthless man," put in one uncle. "I'm tired of my tax money supporting his projects to help the poor in this city. Most of them are there because they got what they had coming to them."

"You're absolutely right about that," said Father. "He needs to stop all this nonsense about giving them a second chance at life. They're making the town an eyesore more and more every day."

"I agree completely," said an aunt. "The other day I was at the supermarket and saw a homeless woman bagging groceries! I don't think I'll be visiting that establishment in the future if they insist on hiring riff raff."

"How did you know she was homeless?" asked Will.

"Well! She had that look about her! You can always tell, can't you?" she huffed. Everyone but Will nodded.

"I don't know what this world's coming to," said Grandfather. "The boy who shined my shoes the other day forgot to address me as *sir*."

"You've got that right," said Father, shaking his head. "A young woman *smiled* at me near the town hall just this morning. They're becoming mighty brazen these days."

"You don't say!" said two women at once.

"No respect," agreed Grandfather. Jed and Jeremiah looked bored and Indiana looked nervous. Blaze was sitting near her.

"Ya'll have to try the new German restaurant downtown," began Blaze. "Have you heard of it? The Frankfurt Palace. You can't miss it. Their head chef has won international awards. I met him when I went there the other night. You should see how they decorated the dining room. It's like stepping into another world. I recommend the pale ale they serve on tap, and then they have a…."

Will began to tune out. He had heard these sorts of monologues before. Blaze would talk about this eatery as though it were the greatest thing any mortal could experience. Everyone would be entertained and fascinated by *how* he said it.

More empty conversation was bound to follow. Will already wished he could go home.

Chapter 3

Will had now been working at the maintenance shop for too long.

He had not studied maintenance or really anything to do with it at university. His focus had been on English with a minor in music. While working his way through school he had once taken a summer job with the campus maintenance workshop. He never thought he'd end up back at such a place until he lost his job teaching high school. That particular private school had been downsizing and his position ended up being assessed as unnecessary.

Every other school he had tried had been a dead end, so he looked at other kinds of jobs. No one had seemed to be hiring. Those who *were* always came up with some reason not to take Will. He had tried a bank but they'd wanted someone with "more experience." Then he had tried a snow cone stand and they had given the job to a sixteen year old and told Will he was "overqualified." The local "Burgers and Fries" establishment had let him down because his father had won a lawsuit for some customer against them. Apparently the customer had found a live frog in her soda. No one knew where the frog had come from, neither did they know who had been more frightened by the ordeal—the frog or the woman. Thankfully both had escaped with their lives, but one escaped with a lot more money than she had had before.

Will had even tried to work as a garbage man, but apparently one had to get in line for such jobs in Dallas. Time and money had been running out, so Will had found work back at his alma mater doing the same sort of work he had done eight years earlier. The maintenance shop sat in the middle of brown open fields of dead grass. A stable for horses was nearby as well as a shallow pond that dried up every summer.

Will spent many hours in the woodshed helping Mr. G with furniture that needed to be built, as well as other miscellaneous requests for fixing things around the university. Mr. G rarely spoke to anyone; his communication consisted of an assortment of grunts for the most part. Will had to interpret these grunts perfectly or he ran the risk of incurring the man's anger. The few sentences he would say once in a while were hard and full of bitterness.

This particular day at work, Will found himself in the woodshed trying not to be bothered by the usual brooding silence of Mr. G.

"Did your daughter enjoy her time at this university when she attended?" asked Will, thinking Mr. G might enjoy talking about one of his children.

Silence. Will kept sawing away at a board. When he finished cutting the piece, he handed it to Mr. G. It didn't fit exactly right.

"You young people nowadays are all as stupid as my lazy, good-for-nothin' dog! Can't you see this is an eighth of an inch too long?" Mr. G shook his head and fumed silently as he continued working. He didn't ever look directly at Will even when he spoke to him. Will knew that he would be upset for at least another hour and he would huff and snort like some wild animal. The air wouldn't clear until lunch hour came along.

Yet this was a typical day at the maintenance shop. Will had gotten used to it after a fashion—as much as anyone can get used to a toothache or a mosquito buzzing in their ear. It still twinged him inside and he often came home worn out more in soul than in body. Mr. G went to some country church beyond the suburbs. Will wondered why. He pitied Mr. G. There seemed to be something evil, spiteful, and unredeemable in a man like that. He treated everyone the same way. Will prayed for him, but he didn't love him. He wanted to love him. Jesus had commanded him to love his enemies. But Will chafed at that command when it came to Mr. G. He doubted if even the man's own wife could love him. But one day Will found out that he didn't have a wife—she had left him. "Help me!" was Will's muttered prayer often throughout the day.

Lunch couldn't have come any later that day. Will went to the break room, took out a brown paper sack, and sat down. His feet ached. The cold kept seeping through his old stained dark green jacket. When would Spring finally come? The grey sky loomed overhead with tints of Will's mood. He looked around him as he ate. At another table sat Mark mumbling to himself as he played some kind of card game alone. Will had tried to sit with him before and be his friend, but Mark had actually told him outright that he preferred to eat lunch alone. No explanation was given. Will had worked with Mark on some projects around the university. Once they had gone together in the shop's old pickup to change a light bulb for the university president. Mark kept mumbling to himself whenever they weren't conversing. Otherwise their conversation had proceeded as follows:

Will: "Nice day, isn't it?"

Mark: "What's nice about it? It's another day of this stupid job."

Will: "Got any plans for the weekend?"

Mark: "Nope. Just going to try to forget I'm alive."

Will: "Sorry to hear that. What's wrong?"

Mark: "Nothin'. Are you done asking questions or what?"

At another table sat Bill. He had his head resting on his arms trying to get some sleep during the break. Bill had previously worked as a salesman but he got depressed and quit. While he was at his job one could often find him woolgathering about being a professional hockey player. Even though he had never learned to ice skate Bill persisted in this ambition, and he was quick to share it with others. Anyone who met him might at first believe that he was already a part of the big leagues just from the way he talked. Yet at the same time he was earning a major in history and a minor in biology, all the while rising and falling in his levels of melancholy.

A girl in denim overalls walked in. She sat down at Will's table and poured herself a glass of cold water.

"Hello, Laura," said Will.

"Howdy," she drawled.

Laura had grown up on a farm for most of her life and didn't know what to do with herself yet. She wasn't in school so she worked at the maintenance shop full time. It was highly unusual to ever find a woman in such a place, but she felt more comfortable there than doing housecleaning work. She was the boss's daughter and because of that she often got paid for not working much. Will had seen her taking naps while on the clock. Her favorite spot on hot summer days was in the horse stable. She also liked to sleep in the truck during the cold season. She always got away with it. If she didn't want to do something, she simply said that it wasn't her responsibility, and someone else like Will or Mark would have to do it for her. In spite of her faults, Laura was the only coworker who actually talked to Will like a real human being. She often went with "Daddy" to a nice eatery for lunch, but when she was around the shop for the noon break she would usually sit with Will and converse for a spell.

"Mr. G seems to be all in a ruffle again," she said.

"Yep. Are you surprised?"

"No siree. I reckon he's about the strangest bird ever came 'round these parts. Even Daddy's 'fraid of 'im."

"I think he must have taught the devil how to treat people."

Laura chuckled. "William Millhouse! Listen to the mouth on you! For shame. You're a fine feller to be sayin' such."

Will smiled. "What are you working on today?"

"Ha!" Laura laughed, "you sure you wanna give me that much credit? Me? Workin'?"

"Hmmm...you have a good point...."

"Ok, alrighty. *If it suits me* I may be helpin' fix some of the bleachers 'fore the next basketball game."
Will offered her some of his raisins which she took.

"Do you have any more ideas about what you want to study?" asked Will.

"I'm thinkin' lately that I've always taken to cuttin' my little brother's hair. Maybe I could go to one of them cosmotology schools. But then I've always loved horses. Daddy says there's loads of money for the takin' if you learn how to train horses. All them rich folk up in Colorado is always lookin' for someone to train the horses they keep on their big ranches. But it's a man's work—that's what they say. But I can train a horse just as good as any man I ever saw."

"I like the latter best for sure."

"I ain't mentioned no ladder, you crazy coon."

"No, I mean I like the second option best—the horses. Latter as in L-A-T-T-E-R. It just means second or last."

"Oh! Sometimes I wish I had all your mind for book learnin'."

"Well you could in a second. All you need is practice. You could start with that book I gave you last fall."

Laura looked at him and smiled. She took a few leisurely gulps of water and then looked at Will again.

"What?" asked Will.

"Mr. Millhouse, I reckon you're just fine. Swell as they come. Don't let anyone tell you diffrent, ya hear?"

Will smiled back. It was the first time in years that any one had admired him.

Chapter 4

Of course it could only be expected that Will's parents disapproved of his job. He could remember the shock on Mother's face when she'd found out he was working at the maintenance shop again.

"This is only temporary work. I'll find something better soon," he had told her.

"You'd better—and quickly. Until then I'll try not to be embarrassed by you. Fancy *me* having a son stooping to such employment."

But Will hadn't found something better. The months kept coming and going without any new opportunities. His parents became increasingly worried. But they had always been worried about him ever since he had come to know Jesus Christ. It had come about years ago in a mysterious way. One day, at the age of 22, he had stumbled across a book in his home. He still had no idea how it had got there, but it caught his attention. It had been *Letters of Samuel Rutherford*, the great puritan of the 1600s who had written from prison. Overcome by curiosity and a desire to explore its pages, Will opened it. His eyes fell upon a short sentence:

Faith may dance, because Christ singeth.

That line had haunted him for a long time, even as he read on, like a strain of music that will not stop playing in one's mind. But there was more. Those letters were full of something he knew he didn't have. And he wanted it. This Christ man whom Rutherford called "my great and incomprehensible, and never-enough wondered at Lord Jesus" had intrigued him. He had suddenly wanted to understand this puzzling obsession of Rutherford. He had gone to a library and found a Bible, and for the first time began reading the New Testament, eagerly devouring the things it had to say about Christ. He had turned out to be dazzling, disturbing, and confusing. And everything he said was full of light.

Months had gone by, and Will had come to a point where he had stayed up nearly all night reading Galatians and thinking. Then something like a white flame had burst in his mind, and he knew all at once that he believed what this book was saying. There had been tears and joy. And Will had found himself becoming someone he scarcely recognized. He had entered into a strange new reality that seemed unapproachable to his parents. His thinking had slowly become drastically opposite to theirs in many ways. So that now they often felt as though he was no longer related to them.

One of the first shocks for them had come when Will invited a homeless man to sleep on the couch in his living room. His name was Douglas and he was in his forties. Douglas had needed a place to stay until he could get back on his feet. He had been trying to get away from bad influences and stop drinking, and a church in the area had helped him find a job. All he had lacked was time to save up a little for his own place.

Will had known that he was taking a risk in inviting someone he hardly knew into his home. Douglas had openly admitted to having spent time in prison twice during his more reckless days. But Will had been happy to take that risk. Douglas had turned out to be quiet and good natured for the most part. He'd gotten up early and worked hard, and even helped pay some of the bills. But somehow Douglas couldn't seem to save any money.

On one occasion Will had been running errands and had brought Douglas along so that he could get some groceries. They had needed to drop off some things Mother had asked for. When they had arrived no one was at home, so Will and Douglas went inside carrying the parcels. Mother had found them in the kitchen.

She had stood in the doorway and looked at them. One could feel the silence spreading through the air like a cold, smothering wave.

"What does this mean, William?"

"Douglas and I brought the things you wanted. What's wrong?"

Mother's tone had tried and failed to conceal something like icy hatred.

"I thought you had tortured and shamed me enough by insisting on letting rabble into *your* home. And now you bring him into *mine*?"

"Mother, I'd like to introduce you to my *friend* Douglas Cooper. Douglas, this is my mother. Please forgive her lack of basic courtesy and respect."

With that Will and Douglas had walked out, leaving an indignant woman behind.

One day Douglas had come home smelling of liquor. This had deeply disappointed Will, and he was forced to confront him about it. One of the conditions before Douglas moved in had been that he would never touch alcohol, since it had wrought nothing but destruction in his past life. Douglas had meekly confessed and promised to never let it happen again, but a week later it had. Up until that point Will had thought a good friendship was blossoming between him and Douglas, yet Douglas had begun to come home later and later. His attitude had gone slowly from affability and contrition to one of hardened bitterness. He had ranted more and more about the injustice of God in not giving him a normal life with a wife and children and enough money. His words had become caustic as he retreated into a victimized illusion of himself.

Will had come home from work one evening to find Douglas's things gone. Some money that Will had kept in his desk drawer had also disappeared. And he had never heard from him again.

Will's parents prided themselves in not saying, "We told you so," but they managed to hint at it in all sorts of other ways. Occasionally Mother would ask with a mocking undercurrent, "How's your *friend* Douglas? Any word from him?" Then she would sip her wine and return to some discussion of the price of Spanish silk.

Ever since Will's plunge into the new life that Christ had given him (his family referred to this as "when Will got strange") his parents had disapproved of much more than his choice of housemates. His wardrobe was appallingly low-budget in their eyes, even though it really was clean, fitting, and functional.

"If I spend less money on clothes I have more to give away," Will kept telling his mother. But she never understood.

Then there was the issue of his automobile. Even Will had to admit that it had "character." Which is to say that it was a noisy little machine with a mind of its own. It had been very cheap and it looked just so. Will kept meaning to have it repainted, but he never seemed to get around to it. There were holes in the floor that would let water splash through while going through a puddle if you weren't careful. There was no heater in it like the fancy new automobiles that his parents drove, and in the winter Will had to put on two or three jackets to survive the cold drafts. He had named the car Mary after a girl he had secretly loved in college. Mary had loved children and Will had admired that about her. As for him, he had never been able to connect with children. He hated to admit it, but he was afraid of them. Rarely was Will more awkward than when he was forced to interact with anyone who hadn't yet reached their teens. Although he wanted to love and understand these little people, he found himself falling short again and again.

"Will, honey darling, why don't you just give up on that silly writing hobby of yours and put that energy into something more…useful?" Mother had asked one day. This was something else his family frowned upon. From an early age Will had been an incurable scribbler, even though he didn't pursue or develop much of this impulse until he entered university. Perhaps it was a silly hobby, but he needed it. He felt God's pleasure when he wrote. His predilection for creating things found its best consummation on the written page. It was probably never anything that would aspire to publication, but it brought him happiness. Somehow his parents were unable to see that pursuing business and law would never make him one fraction as happy as an evening alone with pen and paper. What sorts of things did he write? Will was still a bit shy about what he produced, so for now we will refrain from sharing it here out of respect.

One thing that his family couldn't disapprove of was a certain secret he had kept from them for years. He called it his Dream Meadow. When taking some shortcuts through the surrounding neighborhood he had suddenly come across a small park in the midst of the sprawling concrete. It was like stumbling into an oasis, or seeing a beautiful face where you expected darkness. The park was very simple. Around the perimeter ran a neat redbrick walkway, a few benches, and some trees. A small playground sat playfully in one corner. But in the middle was a sizeable meadow where the grass grew in green velvet. Nearly every night Will would visit his dream meadow. He was always the lone visitor at that hour, and he would take off his shoes and savor the feeling of cool grass under his feet as he wandered.

A moonlit shimmering world makes the blood sing with prayer, and that is just what Will did. He could imagine what his mother would say. "Honey darling, that's not safe!" But what did Will care about safety when he had this dream meadow all to himself? It was there that his soul found a solace and sweetness. Poor Mother. She did not know the deliciousness of prayer. Whether it was summer or winter Will seldom failed to make his way to this sacred place where he met with a man who died for him.

Sometimes Will would sit and write by moonlight. Sometimes he would lie on the grass and gaze at the stars. Once he had been so enraptured that he couldn't bring himself to leave. He had fallen asleep on a bench with crimson joy pulsing through him. When he awoke it was three in the morning and he had gone home refreshed and still glowing with happiness.

His secret meadow held its own strange peace and silence that had somehow escaped from the kingdom of noise around it. Will cherished this. He could often hardly wait to go back each day. The breezes were firm, the trees were gentle, and the stars themselves seemed to favor the place with twinkles merrier than usual. Freedom and life rested on the field like dew, and Will suspected that love had often lingered there in days gone by. Its afterglow was everywhere.

Night has a glory all its own, and Will's dream meadow teemed with it once twilight faded. Even the shadows were friendly. Will saw it all as an arrow meant to point his heart upward to the source. The trees rustled softly and Will worshipped. He was supported through many a dreary day by the hope of going to this meadow of dreams.

Chapter 5

Up to the age of 28 Will had believed his real parents were dead. Ever since he was a child he had known that he was adopted and had been told that his first mother and father had died of fever when he was a baby. The Millhouses had always prided themselves for adopting a helpless little boy. It was the good deed of a lifetime that they felt made them rise above the ordinary throng of well-meaning citizens.

All Will knew about his parents who had passed away was that their names were Peter and Hannah Edmonton. Good strong names, Will had thought. He had often stayed awake at night wondering what they looked like, what had filled their lives and their hearts. His mother must have been beautiful like the rain at dawn. And he was certain that she must have sung as sweetly as her namesake had. The first time Grandfather had read Hannah's song to him from the Bible his heart had welled up with an aching longing.

> My heart is glad in the Lord, my horn is exalted through the Lord: my mouth is enlarged over my enemies; because I rejoice in thy salvation.

He could remember Grandfather saying, "Now that's a song, Will! No one writes songs like that anymore. All these musicians nowadays think they make music. Ha! *This* is music, my boy. Don't you ever…." But Will had slipped into a reverie. He had seen his mother with her hair shimmering and dancing on the wind, her face full of the life of light, her eyes brimming with joyful tears. He had loved her in that moment. He had almost hated God for taking her. The words of the song had pierced his young heart:

> The Lord killeth, and maketh alive: he bringeth down to the grave, and bringeth up.

How could anyone sing such things? He hadn't liked it at first. But then he had thought about the parts that spoke of the Lord making alive and bringing up from the grave. Such absolute power. It had shot him through with frissons. Oh how he had longed for his beautiful mother—for the Lord to make her alive. Surely she would have had the warmth and selflessness his adopted mother lacked.

Will had never seen a photograph of his real parents. Once when he was 23 he had decided to go on a search to find out more about them. All of his research had found him nothing and he finally gave up after a month. Years passed and he thought less and less about them until one day when he was at his parents' house. He had been mindlessly browsing through their library. It was an impressive display of books which they had never read and did not intend to read. An elegant edition of *The History of Western Civilization* had caught his eye. It was just the kind of book in which he might have hidden a treasure map long ago. He took it down and began flicking the pages. To his surprise, between pages 235 and 236 he found a yellowed envelope. Desperately curious, he removed it and read the clear black print. It was addressed to William Millhouse. His heart stopped when he saw from whom it came.

Peter Edmonton.

Scarcely remembering to breathe he sat down and opened it. The seal had already been broken and two pages of neat longhand emerged. In the right corner the date was from eighteen years earlier.

Dear William,
    I still hope and desire to hear from you. Did you enjoy my last letter about your mother? I hope it will help you understand what she was like and why I loved her so much. Before she died she made me promise to take care of you. She wanted to scale mountains and pluck the stars out of the sky for you. She always said it that way. But I was a fool then. I never deserved her. I failed her because I was so selfish. I know I have asked you before but I still have not received an answer and it worries me: will you forgive me? Can you find it in your heart to pardon a man who threw away his youth on sinful pursuits? I want to make it up to you any way I can. I pray to God that you are strong and

healthy and loved where you are. It gives me some consolation to know that you are well provided for. Maybe someday I will be able to see and embrace you.

Hoping for that day, I remain yours faithfully,
    Your father

Will had stood there a long time reading the letter over and over. When he had nearly memorized it he folded it carefully and took it home.

The next day he had gone back to speak to his mother. He had never driven so slowly. The city had never looked so dirty and grimy. The clouds had never been so grey. The sun itself seemed to have withered.

An afternoon luncheon was in progress at his parents' home when he arrived there. Their big drawing room, decorated lavishly with orange tulips, was full of people. He saw Mother laughing and chatting in her favorite lily chiffon. With white diamonds glimmering in her hair she looked, as one lady put it, "like such a regal matron." Venetian lace covered the tables where people hovered over expensive hors d'oevres.

Straight through them all Will strode toward his mother. He did not care how many people were there. He had one question to ask and wanted an answer. An honest answer. He smelled a lie, and luncheon or no luncheon, Will would have the truth.

"Mother," he said, "did you hide this letter from me?"

He held up the yellowed envelope. An unnerving hush suddenly fell over the guests. Grandmother gasped and one of his aunts turned green and excused herself. A blue fire seemed to kindle in Mother's eyes but she managed to suppress any expression of surprise.

"Did you?" said Will.

"Yes," said Mother. She said nothing else. Will asked nothing more. Turning away, he went upstairs to his old room. He shut the door and sat down very slowly on the bed. With his head in his hands waves of hurt and shock seemed to be crashing over him.

His mother had known all along. He had lived 28 years believing a lie about the closest family he had. He wondered what else they had hidden from him. The image of a lonely, desperate man writing him with no response played in his mind. How long had this gone on? How many letters had he missed over the years? Where was his father now and what was he doing? Will wondered and nearly cried. From an early age he had been taught never to cry—that it was a despicable display of cowardice. Ever since then Will could not remember the last time he cried. But now he was near the point where he no longer cared. Even though no tears flowed his face bore an expression that might have broken the heart of anyone.

Mother had found him there after everybody had gone. He was bent over, elbows resting on his knees, staring at the floor.

"Will."

He did not look up.

"Will, I have always recommended to your father that we tell you the truth, but we only had your best in mind. Your mother did die shortly after your birth and her husband was running from the law at the time. He was in no position to raise a child. He was grateful that we were willing to take you. Shortly after we adopted you he ended up in prison for a long time. We don't know exactly how long."

"So you lied to me because he was in prison?"

"We were concerned…that it would bring too much…shame…."

"On the family. Of course."

"We didn't want you to be too disappointed that your father was in prison. We thought it would be…easier on you."

"You lied to me and everyone else so you wouldn't look bad in the eyes of all your pompous friends!"

Mother was silent.

"Where is he now?" asked Will.

"I don't know," she said quietly. "We stopped receiving letters from him when you were twelve. When he finally got out of prison he moved to Alaska. We don't even know if he's still alive, Will."

"And all the letters?"

"Destroyed." Mother almost sounded meek. "We didn't want him to influence you toward—"

"Low tastes? Humble living?"

"That's not what I said."

Will got up to go. He was afraid of what might come out of his mouth next. There were plenty of furious words stabbed through with pain ready to be unleashed. He looked at his mother with a wounded expression of disgust.

"I can't believe this. I can't believe you and Father would stoop so low. You think you're not a slave to sin?"

Will had gone home. There was nothing he could do. His father had probably died a lonely, broken man. And now, the only parents he had, called lies "love." They thought they loved him but it was only pride and hatred and jealousy covered with a thin veneer of what looked like love. This had poisoned everything. Just then he felt that he could never bear to set foot in their house again.

Back at 125 Sunshine Ln. he walked wearily into his dark, quiet home. Once in his room he sat down at his desk and wrote,

> O Lord, my eyes grow dim from sorrow. My companions have become shadows. When will the shadows lift their hands to the light? Where is the dwelling of the light? I am shut in with the anguish of my soul, and will You hide Your face? Even my own flesh and blood have fed me with the bitter fruit of lies. How long will You forget me? How long?

Putting his notebook away in the desk drawer, Will's hand brushed against a piece of paper in the far back corner. It was caught on something. Will carefully dislodged it and unfolded what appeared to be some sort of note. Douglas had written it.

> Will, I'm sorry I've got to leave without saying goodbye. Maybe one day you'll understand. I think I found someone who can help locate the treasure of 125 Sunshine Ln. This is my only chance to strike it rich and get a better life. I need this. All the best.
> Douglas

Chapter 6

It was a few years now since Will had last seen Douglas. He couldn't imagine what had become of the man, nor what had happened to his hope of finding the treasure. Had Douglas found and taken it one day while Will was at work?

The next evening Will was in the market choosing some grapefruit when out of the corner of his eye he spotted a man not ten feet away from him with his back turned. Will knew it had to be Douglas. He had the same scraggly, pepper hair and cap as always. He was even wearing a shirt Will had given him.

"Douglas?"

Douglas ignored him and began walking away. Will hurried to catch up with him.

"Douglas! Wait!"

But Douglas had slipped into a crowd of people and now was disappearing swiftly around a corner. He obviously did not want to speak to Will so Will gave up with a surge of disappointment.

It was another cold March day with a sulky sky. Will stood for a moment wondering why Douglas should avoid him so coldly. At least his mother had not been there to gather more fuel for her sarcasm about his *friend*. Friends were indeed hard things to come by in this city. Will wondered when a really true friend would enter into his life—someone with whom harmony of heart and mind would come as naturally as breathing. The busyness of Dallas specialized in choking out friendships, which, if they are authentic, are fragile treasures that shrivel away without the water of time. Most people make friends with ease; few keep them. Many want the pleasure of society without the care and thought required to maintain a faithful friend. Not a few fair friendships have died from laziness.

Will had longed for a best friend for years. He had one person whom he would gladly call his best friend if only that friend felt the same way. Sonny was this friend, and although he loved Will his friendship only came in spurts of intensity and investment. What Will wanted was consistency and availability, but Sonny never seemed to be interested in making the effort to offer those things.

Part of the reason was Sonny's young family. Like many of Will's university friends Sonny had married a woman he had met in one of his classes. She was a lithe slip of a girl whose beauty did not impress right away, but over time grew increasingly fascinating. After graduating they had married and by now had three children. Ever since their marriage Sonny had found less and less time for Will. Once in a while Sonny sought him out when he needed someone to talk to. Will would come over, and they would sit in Sonny's backyard and sip lemonade.

Sonny never hesitated to confide anything in Will who proved to be a wise counselor and grateful listener. He appreciated Sonny's honesty about life, his commitment to his God and his family. They often laughed and reminisced about their university days. Those days had been lively and golden, full of excitement and discovery. The two friends had played pranks in their dormitory, spent late nights out by lakes with campfires, shared sorrows and challenges, hated their American History professor, adored their Geology class, and discussed many a member of the opposite sex. First there had been the clique of three girls who always sat two tables away from them at the dining hall. Darla, Claire, and Ramona were all beauties in their own elegant way. Will had admired Claire as they both sang in the university choir. He would watch her lilting soprano notes as he stood on the other end of the stands as a baritone. Her wealth of dark curls around a childish forehead had plunged him into his first episode of unrequited love. Some would have called it an infatuation. Whatever it had been, it was certainly an intensity of attention—an admiration that Will knew not what else to call but love.

Then there had been "Vanity Fair." These three girls commanded a certain awe and respect because of their perfect looks, yet they earned their nickname for a reason. Their preoccupation with themselves, their glitziness, their everlasting prancing kept them as little more than a joke in Will's eyes. Sonny had sometimes been tempted to go after one of them but Will, as a faithful companion, had always talked him out of it.

Sonny had never forgotten, since he would have missed the girl he'd married if Will had not reasoned with him so patiently. He often reminded Will of the debt he owed him for his sound counsel.

Just as Will was turning to leave the market Sonny called out to him.

"You seven times son of a gun! You're here! I can't believe it!"

Will walked over to meet him with a wide grin and the friends embraced.

"Will, man, we need to talk! When can you come over? Tonight maybe?" asked Sonny.

"I can do that. But after church. I hope that's alright," said Will.

"Does a chicken use fowl language?"

Sonny had always made Will laugh with his contagious sense of humor. He was a short, balding, round man, and his jokes were often self deprecating. Everything about his jollity was a brisk tonic to the heart. With a fast and flawless wit Sonny found Will to be one of the few who could keep up with his puns and turns of phrase. One moment they would be talking about a recent robbery in the paper and Sonny would say, "The problem with thieves is that they always take things literally." And then there were the many memorable phrases that he coined and said more than once. "Is she single for a season or single for a reason?" "The odds are good but the goods are odd." "She's good from far but far from good." "Never choose a horse or a wife by candlelight."

When Will went to church that night he sat in the middle of the sanctuary on the right side. This was usually the side where he was least likely to end up near children. Again, not that he disliked them; he just didn't know what to do with them. As the prayer service commenced he looked around. Mr. Johnson was sitting in front of him. Mr. Johnson was a hard worker, but often his tongue worked harder than the rest of his body. His slightly nervous demeanor often made Will feel like he was worried that others may be thinking as much about his private affairs as he was about theirs. Mrs. Johnson sometimes came with him, but she usually stayed home complaining of some kind of rheumatism. She had been on the weekly prayer list for a long time although everyone knew that she simply didn't want to come. Besides, she had all the gossip of Dallas Bible Church brought to her fresh every week from her own dear husband.

On the left side of the very front bench sat Lydia Belcher. She never deviated from this place that she considered sacred and devoted to her alone. If a newcomer innocently sat there she would kindly but firmly inform them that they would need to find another seat. "God made me the kind of person who speaks her mind, so I'm gonna speak it," she would say, and she seldom failed to do so. Her large hairdo represented the size of her personality well. Whether or not Will wanted to hear what she thought he could always count on finding out, whether it had to do with puppies or politics.

Sitting behind Lydia were Mary and Steve, some of the most normal people Will had ever met. They directed the hospitality ministry of the church and taught Sunday School to the children. It seemed that they had always been there. Even though they had never been able to have children of their own they never faltered in their commitment to their Sunday School classes. Will watched them interact with the young fry and marveled at their ease and confidence. Everyone spoke well of them—even Lydia Belcher and Mr. Johnson. They sang the songs with gusto, smiling all the while and hardly ever needing to refer to a hymnal.

When the singing was over Pastor Ryan rose and made his way to the front. He looked exactly his age—56 years old. Raising five boys had taken its toll on any last traces of youthfulness, and he wore his gray hair with a calm assurance. His quietly glad demeanor often made Will feel like he had just been speaking to God, or that he was doing so while he listened to you. He opened his Bible and signaled for the congregation to be seated. He was smiling but Will perceived a gravity behind that smile.

"Psalm 115. 'Not unto us, O LORD, not unto us, but unto thy name give glory, for thy mercy, and for thy truth's sake. Wherefore should the heathen say, Where is now their God? But our God is in the heavens."

He paused.

"'He hath done whatsoever he hath pleased.'"

With a gentle heart and conviction of steel he went on to preach about the freedom of God. "When God has acted," he said, "he has done so under no compulsion but only because it has pleased him to do it." It was a psalm Will was familiar with, but something about it haunted him that night. What sorts of things might God be pleased to do? Pastor Ryan had mentioned some that the Bible revealed in the heart of God, but what did Will's future hold under such a frightfully free Lord? He thought about this much while working in the days that followed.

One night a strange thing happened. Will was lying in bed with the window open, enjoying the cool breeze that was blowing in from an oncoming rainstorm. He had just turned off the light and was drifting off to sleep when he inhaled something wonderful. It was the scent of lavender. Nothing like it had ever happened before at 125 Sunshine Ln. There were no gardens nearby and there certainly wasn't any lavender for miles. But there was no mistaking it. As the lightning flashed in the distance some of the sweetest perfume Will had ever known floated into his room.

In his journal he wrote:

> This illusive fragrance: is it some window of heaven that has cracked opened for a moment? Has some universal boundary been torn? The fields of Elysium must smell like this, for it is the fragrance of bliss and innocence. It is the fragrance of purity and...grace. There is some vagrant magic here and I am thankful. Praise be to the Lord of lavender storms.

Chapter 7

Mother's idea was a bolt from the blue. She came to share it on a dreary morning near the end of March. Will woke up and looked out the window at a dour sky that seemed to reflect how he felt just then. Life seemed to be bringing him grey cold more often lately. It was Saturday and he had no plans. His house soaked in silence. The street outside couldn't have been more desolate.

Will lay in bed for a little while wondering what he should do with another day off work. He stared out at the dirty snow that had turned into slush and mud. A lone bird sat still on a scraggly bush near his window, all puffed up and dusted with snowflakes. Will thought of how many mornings he had avoided getting out of bed, gazing out on the ugly world of 125 Sunshine Ln. He wondered about when he had last seen children playing there...or even heard laughter along those cracked sidewalks or from those ramshackle porches. Will hated this dark end of winter. And he hated his house and street more than ever that morning. The house was too big and lonely for him alone. He wished he could wake up to some dear soul rummaging around in the kitchen, or to the smell of hot coffee. Even the sound of someone crying would be a welcome change. Just to know that another life was near, breathing and *living*— that would be lovely. But Will could find no one. Most of the time he liked his independence and privacy. But just now he despised it.

"You're better off without all those rotten housemates," Father had said once with his cold, unsmiling smile. "All they ever did was leave dirty dishes for you to wash." Father had a point, but Will hadn't liked the way he'd said it. The house truly was too large for one person. It didn't seem ken to him anymore. There was a hostility in its silences; a menacing tone to its creaks and groans. It was watching him always with vindictive eyes. Will knew such thoughts were foolish, but they were there all the same. This house didn't like him, and he disliked it at least as much. It might be different if he was able to decorate it better. Blaze had once made it look elegant and fashionable inside, but when he left, all the decor left with him.

Will got out of bed and dressed himself wearily and wandered into the kitchen with its crooked floor. It was going to be cold oatmeal for breakfast again. It wasn't his favorite, but it was cheap. And he didn't have the motivation to make anything more interesting. He had just settled down at the table to read his Bible while he ate when he heard a knock at the door. When had someone last visited him on a Saturday morning? Will couldn't remember. On his way to the door he glanced at himself in the mirror and wished he hadn't.

When he opened the door his mother stood there in her ostentatious white mink coat.

"I do wish you would install a telephone here. You don't know what a nuisance it is to come all the way in this weather just to tell you something."

Will had had a telephone in the house when Blaze lived there, since Blaze could afford it. But in those two years no one had ever called him. Not even his parents. But they had always managed to chide him for not calling them more, even though he had called them plenty.

"Good morning, mother," said Will. "Won't you come in?" She gave him a customary kiss on the cheek as she stepped inside. "So how are you?" Mother ignored the question.

"My! This house is frightful! It scarcely looks as though anyone lived here! Honey darling, you *must* do something with this place. I can't see why you didn't learn anything from Blaze when he was here." The accusing tone was in her voice. He decided to change the subject.

"You had something you came to tell me?"

"Oh, yes. Well, your father has made a new acquaintance at work. His name is...Bill. Bill Rumpel I believe. He's part of the law firm. They got to know each other a bit, and you'll never guess what he found out!"

"What? I give up," said Will.

"Bill and his family are *Christians!*"

Will stared back at her a little blankly.

"Hmmm. Grand. But...I don't understand why *you're* excited about that. I thought...."

"Well it's because Bill has a daughter your age—who isn't married. She sounds smart and talented and she'll be playing the harp tonight at The Cyprus Grill and—"

"You're trying to match me up with a girl you haven't even met?" said Will, trying hard not to sound annoyed.

"Now Will, we—Father and I—simply thought it would be nice to meet her. We'll all go together. The whole Rumpel family will be there, and it'll be the perfect way to get to know a good Christian girl. No one will even know about our intentions. Father didn't even tell Bill much about you. Bill tried to invite us to his church but Father suggested dinner instead. And Indiana is sick, so it'll just be the three of us as a family."

On the one hand Will was touched by his parents' gesture that acknowledged how in earnest he was about marrying a believing woman. But on the other hand he loathed setups. He had experienced enough of them in college to know that they were always bound for failure or worse. Yet this could be a chance for mother and father to hear the gospel from another family, or to perhaps see it lived out. It could be interesting—maybe even fun.

Will agreed to go under the condition that mother and father promise not to say anything awkward about the situation. The restaurant that night was filled to the brim with wealthy people. On a small stage in a corner sat Rachel Rumpel, masterfully plucking away at a beautiful brass harp. She wore a pale green dress of clingy silk, ornately embroidered with delicate pink filigree. With flawless features and golden hair down to her waist, Will thought she might be an apparition. He could scarcely believe the ethereal splendor of her face. Every perfect trill of the harp seemed to be embodied in her.

The rest of the Rumpel family was late. Will was happy to let Father and Mother discuss their next vacation to Italy while he watched Rachel. He could hardly focus on anything else. He found the way she caressed the strings mesmerizing, and found his gaze being drawn again and again to her as if by a star. He was close enough to see her eyes, and now and then she would glance over at him, almost daring him to stare back into those pools of liquid glass. Before long Will had memorized her face. The dimple on her right cheek when she smiled, the elegant contours, the delightfully subtle curve of lips, every shadow shining with angelic light, each eyebrow penciled with fine grace, the svelte nose, the girlish tenderness in her brow, the satin sunset in her cheeks...her hair. Her hair! He did not have enough time to celebrate it. He sat dreaming how he might describe it. Rivulets of gold. No, that didn't quite capture it. Tresses sliding over her neck...streaking down in streams of gold...ripples of gold...with magic light. That still didn't do it justice. Warm magic rippling down her back...glossy miracles across her shoulders...strands of magic...of paradise. He finally took a napkin and wrote: *Her hair—a glowing, rippling, golden cascade of savage silence and wild peace. Her shoulders misted over with a golden cascade roaring silently.*

Then the Rumpels were there, apologizing profusely for being late and making introductions. Sean, the younger brother, greeted Will with the strangest voice he had ever heard. Then there was Bill and his rather corpulent wife Darla. Rachel finished playing her first set and began walking toward the table. Will's heartbeat quickened. Heat rose in his face and he felt almost dizzy. He tensed with nervousness as his mind raced to find the right words.

Rachel saved him the trouble. After a cursory nod and smile to all at the table, she sat down and said, "You may have noticed that I didn't play any Christmas music."

Will hadn't noticed. It was March after all.

"That is because we believe that Christmas is really just a recycled pagan festival." The other Rumpels all nodded gravely.

"Well that's...very interesting," said Father.

"Your playing was beautiful," chimed in Mother. She turned to Bill and Darla. "You have a very talented daughter. You must be proud."

"Oh we certainly are. We're also very proud of Sean. He plays the saw. He's really quite handy with it."

Will didn't know saws could be played. He had used them plenty of times to cut wood at the maintenance shop, but that was all.

"That's so *interesting*," said Father. "I've never heard someone play the saw before."

"Well you will tonight," said Sean. Will thought that his voice sounded like a combination of a screeching owl and an angry penguin. What on earth could be the matter with him? He felt sorry for this twenty year old boy.

"Yes, tonight you can say you *saw* it live," replied Bill. All the Rumpels cackled. Will couldn't decide which was more abrasive to the ears—Sean's voice or his laugh. The latter was more akin to a dying rooster.

"I brought my saw to play with sis during the next set," continued Sean. "And I invited my fiancé Samantha to join us. I hope you don't mind. She should be here any minute."

Just then a woman exactly six feet tall walked through the doors wearing a red dress. Heads turned. She looked like a vision from the stage, and she was headed straight for their table.

"Here she is! This is Samantha, everybody."

Samantha fawned over Sean, which led to Bill fawning over Darla. Darla could certainly not have been on speaking terms with a mirror on her best of days, and Will found himself counting her chins and wondering how on earth Rachel could be related to her. Darla must have decided it was her turn to try her hand at conversation, so she addressed Will who had just finished noticing her third mole.

"Will, you're not married, now, are you?"

Will shook his head.

"You can't be having a long list of things this woman's gotta have. That's my advice. Too many young men looking for someone perfect these days. You'll thank me later. Just throw away that list you have."

Darla looked very pleased with herself. But Will did not looked pleased about anything. He nodded politely, and that was all. People assuming and offering him advice without knowing him—*that* was one of Will's great vexations.

Mother sensed Will's irritation and tried to rescue the conversation by asking how Bill and Darla had met and married. It turned out to be a depressing narrative about how they had both been lonely and desperate, and had simply decided that it was a sensible match. But this ended up causing Darla to criticize Bill for not having been more romantic in their courtship, and Mother tried again to bring up something happier.

"So where did you honeymoon?" asked Mother with an anticipatory smile. It turned out that Bill had never been a good planner, and he had forgotten to organize anything for their honeymoon. They had ended up at his parents' house, listening to his father snoring in the next room.

Will thought he should make an effort to change the subject. He turned to Rachel.

"I'd love to hear about which church you're a part of."

"We attend the First Church of Christ, Scientist."

All the Rumpels nodded gravely. And Will felt dyspeptic.

After his parents left him at his doorstep, Will went into his big, dark, empty house. No one was waiting for him, and he went to bed early.

Chapter 8

Then there was the affair of the dream.

Will didn't usually remember his dreams. He wasn't prone to nightmares, but his dreams weren't always very positive either. Whenever he woke up and actually recalled a good one, he would try to write it down in his journal. The last one had not been worth recording. It had had something to do with crocodiles, his shoes, and somebody from work. He had heard that some people flew in their dreams. They started running, put out their arms, and then somehow began to soar like a bird. Ever since then he hoped that he would be able to fly, but it never happened. At least Will's dreams were never predictable and boring like Blaze's. Blaze only ever dreamed of designer clothing and expensive food, and he loved to tell Will all about it.

One night Will went to bed and tried to ignore the howling of the wind through the attic. He stared at the ceiling, tried reading, and then began to smell lilac perfume wafting in from outside again. With that scent flooding his room, he finally fell asleep well past midnight.

He dreamed that he was at a carnival, and had just stepped off a Ferris wheel. That part of the dream was very clear. The carnival was not familiar, and everyone ignored him. He stood there watching the faces go by, flowing past him like a river.

Then came a surprise. He noticed a little blond ponytail of a girl standing with some adults. There was something about the shape of her head that caught his eye. It seemed familiar yet foreign, and it sent a throb of gladness through his heart. The girl's head turned around. She looked over and saw him, and a light of recognition rippled over her face. She dropped the doll she was holding and ran toward him ecstatically. He found himself crouching down to receive her flailing arms in a firm embrace. She hardly slowed down before the collision, and he was staggered by a rush of awful happiness. Then she stood back, and he grasped her by the shoulders and said, "Let me look at you!" It was the most natural thing in the world. He met her shimmering eyes with his own searching ones, cupped her small head and shining hair in his hands and kissed her forehead with a hearty smack. Then a bearded man in a brown suit looked down at them and said with a big smile, "It's proof! It's proof, I tell you!"

"What is? Proof of what?" said Will.

The man said something, but the roar of the crowd drowned out his voice and Will only saw him pointing upward. Then he looked and saw that the girl was gone. Her face was fading from his memory. Suddenly he was in a dark forest, looking for her. A storm broke out and still he searched as the rain fell. He didn't know why but he had never known a happiness quite like that fleeting encounter. Without warning the rain turned into liquid light. It seemed to be moonlight that was coating the world around him. Everything was silent as the trees began to glow. Will started when a woman's voice broke the quiet.

"It lives. It shines. It rings."

He could hear her but could not see her. The falling moonlight was warm and he was unable to speak. He wanted to ask the voice what it was talking about. And he wanted to see who it was. He ran toward the voice and slipped down an embankment. Losing his balance, he slid into a river which was glowing as well. The luminescent water was beautiful, but he felt himself sinking. This water was different, and no matter how hard he tried to swim, he felt himself slowly going under. Just when he thought he might wake up in a cold sweat of desperation, he gasped and found that he could breathe under this water. He was floating in pale light. Bubbles gleamed and fish swam by. He put his hand over one of the bubbles and found it to be hard like a glass ball. Then he reached out to touch a lazy fish and his hand went straight through it as through a phantom. He decided to swim deeper and explore. The liquid light felt like breathing autumn air. Then the same woman's voice began to sing:

"He paints in fairer lines. He paints in fairer lines."

The current grew swifter, and a distant roar was getting louder. He knew what was coming but was not afraid. He let the river plunge him over a precipice and felt no fear. Landing lightly in a gleaming lake, he saw stone steps leading out and onto the shore. As he came out of the water he saw the young girl from the carnival. She was laughing and waving as she skated across the lake, for it was now frozen. Will rushed out on the ice to follow her and then he awoke.

Try as he might, he could not drift back into the dream. He wanted to more than he could explain. With half-conscious bewilderment he felt happier than he had in a long time. He knew he should get up and write down the dream before he forgot, but he didn't want to stop trying to fall back asleep so that he might continue where it had left off. His hope proved futile. But in spite of that, Will got up the next morning refreshed and pleased. He remembered the dream, and the details were still amazingly vivid. It was a memory that he would return to for a long time.

Chapter 9

Will could never understand the affair of the dream. It haunted him and left him with a strange pang when he remembered it. He was thinking about it one morning in early April as he got ready for work. Trudging through his morning routine, he was not looking forward to another day with Mr. G. *Maybe I'll get called out on a work order with someone else,* he thought. That was one of the wispy hopes that kept him from quitting work altogether.

Mr. G was still drinking his coffee and reading the newspaper when Will arrived.

"Good morning, Mr. G," he said.

Mr. G didn't say anything. He did not even acknowledge that anyone had entered the building. Inwardly Will braced himself for another day of awkward tension and clocked in.

By the time lunch rolled around Will was ready to throw in the towel and not look back. He had upset Mr. G yet again because he'd put the hammer on the wall in the place where the level was supposed to hang. Mr. G huffed and puffed and grunted and there wasn't a thing Will could do about it. He had wanted to say something impertinent but he knew it would only serve to make matters worse. Will walked into the break room and brought his lunch bag down on the table with a little more force than usual. Laura came in just in time to see his face and hear the thud. She walked right over and joined him.

"What's eatin' you today?"

"*You* ought to know. Guess."

"Laws, I can imagine sure as shootin'! That ole crank of a G ruinin' your day again? You oughtn't be lettin' the likes of him get under yer skin."

"You should try it sometime. It's not as easy as you think."

"I betcha *I* could ignore him and all his tantrums 'bout nothin'. That big grouch can't scare *me*. My gramps used to have a fair sight bigger conniptions than ole G ever has. He'd just rage like a rabid hornet, cursin' and yellin' at the slightest provoca…provocativation."

"Provocation."

"Right. Well he thought I's dumber than a box of hammers, but I learned to stand up to him early on. I wasn't about to let an ole crosspatch like that spoil my fun. You gotter get thicker hide and stick up for yerself more, Mr. Millhouse."

"Easy for you to say. You're the boss's daughter. Besides, you've never actually worked with Mr. G, so you've got no place to speak."

"Tell you what, then. I'll take your job for the afternoon and you take mine. We'll do a little switcheree on Mr…. Say, what does G stand for anyways?"

"As far as I'm concerned it's 'Grouch' or 'Grump,'" said Will. "But since when are we allowed to switch roles in the middle of the day?"

"*I'm* the boss's daughter. I can do anythin' I want," said Laura with a wink.

So it was that Will found himself in the work truck on his way to move a desk out of one of the faculty offices, while Laura intrepidly submitted herself to Mr. G as Will's replacement for the day. Will was happy but also worried that Laura would not turn out to be as brave as she boasted.

After loading the desk into the pickup he began heading back to the shop. The few signs of Texas spring were beginning to show themselves. He filled his lungs with the crisp air streaming through the window and was glad. The sun was shining in cheerful earnestness and birds sang in the budding trees along the bumpy road. Driving as slowly as he could to savor his time away from the shop, Will whistled and hummed. About half a mile away from the shop he spotted a lone figure in the distance. As he drew closer he could see that it was a child walking along the road next to a field of dandelions. This part of the road was lined with blooming magnolia trees and the late sun spangled the ground with leafy shadows. The child heard the approaching truck and stopped to turn around.

Will could now see that it was a young girl. She looked lost. Never before had he seen a child on this dusty road leading to the maintenance shop. He slowed to a halt and looked out at her from the window. Her face was pale and her cheeks streaked with tears. Will guessed that this blond waif couldn't be more than 12. She wore a plain blue dress and she carried nothing with her. Blue eyes squinted up at him and Will wondered what he should say. He tipped his hat and forgot to smile as he said, "Howdy, miss. Are you lost? Do you need some help?"

At that moment something terrible happened. The girl's eyes widened, as an expression of terror swept over her face. Will, confused, looked behind him to see what had caused this small creature so much fear. But there was nothing. By the time he glanced back the girl had fled and was running with all her might out into the east fields. He saw her stumble and fall hard, then get up again and keep going.

"Hey! Wait!" he called after her. "It's alright! I won't hurt you!"

Still she did not look back. Will knew those fields were filled with rattlesnakes that would be emerging for the spring sun. He and his coworkers always carried a gun when they cleared those fields. If he didn't go after her now she was bound to upset a snake in her reckless haste. She fell again as he threw open the door and took off toward her, calling, "Stop! It's dangerous out there!"

She paid no heed. Being a fast sprinter, Will caught up with her swiftly. When she heard him approaching she looked back and the hem of her dress caught on a thorny bush, pulling her off balance as it tore. Down she went with a little cry. In a moment Will was standing over her and trying to help her up. Even though she had suffered a bloody elbow and a scraped knee, Will was relieved that a rattler had not struck her. The girl accepted his help and stood to her feet bravely. More tears were glistening on her cheeks.

"Who…are you?" she said, still breathless, still afraid.

"My name is Will. Will Millhouse. What's yours?"

Her eyes grew wide again.

"There, there, miss. I told you it's alright. There's nothing to fear from me. I wanna to help you. Whad'ya say we get you back home? Where are your folks?"

It hurt Will that this delicate child kept staring at him as though he were a ghost. How could he be so frightening to her? He waited and then asked again.

"Will you at least tell me your name? Please don't look so frightened," he said.

"Cris...Cristina," she said after a moment's deliberation.

"Good. Now, Cristina, let's get back to the truck. I don't want a rattlesnake to find us. They seem to have their family reunions in this field. Then I can drive you home."

"Will you carry me?" she asked.

This surprised Will. He had carried babies once or twice but never a child like this one. He raised his eyebrows.

"Are you sure about that? I thought you were afraid of me."

"I am, but I'm more afraid of snakes. Please carry me."

Smirking, yet still unsure of himself, Will lifted her up and started back carefully. With her arms around his neck she looked up at his face and commenced to study him intently. He glanced down at her a few times and, as he did, she would glance away, pretending to look elsewhere. Once back at the truck he set her down. She looked slightly dazed, but at least she no longer wore that expression of terror.

Will looked at his watch. It was almost time to clock out for the end of the day. With a little more coaxing the small girl got into the truck and they drove up to the shop's main building.

"Follow me inside. We need to get those scrapes cleaned up. There's a first aid kit we can dust off somewhere."

Laura was sitting in the break room when they entered. She did not seem to be in her usual chipper mood.

"Hello, Laura! You're finished early."

She nodded. "It kills me right good to say it, Mr. Millhouse, but you were right and I was wrong."

Will couldn't suppress a grin. "Oh? Mr. G was too much for you after all, eh?"

"That man is so wretched.... I did everything he wanted faster'n a frog's croak and what thanks did I get? All's he could do was grunt and snort 'bout how I done left the saw on the work table 'stead of hangin' it up where it belongs."

Will bit his lip and tried to look empathetic but failed.

"Well that's a shame. I was hoping you two would hit it off and I could take your job every day. I had a swell time. And look what I found in the process. This is Cristina. I need to get her cleaned up and take her home. She's a little lost and fell in the field a couple times."

"Hello there, miss Cristina. Pleased to meet ya." Laura held out her hand with warm smile. "The bandages and such should be in the cupboard over that there counter. Here, Cristina girl, have a cookie. You look mighty hungry."

Bandaged and feeling a trifle less rumpled, Cristina got into the car with Will, and they began making their way down the dirt road toward the edge of the main university campus.

"Now how did you manage to get lost, Cristina?"

"I don't know. I don't even know how long I've been lost. All I remember is waking up on the grass by the side of the road. I was so scared. I cried for a long time because I didn't know what had happened or where I was. Then I finally started walking…and then you drove up."

"That sounds awful…I'm so sorry. Do you remember where you were before you woke up on the grass?"

"I think I was in my bed. And I think there was a thunderstorm," she said.

"Huh. Strange. What a confusing ordeal. Hopefully you know your address?"

Cristina hesitated. "It's on Walnut Street…I live on Walnut Street…number 15. There's a big weeping willow in the front yard. We live out in the country a little ways from the city."

"Alright. I think I have an idea of where that might be. We can at least ask around. Will your mother and father be home?"

"My aunt and uncle will be there. But my parents are dead."

Will winced inside. "I'm sorry to hear that," he said. A few moments of silence followed. Will could see out of the corner of his eye that she was studying him again. He felt the scrutiny of her inquisitive gaze and he wondered what she was looking for. The sun would be setting soon and they needed to find her house before dark.

Pulling up to a drug store, Will hopped out to ask the proprietor to point him toward Walnut Street. The man was very helpful and ten minutes later they entered the driveway of an old, broken down house. Will double checked the number on the mailbox and let Cristina out. They stood there looking at a place that appeared nothing short of haunted.

This makes 125 Sunshine Ln. look like a palace, Will thought. What he said was, "Are you positive that this is the right address? It doesn't look like anyone has lived here for decades."

He looked at Cristina who said nothing. That wide eyed horror that he had first seen on her face was returning. All at once she bolted towards the front door, calling, "Aunt Grace! Uncle Ben! Where are you?!" Frantically she pulled on the door but it would not open. She rushed to the window and looked in through the broken glass. All she found were cobwebs and dusty darkness.

In the fading light she made a pitiful picture, finally bursting into desperate tears. The winds of twilight were beginning to stir in the tall grass, and the crickets were striking up their oblivious music. Then Cristina turned around and looked into Will's eyes with her own shot through with hopelessness.

"Oh God, help her," he whispered. And he went over to where she had sunk to the ground with her back against the wall of the house. Sitting down beside her he wished he knew how to comfort her. How could he know how to speak to a child who seemed to have lost everything she had? He did not even know what to say to normal children. And here was this girl below a purple sky surrounded by the shattered pieces of what seemed to be her existence.

"I know…this is the place," she said in a voice that wavered from the throbbing of her shaken heart. "But I don't…understand what happened. Before I got lost this house looked almost brand new. See? There's the weeping willow just as I said."

"I don't understand what's going on either, but we'll figure it out. You can count on me." Will hated how trite his words sounded. He shouldn't have said anything. Then he looked up at the blossoming stars and whispered, "Lord, we don't know what to do."

A moment later they saw a man with a lantern making his way toward them. "Hello there?" he called.

It turned out to be one of the neighbors. He did not recognize Cristina and he confirmed that the house had been shut up for 24 years.

"You'll only find bats and spiders livin' in that place. Maybe a ghost or two."

No aunts and uncles of their description lived in the area that he knew of, and he assured them that he had never seen Cristina before.

"Good God, missy! You look a sad sight! Everything alright here?"

"God," said Cristina distinctly and deliberately, "is not good."

Chapter 10

"Do you want to keep looking or should I take you to the police station and see what they can do?" asked Will when they were back in the car.

Cristina only shook her head and looked disconsolate.

"This is all so strange and mysterious to me," Will admitted. "I hardly know where to begin. Don't you have any other friends or family we could look for?"

The small child stared out the window at the moon, feeling betrayed by life. Was she crazy perhaps? Will wondered. How could she possibly not remember how she got lost? Or was she lying and really had no family at all? Maybe she was an excellent actress and this was some sort of scam. But Will doubted that possibility. Her heartbreak appeared more real than any he had ever seen. And besides, she had run away from him at first in fear. It was difficult to question her sincerity. But what was to be done?

She finally spoke. "My grandmother lives not too far from here. All I ever call her is Naomi because she asks me to, but Gran says that it's not her real name…and I don't know her real name. I don't know her address but I might be able to tell you how to get there from here. Gran and Pappy take me to see her all the time."

"Ok, but do you know any telephone numbers we could call?"

She shook her head and said, "My aunt and uncle never wanted a telephone. They always said it was too modern for them and they'd rather be seeing people face to face when they're talking. Besides, it's awful hard for me to remember things clearly right now. And I'm only eleven, mister."

"Fair enough. We'll try finding Naomi then. But don't you need something to eat first? That little cookie from Laura wasn't enough. I don't want you to go fainting on me." Will smiled, trying to cheer her up the smallest bit.

Her countenance remained unchanged and she said, "How can a soul in a wasteland of sorrow think of food?"

"Good point," said Will. Cristina did not see the twinkle in his eye. "You're having a Jonah day indeed. Do you feel buried in a graveyard of despair?"

"That's not funny. You don't have to be so dramatic."

Will cleared his throat. "Yes ma'am. My mistake. But you really should eat something," he said as he started up the engine. "I know just the place. It's a little diner close by. I only go there on special occasions…and when I find lost girls. It's called *Esther's*. Heard of it?"

Cristina had not. A minute later they rolled up to what looked like a small, red barn that had been turned into a room filled with round tables and warm light. Cristina did not want to go inside so Will ordered BLTs with french fries and a couple of milk shakes, and brought them back out to the car.

"Here you go, lost girl. You can't tell me that doesn't smell delicious."

Cristina was famished. She hesitantly took a sandwich and began to eat.

"I can't pay you for this, mister. I hope that's alright."

"Hmmm…an eleven year old who is lost without money. I've a penchant for swindling helpless children out of money but I'll make an exception this time around."

Cristina remained as solemn as ever. The two ate in silence for a few minutes. Will did not want to keep her from eating so he asked no more questions. When she slurped up the last of her milkshake he drove back to the old house on Walnut Street so that she could direct him from there to Naomi's house.

"You ready?"

"I think so. It's going to be harder now that it's dark, but I'll try," she said with a brave sigh.

"Here we go."

Cristina seemed fairly sure of herself on the turns. Only twice did she hesitate, and she only made them retrace their steps once.

"We're almost there. This is the last turn—right."

"Whad'ya know! My mother lives in this neighborhood too." said Will.

The little girl looked at him askance.

"Slow down. It's that one right there," she pointed. "The one with the two lamps and the fountain. It looks like someone is actually there! Swell!"

Will stopped in front of the home and turned off the engine. He sat in silence for a moment and then looked at her. Taking a deep breath he said, "I don't know how this is possible…." He paused. "It's just that…well…."

"Yes, sir?"

"Well you see…this is where my family lives. Are you sure you didn't get mixed up on the turns back there perhaps?"

"I'm sure. Although it looks a tiny bit different—but this is where Grandma Naomi lives."

"Well there has to be some mistake somewhere," said Will, scratching his head. If you want to go in and see, we can do that. But I don't know if you want to meet my family. And I have no idea what they'll think of all this."

Fear began to creep back into her eyes and spread over her brow. *Or was it fear?* Will couldn't be sure of anything anymore. He was starting to feel a little crazy. Things were getting more uncanny by the hour.

"Now don't fret yourself over this," said Will. "Let's go in and see if Mother and Father have an idea where your grandmother might be if she's close by. We'll get to the bottom of this yet."

Just then the front door of the house opened and Mother stepped out and waved. Cristina's eyes lit up, and before Will could blink she had dashed out of the car yelling, "Grandma Naomi!" Mother instantly stiffened with surprise and realized that this child coming toward her was not slowing down. Bracing herself indignantly, Mother stood her ground as the girl came crashing into her with a hug. She did not return the embrace and had no intentions of doing so.

"What is the meaning of this?!" she sputtered. "William Auden Millhouse! You get this…this…just get her off of me! What in the blazes is going on?!"

As soon as Cristina heard this she instantly let go and backed away from Mother. That silent horror had come back into her eyes with a vengeance.

"Naomi?" She whispered plaintively.

"I have no idea who you are talking about, missy. Have you lost your brains? I've never seen you in my life! Someone ought to teach you some manners. This is *not* how you treat strangers. God in heaven! What's gotten into you, Will? Where did you find such a stray, homely thing? Look at her! She's straggly and looks to be half crazy."

Will was beginning to feel frustration stirring inside him. The last thing this poor girl needed was his mother's biting tongue that knew no grace or love.

"That's enough!" Will's voice boomed. "Mother, this is Cristina. She's lost and I'm trying my best to help her find her home. She only thought for a minute that you looked like her grandmother. That's all. She's had a long day, it's dark, and she's just confused. Can you try to help us for a moment? Do you know anyone around here that could be a grandmother to this girl? She says she comes to visit all the time. Does she live alone, Cristina?"

Cristina did not answer. Instead she stood by Will in shock. She looked up at him and said, "It doesn't matter anymore. I'm not confused. We're not going to find another Naomi."

Will crouched down and looked into her face. "Hey, there, there now. You've gotta help me. I'm doing my best but you can't be making it harder on yourself than it already is."

"Besides," he whispered, "you wouldn't really want her for a grandmother anyway. Don't go wishing that on yourself." He smiled, but she did not smile back.

"I didn't choose any of this, mister. All I know is that this is Grandma Naomi. But she's very different inside."

Will began to wonder if this was why people had a hard time believing children. Was this some extra imaginative child who was playing games? But she was not enjoying this any more than he was.

Suddenly the girl took on a firm tone. "Look, mister, you can think what you want but I'm *not* batty. I haven't even gone mad. You don't have to believe me and you probably won't, so we should go."

"Well then I guess I'm the one who's gone mad because I sure feel like it right now. Let's go then."

"What's going on here?" Father had just stepped out in his bathrobe.

"We were just leaving," said Will. "Goodbye, Mother. Sleep well, Father. I'm going to find this girl a place to stay for the night."

Back on the road in Will's old automobile, they both took a deep breath and sighed at the same time. The wind was billowing in through the windows, pure and fragrant, and not a cloud veiled the sheet of diamonds above. The waif in the passenger seat was pale as the moonlight. Her face still carried a burden that knit her brow. Will figured that she must be thinking hard about something.

"There's not anything else we can do tonight, so I think it'd be best if I take you to Sonny's house to sleep."

"Who's he?"

"My best friend. He has three children and a wonderful wife. They'll take good care of you."

"Why can't I stay with you?"

"You mean you're not afraid of me anymore?"

Cristina shook her head.

"Well if that ain't the cat's whiskers!" With a broad smile he said, "I don't feel half as crazy anymore! But we've got to be sensible in any case. Everyone knows that an established old bachelor like myself doesn't know a thing about taking care of little girls."

"What's there to know? You've taken care of me this whole time."

"But…you see…" The car rattled over some bumps. "Folks just wouldn't find it proper."

"I don't want to stay with anyone else. I'm tired and I don't want to meet any more people."

"I understand, but I've made up my mind. You'll be just fine, I promise."

When Cristina saw that there was no use in arguing she folded her arms and sulked. They stopped at a quaint blue Victorian house in a tidy neighborhood. No lights were on inside but Will still went to the door and rang the bell. No one came. Sonny's car was not in the driveway either.

"I don't understand what's going on," said Will as he reluctantly got back into the car. "Where could they have gone at this time of night? This has never happened."

A little smile crept ever so softly onto the girl's face, like a shy doe peaking out of shadows. It was the first one Will had seen her wear and he thought that it became her. She looked like a different person. Part of that smile stole into her eyes like a bit of fresh dew.

54

"You think this means you're gonna have to stay with me, don't you?" said Will.

And they drove to 125 Sunshine Ln.

Chapter 11

Will awakened to the sound of rummaging in the kitchen. Drawers and cupboards were being opened and closed. Glancing at the window he could still only see darkness. *What in the name of sense was this child doing now?* he thought. He hoped he would not have to repeat the events of the day before. Thankfully it was Saturday, so he would have time to figure out what to do with Cristina.

"Hello? Everything alright?" he called.

"No!" a small voice answered back.

Will got up and went to the kitchen. He found Cristina standing on a chair peering into one of the cupboards over the sink.

"I can't find anything to make coffee with," she said. "I wanted to get up early and have your coffee ready when you woke up."

Will smiled. "That was very thoughtful of you…but I'm afraid I don't drink coffee. That's why I haven't got anything for making it."

Cristina sighed. "I should have known. It's just my luck. My aunt says that anyone who doesn't drink coffee isn't to be trusted."

"I guess you're stuck with an untrustworthy fellow then. May God help you," said Will solemnly.

Cristina got down from the chair. "I don't like coffee much either. But I wish I could have made you something."

"Well tomorrow morning before church you can make me some toast and a fried egg if you want." He paused. "That is…if we haven't found your aunt and uncle yet."

"What's the plan for today then?" And the two of them sat down at the table.

"I'm still trying to figure that out myself. Have you got any suggestions?" asked Will.

Cristina shook her head—a little too nonchalantly, Will thought.

"Don't you have any friends we could look for? Other aunts and uncles?"

"I have friends but they all live in my neighborhood. If my aunt and uncle's house is abandoned then they're probably not there either. But if you want we could go back. All my other relatives live in Kentucky. By the way, my room smelled so nice, like a perfume store."

"Oh, that's because I put you in Blaze's old room. He uses a lot of cologne."

"Blaze who?"

"Blaze Thunder."

"Really? *The* Blaze Thunder?"

"I guess. Why? You know him?"

"I've seen his pictures. He's a swell actor. Grandma Naomi loves him. She thinks he's a real knockout."

"That's strange…I never would have guessed there would be two Blaze Thunders in the world who are interested in acting. The one who is my friend hasn't actually started acting yet. He wants to, though."

"Do you have a…lady you're going steady with?" asked the girl intently.

"Say! You're a curious thing today. Why do you ask?"

"Oh, just wondering."

Will looked at her and realized that not a trace of fear remained in her. She seemed to have a glint of something in her eyes that he could not quite understand. Her hair was still tangled and her dress needed to be washed and mended. But there was life in her face.

"Well, nosy lost girl, I'm not courting anyone, no."

"I guess that's good. Uncle Ben says that all the trouble in the world that's not about money is about women."

"I suppose your uncle's not far from the truth. But if you *do* find the right woman, let me know."

"I will. You can count on me, mister."

"Good. But you need to tell me about your school. Which one is it?"

"Franklin Elementary." Cristina's expression faded and she looked at the table.

"What's wrong now?"

"I...I don't think we're going to find help there...but you can try if you really want to."

"Why do you say that?"

"It's...hard to explain."

"Try me," said Will.

"Do I look...strangely familiar to you?"

"What's that got to do with it? Are you trying to change the subject?"

"Just answer my question," she said patiently.

"You're a demanding little creature, aren't you?"

"Well do I look familiar?"

"Not a bit, why?"

"Because you look very familiar to me."

"Really? Who do I remind you of?"

"Someone...who is important to me," she said quietly.

Will frowned. "Then I shall try my utmost to live up to whomever this person is." He looked out the window and said, "We need to go soon. I want to see if Sonny is back and get a few groceries. We should buy you some clean clothes to get you through the weekend too."

Sonny and his family were not at home. Cristina made a poor effort at concealing her delight at this providence, while Will was frustrated again. Since there was nothing else he could do, they went to the butcher and bought a pound of bacon, stopped by the bakery for a loaf of bread, and got cheese, eggs, and butter from another shop. At a small market they acquired a pound of cucumbers.

"Do you always cook for yourself?" asked Cristina.

"Almost always. I'm afraid I'm not the most interesting cook. But I survive alright and keep up a good constitution."

"And you eat all alone?" She looked almost pityingly up at him.

"Yes, usually."

"I'm sorry."

"I am too sometimes, I'll admit. Come on, lost girl, let's get you some new duds."

And so it was that Will ventured out into the world of women's clothing for the first time in his life. *Blaze should be doing this*, he thought. But then again Blaze would end up taking them to some place that charged a fortune for something that looked more queer than pretty. There was only one place he remembered because he had ended up there with his mother and sister one day: Gardenia's Boutique, which was on Main Street. As they rattled along in his car on the way Will could see Cristina smiling up at him out of the corner of his eye. This time when he turned to look at her she didn't glance away. She met his gaze with a diffident friendliness that transformed her whole countenance. It was one of those smiles of closed lips, yet utterly sincere.

"What?" asked Will.

She shrugged her shoulders. "Nothing."

Then they were at Gardenia's. Will was nervous. What did he know about buying dresses? He hadn't a clue what he'd say if someone who knew him turned up. He suddenly regretted the whole idea. She had not requested it, so maybe he could back out with some casual excuse and borrow some dresses from Sonny's daughter.

But there she was, staring out the window, happier than he had ever seen her. All unconsciously she reached over and clasped his hand, and his heart played its first trick. With bright eager eyes she said, "Are we going into *that* shop?"

With the stealth of a panther, some kind of joy had crept up and pounced on him. It seemed to come from out of nowhere, like a seed that sprouts overnight when you never knew it had been planted. This natural gesture, this unwitting touch like velvet woven from threads of flame furtively stole its way to his soul. He could not find it within him to back out now.

They got out of the car and approached the boutique. As they drew closer Will noticed how tastefully the shop window was decorated. Fresh flowers were everywhere and many of the styles and patterns on display reflected the floral spirit of spring. Will suddenly saw everything with new eyes. Before, he had viewed clothing stores like this one as cauldrons of vanity which drained away ludicrous amounts of money from his family's coffers. But now it was a land of potential consolation for a homesick girl.

Cristina was wild over the selection. Aunt Grace had always made her dresses, and she never had dreamt of being able to have one from a store. Will told her to pick out two—whatever she liked.

Just then a gigantesque woman walked past them. Sonny would have said that she looked like she was "haunted by broken chairs and mirrors." She waddled to the counter and began fussing that the dressing room was not "roomy enough" and that they didn't carry anything her size. After rudely insulting the proprietor, she stamped her way out the door and dropped her hand bag, scattering a pound of caramel candies over the floor.

Will smirked and let out a little chuckle. "Do you think she's headed for the tent store now?" he whispered to Cristina.

"Shhhh! You're not supposed to make fun of those kinds of people, mister!" she whispered back with a reprimanding expression.

"Ahem…yes, of course, pardon me," said Will, instantly sobering.

She held him with her stern gaze for a moment longer and then slowly smiled a most wholesome smile. She began to giggle.

"This is no laughing matter, young lady." Then he smirked. He couldn't help it. She was still giggling, and it was contagious.

Chapter 12

The next few hours were filled with wonder for Will. For the first time in his life he felt like he was actually enjoying the company of a child. And it was evident that Cristina enjoyed his. He had spent far more on those two dresses for her than he had ever spent on any clothing, but it all had a sense of rightness about it. They had agreed upon a sensible everyday dress of creamy yellow with a fitted waist. Then they found a Sunday dress of purple taffeta with a flourish of scarlet filigree about the neck. The middle tied behind in a black bow, and they had both adored it instantly. With new stockings and a few other articles they had left in high spirits and ate lunch together at Carmen's Cafe. There they discovered that they both didn't like raw onions or mustard on their sandwiches, but they loved extra tomato. Will realized that he could make her laugh with ease, sometimes even when he wasn't trying.

Just when Will had finished saying, "Have a carrot, stick," Mr. Johnson entered the cafe and came over to their table.

"Howdy, Mr. Johnson! How do you do?" said Will. He stood up, they shook hands, and he turned to Cristina. "Allow me to introduce you to Cristina. Cristina, this is Mr. Johnson from my church."

"Pleased to meet you, Mr. Johnson," said Cristina. It was the way she said it that made Mr. Johnson dislike her from the start. The tone was too mature; she was too articulate and sounded much too intelligent for a child. Preco—... he knew there was some accursed word for that sort of youngster, if he could only remember it—and he did not approve of such. Besides, what business had a child in speaking to him before being spoken to? Mr. Johnson barely nodded to her and looked at Will with a bit of surprise.

"I say! I don't recall ever having seen you like this in the company of a child. Who on earth is she and where does she come from? I've a premonition she's not from around these parts."

"Well Mr. Johnson, I'm afraid it's a long, rather strange story. We're both not sure what has happened, but her family seems to have disappeared, and she herself doesn't remember how she got lost."

"Have you notified the proper authorities?"

"I haven't yet. You see, she was rather frightened at first and I think it would have made it worse if I had turned her over to the police. I took the duty upon myself to see her safely home."

"Sounds like quite a pickle, I'll say. She doesn't seem to be from a poor family, that's certain. Dresses like that don't come cheap. Perhaps there'll be a handsome reward for returning her."

Will and Cristina looked at each other, eyes glinting with a secret, silent amusement when he said this.

"You ought to notify the police straightaway. There's bound to be word out by now about a missing child. Where's she staying in the meanwhile?"

Will explained and thanked him politely for his advice.

"That's mighty queer I s'pose. A little girl staying with a bachelor like you's bound to make talk."

And it did make talk, but only because Mr. Johnson ensured that such talk was made. Little did they know that by the time they stepped foot in Dallas Bible Church the next morning nearly everyone would already know that Will was "keeping" a young child. Already some had imagined that Will was planning to adopt her "without having a wife to help raise the poor thing!" Others surmised that it was all a ploy to find a spouse. "Women love a man with children," averred Lydia Belcher. And Mrs. Williams said vaguely, "Isn't that just like a man?" Almost none of what Will had really said had come through to his fellow congregants.

The first comment to Will when they entered came from Lydia Belcher.

"Now Will, I suppose it's none of my business, but you shouldn't be trying to hide this little girl from the police."

Will patiently explained that he was hiding nothing, and that they had notified the police on Saturday afternoon. The police didn't know anything about a recent report of a missing girl. They had said that they would be on the alert for any notices, but until then it was best for Will to keep her. If nothing appeared in a week and no relatives could be found then they would try to find her a good adoption home.

"We want you to feel very welcome here," said the Daltons to Cristina. They looked at her admiringly and took their seats.

Cristina went off alone to her Sunday School class rather reluctantly. Will noticed that she made the other children in her grade look a little plain. She wore her new dress with a graceful distinction and he felt proud. But why should he feel proud? Silly thought. She did not belong to him; he shook his head and drove away the sentiment.

During the Sunday School hour he found it difficult to focus on the discussion. He wondered what she thought of her class and how she might be getting along with the other kids. Was she making new friends? Did she miss him? Because he was, in spite of the dictates of reason, missing her. He kept glancing at the clock. What were they discussing? Oh yes, something from James about the tongue. Mr. Bryant was pontificating and revealing his ignorance of the actual text before them. This was enough of an excuse for Will to step out early. Ten more minutes and Cristina would be back. He paced the foyer and wondered what on earth was wrong with him. Cristina was about to disappear from his life all too soon. He could not deny that her appearance had banished his loneliness. Her advent had set him stumbling into some alien spring where the colors were sweeter and the air brighter. But this was all nothing but folly. Taking a deep breath, he dismissed his thoughts and entered the sanctuary.

People were just beginning to wander in. He took his usual place and waited. Five minutes passed and he was beginning to worry. The service would start at any moment. Nearly everyone had sat down and he could see pastor Ryan getting ready to take the pulpit.

Then Cristina flitted into the doorway. Her face was flushed and she was near. Will could see her looking throughout the room eagerly, intently searching for someone. Then all at once she saw him—*him*! William Millhouse!—and her face splashed with joy like a brook breaking into sunshine. Will smiled and waved as she scampered towards him. But in his heart something was aching.

He had never seen any other little girls act like she did, with such poise throughout the service, crossing her legs with elegance and calm. Will knew that he should be setting a good example, but he could not wait to hear how she had fared in Sunday School. He drew out a notepad from his jacket pocket, wrote, "How was your class?", and then put it down next to her with a little nudge.

She took the pen and pad silently without looking at him and wrote, "Terible. I'm never going back again."

A few more notes were exchanged and Will learned that Fanny Boswell had been mean as dirt to her. She had told Cristina she could not sit next to her and then made fun of her dress in front of the whole class. *Probably because Fanny could never afford such a nice, stylish one*, Will thought. Cristina had spent most of the class period trying not to cry. On their way out in the hallway a boy had stepped on her toe—on purpose, Cristina asserted. Running outside behind the church, she had given way to tears. That is why she had been late.

An old woman behind the two correspondents cleared her throat meaningfully. Will ignored it. The sermon did not seem important at present. Outrage was boiling up inside of him. This small, lost girl had been mistreated and crying all alone with not a soul to comfort or care. If only he had known and been able to offer his shoulder. Pity and indignation slashed through his heart as never before and his pulse roared. Even though he could scarcely keep from shaking he managed to write, "I'm *so sorry*. I won't let it happen again." Glancing down at her, he saw a stoical face, but a solitary tear trickled down from her right eye. Almost instinctively he put his arm about her, she leaned into him, and in that moment he felt like a new man.

At the end of the service Will spoke with a few friends including Sonny, who apologized for having been out of town with his family when Will had needed him. He met and welcomed Cristina warmly. A few other people said hello to her and later huddled together in hushed tones.

Pastor Ryan greeted the two of them at the door. Cristina had liked his voice and tender smile during the sermon, so she smiled generously and confidently up at him. Because she was not yet aware that this was one of her most winning qualities, the unconscious beauty of it left many people humming in their heart and thinking of starlight.

"This is my mystery girl, Cristina," said Will. "I found her on Friday and it beats me what's happened to her. She's lost and it looks like her relatives are lost too."

Cristina and the pastor shook hands. "Howdy, miss! Pleased to meet you. I'd be pleased to meet you a dozen times a day!" She grinned back sweetly with a steady gaze. "I don't know, Will. Looks to me as if she just stepped out from a frame. You're one blessed son of a gun. God isn't in the habit of doling out pearls like her to just anyone, you know."

"Well *I* may be blessed, but let's hope she doesn't feel cursed to end up with a mossy old bachelor like me."

Cristina shook her head passionately and beckoned for pastor Ryan to bend down so she could whisper something in his ear.

On the way home, after a bit of coaxing, Will finally got her to tell him what she had whispered.

Flashing a timid smile, she said, "*I'm* the blessed one."

Chapter 13

Will woke up tired on Monday morning after a sleepless night thinking about what to do with Cristina. At one in the morning, by some impulse he did not yet comprehend, he had lighted a candle and tiptoed into Cristina's room. She needed to be checked on, he told himself. What he saw was a more peaceful scene than he could have imagined. Her long hair, curling at the ends, was scattered around her face, gleaming in the soft light. Standing there silently he marveled at her face which appeared more serene than the songs of newborn angels. His feet felt jubilant at the sight as he listened to her soft breathing. Then he prayed in his heart:

O Lord, hide not your face from her, lest she be like those who go down to the pit. Let her hear in the morning of your steadfast love. Adorn her with salvation.

How long he stood there watching and praying he knew not. Time seemed tangled up. If he had been able to write in his journal he might have written, "I have been wading in eternal shores. I have been breathing the Elysian air of ages gone by. I have been kissed by the wandering winds of paradise." But Will could not write just then. He returned to his room and knew that this surprising joy must be returned and relinquished. To where he did not know. Grappling with disappointment, girding himself up for loss, he prepared himself in his heart to say goodbye. It was not for him to ponder a life that included Cristina. He must not presume that this strange encouragement would last. He steeled his soul against the clamoring objections and resolved to do what needed to be done. Cristina would be given up to a family to be cared for if she could not find her own.

Yet he knew it would be a lie to deny that everything within him rose up against the idea. His thoughts tore at each other for hours and sleep fled from his eyes. Even worse, he could not fully account for any of these sentiments. He hardly knew this little woman. Three days ago she had been a complete stranger to him. But his heart had its reasons that reason could not begin to know. Reason seemed to be just out of reach, or too weak to steer a straight course, and Will resented it. Whatever Cristina was, she was a child of mystery. Her entire situation hung before him as a baffling enigma. And her very person seemed more and more to be the harbinger of some secret that he was almost afraid to discover.

The following week transpired as follows, according to Will's journal:

Monday, April 7, 19__

Went to work this morning, hesitant to leave Cristina alone. She said she'd be fine. Came home to find her surrounded by a pile of my books, engrossed in one of my favorite novels, still in her nightgown. She'd lost track of time and felt bad that she hadn't tried to get dinner ready for me. I said it was fine and I wouldn't have expected that of her; she's a guest. She says she has a bad habit of reading; she could read all day if someone doesn't make her do something else. I said that was probably a good thing. Her reading level seems to be far beyond what I would have anticipated for someone her age. She used to love climbing up the weeping willow in her yard to read for hours. Then she said that her grandma Naomi always reads the Bible with her. Then she said that Naomi always tells her, "Don't ever forget where the dwelling of the light is, Cristina. It's in the face of Christ." I was shocked. I think she noticed, but I didn't explain why. It is the unchanciest of things. It left me reeling inside for some time. What do I make of such a thing?

Tuesday, April 8, 19__

I asked for the afternoon off at work and went home for lunch. I found Blaze and Cristina in the kitchen making something delicious. Cristina had borrowed a cookbook from a neighbor and Blaze had happened by and saw her through the window. She said she knew he was Blaze right away and let him in to get his autograph. Now I have Blaze's awkward, untidy scrawl on the flyleaf of my Greek grammar. C hoped I wouldn't mind and said it might liven up the grammar a bit. Blaze laughed and teased and said he couldn't refuse a little girl such a request. Over lunch C and I listened to Blaze talk as his propensity dictates—on and on. At one point our eyes met and we exchanged a bit of silent, sparkling laughter (at least that is what appeared in her eyes) over Blaze's drawn out monologue concerning the merits of Italian fashion. He likes the dress I bought C and I think he was sincere. He ought to, since I had to dip into my savings for that shopping venture.

After lunch we all drove to Franklin Elementary (Blaze came along because he *still* doesn't have a job. He seems quite taken with C since she is convinced that he really is a picture star). The school was a dead end. No one recognized C, nor did she recognize anyone except the principal and two teachers. They had no record of her enrollment, nor did they know who she was. Strange it is. Then we drove to the police and asked if there was news. None.

Wednesday, April 9, 19__

Mother heard from a friend of Blaze's mother that I am keeping a young girl. First she went by the house while I was at work and told C that she wasn't wanted there and her son had better things to be doing with his time than offering charity to riffraff and that she'd better be going somewhere else. After leaving C in tears she found me at work and demanded that I come to my senses and get the girl out of my house and get on with my life. She could fuss down the side of a barn. It was a sad day and I tried to be patient with her.

Yet how it angered me when I found a hurting C when I got home. I hit one of the walls hard, and when it hurt me more than it did the wall C had a difficult time suppressing a smile. She said I should pray for my mother and I said I was tired of praying for her; she's beyond hope and God hasn't listened to my prayers over the years. C said that was a fine attitude to have and ranted a bit about how I might as well be one of those yellow fellows in China who doesn't know a whit about the power of God. Then she threatened to become a philanthropist if I didn't pray that very instant.

I asked her if she knew what a philanthropist was and she admitted that she didn't but it sounded bad. So I relented and we both knelt down and prayed together right there on the sofa. She ended it by adding, "And please help Mr. Will's unbelief. Amen."

Thursday, April 10, 19__

Another miserable day with Mr. G. Laura asked about C and said that I need to stop dragging my feet and put her up for adoption. I think she's right, but another part of me dislikes the idea. When I got home C had dinner ready. I'm not sure what to call it, but it was tasty even though she overcooked the green beans. She had somehow convinced Blaze to bring her some coffee and we drank some with lots of milk and sugar for dessert. She says she can trust me more now that she's seen me drink a cup of coffee. I made the mistake of asking her what she thought of me putting her up for adoption, and she got very quiet and sulked through all the dishwashing. She seemed like she wanted to say something but couldn't work up the courage. I told her it was the right thing and it had to be done, and she would end up somewhere wonderful. She didn't say much but made it very clear how little she thought of the idea.

Friday, April 11, 19__

Ran into Lydia Belcher and she told me that the longer I keep 'the child' the more it will hurt my reputation. People have already lost respect for me in the church, she says, and I need to give her up. I asked her why such a thing would hurt my reputation, since the Bible tells us to take care of widows and *orphans*. She sputtered and said that it was all right and good for *families* to do so, but bachelors just don't do that sort of thing. "It's simply not done. Folks think it queer." I looked her in the eyes straight as a dart and told her it didn't matter what folks thought and she should come up with better reasons. She suggested letting the Daltons adopt her and I said I'd think it over. I told Cristina about the Daltons over supper and tried to explain what great parents they would make for her. She got quiet again and said she'd lost her appetite, so she left more than half of her plate untouched. I kept talking about how nice the Daltons were and she finally looked daggers at me and said that if I said one more word about the Daltons then she'd just as well run out into that field of rattlesnakes again and ask one to bite her. She stomped to her room and set about reading a book tempestuously. I felt bad and went to Sonny's for some marshmallows. She told me once that she loves them in her coffee. So I made some good strong coffee and took it to her with the marshmallows bobbing on top. I think just the smell of it put her in better spirits.

At about 2:30 in the morning I was awakened by a faint sob and I went to Cristina's room to see what was the matter. With tear-filled eyes she looked up at me and asked if I would hold her for a while. She missed her grandparents and Naomi and her best friend Marley. And she said that she would not forgive me for giving her away. I said that she wasn't mine to give, and she said, "Don't you understand who I am?" She kept repeating that through sobs. I wish I knew what she meant. I asked her and she only buried her face in my nightshirt and wept harder. My own eyes spilled over and onto the small head beneath mine. It was not until that moment that I began to understand the weight of the psalmist's words more fully: "As a father pitieth his children, so the LORD pitieth them that fear him." He knows our frame. He remembers we are dust. The dusty little frame in my arms made me understand Him. There is something about the girlish tears that cuts to the heart faster than anything else. I cried too, knowing in my heart that I didn't want her to leave. Everything sane and insane within me despised the thought. I hugged her tighter and she asked me to pray for her. "It's so hard to love God right now…to trust Him," she said. I tried to pray, but a sudden panorama of glory opened up before the eyes of my heart. I was being changed somehow and I cannot explain or remember it enough. It struck me with unquenchable fear and terrible force that my Master invented this child. And her smiles, her moods, her flowing saline splendor are merely a particle of what He is infinitely. What on earth is this God who fashions girls like her? I cannot fathom the reality—the unveiled, soul-tearing, blinding reality of such a tender God.

Saturday, April 12, 19__

It's done. Went to the Daltons today with a heavy heart and not a few misgivings. They are ecstatic about receiving C into their home. I will be taking C to church tomorrow and they will take her home from there. C received the news much more meekly than I expected and said she respected my decision even though it made her terribly unhappy. All the same, I'm afraid of what she might do. She's passionate and willful, and prone to do something rash.

Sunday, April 13, 19__

Today she was lively enough, but I could sense that most of it was a front. She actually spent time in the bathroom primping, which she never does. I could tell that she knew she looked prettier than usual, wearing her Sunday dress again proudly. I complimented her sincerely, and she looked back at me with a smile that was like a hug and a kiss. But then she said haughtily, "Well I hope it hurts you all the more to lose me!"

At church we wrote a few notes back and forth again. She asked, "Are you *sure* I don't look strangely familier to you?" I thought a long time about it and finally wrote back, "I don't know." Right away she scribbled, "Then neither will I tell you by whose authority I do these things." I asked her why it even mattered if I found her familiar. Then she wrote, "Because I think you're my father." I said it was impossible, and she said she wasn't going to try to convince me; she didn't want a father who doesn't recognize or want his own daughter anyway.

Monday, April 14, 19__

I will admit here what I shall not admit to anyone else: I feel miserable. I know now that giving away Cristina was the worst mistake of my life. The house is back to its lonely emptiness; life has gone out of it seemingly. And just as well. Mr. Perry informed me today that he has sold the house to some big business contractor. I have two weeks to move out before they demolish it.

Chapter 14

Will found that returning to life as it had been meant returning to a flat, rather colorless existence in comparison. He did not like this. He did not like that his contentment hinged upon a little girl who had appeared out of thin air. Somehow he resented any dependence on her for joy, for was his joy not complete and full in God? But Will still had much to learn about means of grace. He, like many before him, would sooner or later come to understand that God paints his perfections upon the panorama of one's life with many different palettes. He reveals himself in quiet, unexpected places—sometimes even outside of books. Will would one day discover that the God who works wonders often prepares his children to receive them by a drab dose of desert.

And so it was with Will. The hours at work dragged as though through quicksand. When he got home he found no tantalizing smells wafting from the kitchen; all his books were where he had left them neatly on the shelf; the lone clock over the mantelpiece seemed to tick louder than ever before. He found the leftover coffee in the pantry and breathed in its keen scent, but did not brew any. It didn't seem right to drink it without Cristina. Some evenings he found himself too weighed down by sadness and regret to eat, so he went to bed early. Yet when he tried to sleep his mind wrestled with wonderings. How was she faring? Were the Daltons treating her well? Did she miss him? Was she hurting with no one to comfort her? Would the Daltons know how to handle her moods?

Every hour seemed to bring a frantic impulse to drive to the Daltons for a visit, but he resisted heroically. He convinced himself that it was better this way—that it would make the transition easier for both of them. *It's out of respect for the Daltons, to give them a chance to win her trust and affection,* ran his noble thought. Whether he had confused nobility with stupidity, the reader will have to judge.

The first week passed and Will skipped church. He did not want to aggravate things by seeing Cristina there. Monday came and he decided to begin packing. Until he found another place he supposed he would have to stay with his parents. When he went into town everyone he happened to see told him he had done "the right thing." Mr. Johnson and Lydia Belcher had other remarks as well, but Will listened not, for he was preoccupied with thoughts of a fair haired girl. Much of this was involuntary, and Will had trouble explaining it to Sonny two nights before he had to move.

"There's something about her...I've never experienced anything like it. It's embarrassing to be so affected by a little girl I only just met."

"I think I can imagine because I have two daughters. Those little rascals really can worm their way into your heart before you know it. It didn't take long before I would've sold all I had to see one of them again—if that was ever necessary," said Sonny. He took a long draught of lemonade.

"But Sonny, this isn't my daughter we're talking about. It may feel almost like it, but it's *not*. That's why it's strange and everyone else would laugh at me if they had an inkling of the truth." Will paused and looked up at the night sky.

"It's as though God has been tinkering with my heart. I don't know how else to explain it."

Sonny looked at him empathetically. "I suppose God does those things now and then. He's got the right to anyway."

"The problem is that I'm haunted by the mystery of her."

"*I'll* say. The whole thing with her missing family is stranger than Dick's hat band."

Then Will told him about what she had said in the wee hours of the morning through tears, and what she'd written during the service. He had kept the slip of paper and pulled it out of his pocket to show Sonny.

"There it is, plain as print. What do you make of that?" said Sonny.

"It's nonsense. Impossible—as I told her," said Will. "But part of me wants it to be true...thinks that it could be true." He shook his head.

"Well, my friend, there are much worse things you could be doing than wishing you had a daughter. I think it's a natural thing—only not all that common for bachelors I'll admit. But hang what everyone else says. *I* think you would've made a better father for her than Mr. Dalton."

Will smiled and sighed. "I only wish I could find out why a child would say a thing like that and mean it. She was dead earnest."

Sonny didn't have a clue either. There are some things in life that cannot be settled even on a beautiful spring evening with glasses of lemonade.

Will drove away from Sonny's with his heart weighed down and a desperate need to pray. He decided to go straight to his dream meadow. There he settled down on a bench and thought and prayed and wrote. The night air played whimsically in the treetops and drifted lazily through his hair. The tang of blossoms floated and danced lightly on the breezes, and Will felt refreshed. He had never taken Cristina there and now he wished he had. They had never even talked about its existence.

Some frogs croaked in the distance. Not a soul had found its way to the meadow but him, and in the peaceful solitude Will wrote from his heart.

> I miss her. There was something about knowing the child that made me more childlike every day. Her quick wit, the way she ran to greet me once with terrifying speed, ready smile, wholeheartedly abandoned to joy and welcome, the way she shook hands with exaggerated dignity at times, or the tilted head and creased brow as she listened to me—it all still calls to me, echoes about me. Who is this fair bit of wonder? This child of shower and gleam? How did she leave a gaping void in such a short time? O God, what am I to do?

Just then he saw a shadow flitting from behind him and he heard footsteps. Whirling around he discovered it to be the very girl of his prayers. He sat there watching her approach, a bit stunned, not knowing what to do or say. Was this an apparition? Before he could decide she had taken a seat beside him solemnly and set a small carpetbag at her feet.

Without looking at him she said simply, "I ran away."

"I suppose I ought to scold you."

"Yep."

"The only trouble is, I've a got a notion to rejoice."

"That wouldn't be proper." She continued to stare at the grass.

"Well of all the geese!" said Will.

A little shadow of a dimple began to grow on her right cheek. She was trying not to yield to a smile, but the smile was gaining the upper hand.

"I put flowers in my hair for you," she said. "I thought maybe you'd decide to keep me if I did."

Then Will hugged her until her bones almost broke and two of the flowers fell out.

"You little whiffet! How in the black cat's name did you find me here?"

She leaned back on the bench and said casually, "Grandma Naomi takes me here once in a while because she likes to remember you. She told me how you used to come here before you died. I just figured you'd be here when I didn't find you at home."

As Will sat there agape, Cristina explained why she had been so afraid when she first saw him. She had always had a photograph of her father on her dresser at her aunt and uncle's. Although it was black and white and faded, she had memorized that face better than her own. That day when he had stopped to ask if she needed help she had recognized him instantly, and, thinking that he was a ghost, had run from him in a startled panic. After she had realized in confusion that he wasn't a ghost and had no harm in store for her, she had immediately begun to study him and warm up to the idea of sharing her father's company—the father whom death had taken from her before she had turned one. He even had the same name. Her last name was Millhouse too. Naturally she thought she might be a little crazy and was not about to tell anyone. Then she had snuck into Will's bedroom one day while he was at work and opened his journal. She noticed that the date was 15 years before what it should be. She had confirmed the year when Blaze came over.

"And that's when I knew that the only way to explain it all was that God brought me back in time to you for some reason. Naomi really is your mother, but it's obvious God hasn't changed her yet. Don't worry. She's going to be a wonderful, godly grandmother one day,…dad." She tasted the last word in her mouth hesitantly. "May I call you dad?"

Will thought hard for a moment in silence. Frank, hopeful eyes stared up at him.

Slowly he nodded and said, "But only if I can call you froglet."

Never mind that he had just heard his early death predicted. Never mind that he had just heard a tale so far-fetched it would make a politician blush. Never mind the Daltons and everything else. She wanted to call him dad!

"Ok, dad!"

"You look like you need a cup of hot coffee with marshmallows. Let's go home, froglet."

Home they went. Cristina had much to tell about the Daltons and Will had plenty to tell about his miserable week and the upcoming demolition of 125 Sunshine Ln. The Daltons had turned out to be excessively normal. "Some spice got left out of the recipe," averred Cristina. They also had a proud cat named John, and who ever named a cat John? But they were kind and generous and thoughtful and warm. All in all they were good people and Cristina was grateful for their generosity.

"But they weren't…*you*. You understand, don't you?" she said.

"Perfectly. We must forgive many people that fault."

"Mhm!" Cristina smiled and sipped her coffee.

"Now, my daughter, what's a man to do when he finds out he's got a magnificent daughter but he's never known a woman? I feel nearly like the blessed Mary herself!"

"I don't know. It's never happened to me either."

"Cristina Millhouse, have I ever told you you're a good egg?" He looked up at the ceiling and said, "This Cristina girl, she's a dandy egg."

Cristina giggled and slurped up a marshmallow.

"Cris, I'm right tipsy with joy at the moment! I scarcely know myself. When have I ever talked this way? I'm amazing reckless just now. I'm bound to do something outrageous! Down with moderation! I think Reason already said farewell."

Will, who had stood up, plopped back down in his chair and ran his fingers heedlessly through his hair. His eyes were shining.

"What'll we do, frog?" he asked. "We've got two days to move out. We could go anywhere, do anything. Whad'ya say?"

"We could find a house in a nicer part of town," she said simply.

"No, no, no, too conservative. Think bigger, Cris girl. Think farther, wider."

"Amarillo?"

"That's better. But you can dream larger, can't you? Let's be outright bombastic. Shoot for the stars, girl. I feel like I've been handed a million dollars. We could go to—"

"Alaska!" said Cristina and Will at the same time.

Chapter 15

Sonny's offer to stay at his place while they prepared for their trip could not have been more welcome. Will and Cristina packed up the house and had a yard sale to get rid of anything that might weigh them down. "Casting off that which doth so easily beset us," Will called it. But his books could not be cast off; it was a parting which could not be borne. So he decided to store most of them at his parents' house.

"Will there be libraries in Alaska?" asked Cristina.

"I certainly hope so, Duck," said Will. "If there aren't you can bury me in a glacier."

Cristina smiled. Ever since she had run away dad had been a little crazier than before…in a whimsical, endearing sort of way. She liked being nicknamed Duck and Frog and whatever other names dad fancied at the moment. He seemed freer than ever, and his heart had become softer than rose leaves. There was more laughter and radiant love in his eyes every time he looked at her.

They bought four fat second hand suitcases with the yard sale money, and decided to call them "telescopes" for the fun of being old fashioned. Every so often Will would call to Cristina, "Cris, my girl, have you seen Saturn's rings yet? How 'bout Venus? Let me know if you see a comet and we'll name it after you."

Blaze came by with two new dresses and a sweater from some store with a name Will couldn't pronounce. They were amazingly sensible looking items for someone like Blaze to buy. Cristina beamed and Will felt a little jealous, but after she put on the lavender one he forgot all about his jealousy and was lost in the pride and wonder of the moment.

"I can't decide if she's real or not, Blaze. What do you think? I've seen her eat, but I don't know if spirits have advanced in their abilities since Jesus' time. But don't you dare twirl about in that dress, Cristina Millhouse! We mortal sops can only behold so much glory and live. When we get to Alaska you can twirl all you want and I shall die having arrived at the threshold of heaven."

Who was this father of hers? She did not completely understand him. But she loved him.

The Daltons were somewhat forgotten for a while in the bliss of the new discovery. Cristina had left a note explaining her travel through time and that Will was her rightful father. We cannot blame them too harshly if they had trouble believing it, and Mrs. Dalton suspected that the child might be "a bit unhinged, as homeless children tend to be." They bore the loss valiantly, but Will was implicated in the fishiness of the whole situation and they never treated him the same afterwards. Even though the Daltons kept their opinions to themselves they had to somehow explain how they had lost their adopted child. The gossip flew and Mrs. Johnson had a spicy earful that week.

"Where there's smoke there's bound to be a fire," said Lydia Belcher meaningfully. "I knew there was something queer about that child the moment I saw her. And what does a boy like Will imagine he can do for a brainsick girl?"

"Saints preserve us!" was Mr. Johnson's original remark.

"What in the name of sense!" said Mother when Will came by to visit. "Is what Blaze's mother told me true? Have you completely lost your mind?"

"I think so. And out of all the things I've lost in life, it may be the one I regret the least. Good morning, dear mother."

Giving her a kiss, Will slipped past her into the house and found his sister Indiana. Together they went up to the attic and sought out some of her old clothes from when she was Cristina's age. The moth balls had preserved them, and Will was thankful to find some jackets and other articles for the winter. Indiana bequeathed them to Will in a bit of a daze, thinking about as much of his sanity as Mother did.

"How do you plan to…to travel and live without income?" Mother blurted out.

"*That* is a good question," said Will. "But as a wise man once said, 'Don't be anxious about tomorrow, for tomorrow will be anxious for itself. Sufficient unto the day is the evil thereof.' Farewell, my beautiful mother."

When the day came for 125 Sunshine Ln. to be demolished, Will and Cristina took a picnic lunch in a basket to watch. They ate their sandwiches across the street while the workers tore down the building. Will had an inkling that he should feel a bit of nostalgic regret at the sight, but he didn't. Instead he went right along feeling like one of the happiest men alive.

"Cristina?" he said with his mouth full.

"Yes?"

"Nothing. I just wanted to make sure it was you."

"Who else would it be?"

"Psyche."

Cristina did not know who Psyche was, but it sounded nice. This was often dad's way. Then they might be silent for the next thirty minutes, but both of them knew they were quietly basking in the other's presence.

"Let's get some ice cream to celebrate," said Will.

"What are we celebrating?"

"You think up something on the way. I'm sure it'll be a good reason."

And off they went.

After licking chocolaty sweetness from the corners of their mouths the two of them got a big map at the general store. They went back home to Sonny's and started planning their route to Alaska. By the time they had gotten to Washington's coast Sonny's phone rang. Mr. Perry was calling for Will. He said that the demolition crew had found something in the rubble—a metal box that he must have left in the house by accident. Will hadn't any idea what it might be so he and Cristina went down to the site to find out.

"It's as heavy as a lead brick," said the worker as he plunked the box down on a bench. Will borrowed a hammer and broke the lock. Opening the lid, he found a gleaming standard gold bar. It was the treasure of 125 Sunshine Ln.

"Sir, I think this belongs to the new owner of this land. It's not mine, I'm afraid," said Will.

"I *am* the new owner of this land, son. And I think it's only right for Mr. Perry to have it. He just didn't look hard enough. It's only fair."

Will took the gold to Mr. Perry and congratulated him.

"You're a rich man now, Mr. Perry! They found the treasure of 125 Sunshine Ln.! Can you believe it?" said Will.

After the initial shock of such news Mr. Perry said, "Now Will, I don't know if I'm more surprised by the treasure or the fact that you haven't run off with it to Mexico by now."

"Why Mr. Perry! I thought you knew me better than that!"

"Oh I knew, but this is something I ain't ever thought a Christian capable of. I want you to have half of it— There, there now, don't interrupt me and don't try to talk me out of it. I've made up my mind. I'm not as young as I once was and I couldn't spend that much money even if I wanted to. If you're as honest as you've shown yourself to be today then there's a high chance you'll do a lot more good with this gold than I will."

It was difficult for Will to believe that Mr. Perry would follow through with his word, especially when he cashed in the gold bar and saw how much it was worth. But the next day, true to his promise, he came to Sonny's door with a chubby envelope and a smile.

"Cristina! Would you look at this!" Will fanned out the stack of bills rashly. "I feel like a bootlegger's wife! And I'm neither married nor a woman!"

He handed Cristina half of the stack. "There, that's yours. Give it all to the poor if you want. I'm already planning to spend most of my half on you."

"We have to count it all carefully and keep an account of all our spending. And we've got to make a budget," said Cristina.

"Sonny, aren't you glad I've got someone with me to talk sense and keep my head from flying off too far?" said Will.

By Sunday they had all their telescopes packed and ready. The route to Alaska was set. They would be taking the train up through the panhandle, cut across the corner of New Mexico, and then up through Colorado. Once they reached the crossroads at Cheyenne they would head west across the southern part of Wyoming, up through Idaho, across a bit of Oregon, and finally reach Seattle. From Seattle they would take a boat to Kenai.

"Once we reach Kenai we'll ask about my father, and then we'll find ourselves a quaint little house and buy it. We'll have more than enough money to do that now. Tomorrow morning is the day. We'll buy our Union Pacific tickets and be off to fairer lands." Will made a grand, sweeping gesture.

They went to church together and managed to resist the urge to pass notes back and forth during the sermon. Everything was working out so perfectly. Will would not miss what his reputation had become in that church, in spite of his attempts to clarify the gossip. Pastor Ryan was frustrated too; he had expected more maturity from certain members.

The time for prayer came and it was announced that Mr. Johnson had just lost his job. His wife was more sick than she had ever been, and he would now be unable to pay a large debt he owed in medical bills. Never had Mr. Johnson looked so disconsolate as the congregation prayed for him. His hair was stragglier than usual and Cristina noticed a hint of tears in his eyes.

That evening Will and Cristina sat on the porch of Sonny's house under the tender Texas sky and watched the fireflies. Their occasional conversations were not always profound, but they profoundly thrilled Will. They sometimes spoke of music, and he sat there, his soul dripping with music as though she had splashed some of herself—the incarnate dancing-tune that she was—on him. He saw her as one of Heaven's purest melodies. For if she was not an angel herself, she must have been an angel's song. In all his life he had never experienced the ardent fondness a husband feels for his wife, nor the instinctual gentle devotion a father has for his daughter, nor even the admiring affection that rises up in a son towards a mother who loves in sincerity and truth. And now all of those sentiments came crashing, bounding into his heart towards this lost girl with the golden hair. Was he a fool? If this was folly he would welcome it with open arms. He whispered an old bit of poetry:

> *Seek not afar for beauty. Lo! it glows*
> *In dew-wet grasses all about thy feet;*
> *In birds, in sunshine, childish faces sweet.*

Cristina nestled up next to him and leaned her head on his shoulder. The natural perfume of her hair flooded his senses. A stray tress blew in the breeze and brushed his cheek. Such are the moments when distant dreams seem nearer, and grace trickles in and springs praise from a torn heart. Will could almost hear the Spirit of the living God whispering, "She is lovely, she is pure, she is commendable, she is excellent, she is worthy of praise. Do you trust the one who made her? He is at your right hand; you shall not be greatly shaken. He is the stronghold of your life. Of whom shall you be afraid?"

"Froglet?"

"Ya?" said Cristina with a yawn.

"I've been thinking about Mr. Johnson. What we have left from the treasure money should be enough to pay his debts."

Cristina sat up and looked at him. "You're really serious? You want to give him all our money?"

"He needs it more than we do. And if we're going to love our enemies we might as well start with him."

Cristina looked off into the distance a little forlornly.

"This is partly *your* fault…," said Will with raised eyebrows.

"Is that so?"

"'Tis. Just seeing you makes me more generous than I've ever been. I have a daughter! And not just any daughter—*you*! God has filled my cup to overflowing on this earthly sphere. What is money to me now?"

Dad had a nice way of blaming you, Cristina thought. And she had to admit he was right. She was proud to have a generous father, and she fell asleep feeling wealthier than the day before.

Chapter 16

Getting ready for a cross-country adventure, Cristina decided, was jolly. She and dad stayed up late musing about what they wanted to see along the way and what kind of house they would find. They both were excited to see moose and snowcapped mountains and the famous northern lights. Together they wrote a letter to Will's long lost father and sent it with only his name and region, hoping a local postman might know where to take it.

Will had a few last loose ends to tie up before he left. First on the list was Mr. Johnson. After handing him a wad of cash that left him tongue-tied Will wished him well and said goodbye. Then he went to the maintenance shop one last time to bid his coworkers farewell. He whistled along the way, knowing he had done the right thing, and happy that he had his savings to fall back on. It should be enough for the remainder of the journey and food along the way. Laura was the first to greet him in the break room.

"If you've come to say goodbye to Mr. G he ain't here."

"Why? He's always here on Tuesdays."

"The mean ole' fool was robbed blind. While he was at work some troublemakers cleaned out his house of ever'thin' he owned. The little family he's got livin' ain't wantin' nothin' to do with him—and do you blame 'em? I reckon he got what he had a comin' to him. They even took the doors off the hinges and ran off with them too."

Will shook his head in astonishment. "I don't know what to say. That's some sad news."

Without lingering too long, he wished everyone good providence and was off. He was riding Sonny's bicycle because he had already sold his car. It had been hard to part with, especially for the little money he was offered. Now he sailed down the road with the wind in his hair and the rear wheel squeaking as he thought hard about Mr. G. When he got home to Sonny's, Cristina was waiting for him on the porch with her nose stuck in a book. Then all at once she was close and he was twirling with her, scattering day.

"You're an antidote to anxiousness, you know that?" said Will.

Her only answer was the laughing silver sunrise shining in her eyes. A girlish nimbus seemed afire around her entire form and Will was happy.

Then: "I missed you, dad." Only four words, but words that sent his soul soaring to alpine heights. Right then and there the most appropriate thing would be to turn and write a song. But she was already towing his hand houseward with hurried speech—she had made dinner with the help of Sonny's wife. She couldn't wait for him to try it.

Inside he listened to more chatter about how she had nearly forgotten to stir this and add that, how she had chopped the onions without crying (with much pride in her voice), and how the dessert had turned out *so* splendidly. Yet all the while those four words still rang in his heart. As he took his first bite after saying grace she gazed at him with a do-you-like-it? expression. He smiled back and nodded. Oh, but the best flavor was still in her words. Had she really missed him? He knew that memories like this would weigh upon his mind like giant diamonds aching to be set in the inferior gold of prose.

"I'm very close to knowing how Mary felt," said Will.

No one at the table had the foggiest idea what he meant. He cleared his throat and exclaimed, "Talk about ambrosia! Of all the feasts of Lucullus! Ye gods, thy table is spread!"

Everyone laughed, and Cristina savored the sense of accomplishment. What transpired while they ate was a friendly philosophical debate with Sonny and much discussion of how they were going to live in the wild frontier of Alaska. Then the family gradually began wandering off to bed. Will volunteered to do the dishes.

"No father has ever been shot while doing the dishes, Cristina. It's a well-known fact."

"I'll dry then," she said. And they went to work. After a few minutes, while scrubbing the bottom of a pan, Will told Cristina about what had happened to Mr. G. Then he explained all the reasons why no one would probably ever help the man.

"My point is that Mr. G is such a miserable dreg of humanity that when he dies no one will come to his funeral.

Instead they'll write letters saying how much they approved of it."

"That's pretty bad," said Cristina gravely. "It sounds like you're gonna have to give him your savings to show him what God is like."

Will forgot about the pot in his hands and looked down at the child standing next to him. Her face was earnest as she returned his gaze with lively blue eyes. She made the little white apron she wore look like a queen's gown. Cristina's soul suddenly thrilled with admiration. There stood her very own *father*, tall, with the yellow light accenting his strong features. His eyes alone said more things than she had ever known eyes could say. Just now they had turned glassy, as though something like love itself were about to spill out. His brow shifted and a tear strayed down his cheek. Most would have shrunk awkwardly under the intensity of his gaze at that moment, but Cristina only basked in it and stored away the warmth in her heart.

"Well if I ever!" exclaimed Will suddenly. "How *dare* you twist my arm, you persuasive old mill-hopper!" But he was smiling from ear to ear.

"Come 'ere!" and he darted to tickle her with wet, soapy hands. She squealed and dodged, and the chase began. He finally tackled her on the sofa in the living room.

"Shhhhhh!" whispered Will as she squirmed and giggled uncontrollably. "You'll wake the whole house!"

Later that night Will stayed up to write. His whole being felt full and more alive than it seemed possible to feel. "My heart is expanding," he wrote.

> Who is this child? I find myself baffled again, searching for some clue to the change, the wonder. Trying to describe the sound of her face is difficult. It is like trying to taste moonlight or recount the mirth of a sunrise. Simply being near her infuses me with innocence. Am I actually to believe that You have tampered with Time to bring her to me? The world scoffs at the notion, yet I hesitate, remembering Zechariah's folly and Sarah's laughter. For this is not much more impossible than the birth of Isaac.

This unfolding wonder is Your gift. And it is a fringe of Your garment. I often feel frightened—afraid because You whom I have come to know seem to have dilated beyond the limits of my mind and conventional theology. It is very similar to the feeling that overtook me when I came to understand and accept the truth of Your absolute sovereignty. For she is like a panther, tiptoeing about devouring small views of God, pouncing on the stingy gods, the loveless gods, the gods who are not lavish beyond one's wildest dreams. What exactly should I do when a young maiden builds siege works around what I thought was orthodoxy? When she pelts it with impossible smiles? These are growing pains. And You are gently expanding my heart with this smallest of creatures. Your strength is in her weakness, and my weaknesses are being demolished.

The next day was bright and burgeoning with blossoms. Spring was pushing in so strong that Will and Cristina almost felt shoved. It was their last day in Dallas before they headed north. They had postponed things long enough. There was a lot to do.

"I suppose I'll be hopping on over to Mr. G's house to give him the last of my savings," said Will. "Are you sure about this, you generous daughter o' mine?"

"Positive," she nodded. "Besides, what's the point of being a Calvinist if you can't trust God to provide for little things like food and train tickets?"

"There now! Where on earth did you get such an idea?"

"I read it in one of your books," she said.

"This one! She's full of wonders!" said dad to the sky. Cristina looked up at the sky too, and then she felt arms around her tight and a peck on each cheek. Then he was off on Sonny's bicycle.

By the time Will had finished all his errands it was time to head to the house of Pastor Ryan. He had invited them to a small goodbye party with some friends and relatives. On the way there with Sonny's family Will told them how it had gone with Mr. G. He had been proud and hardly muttered a "thank you" when he took the money Will offered him. Will had not even expected any words from him at all beyond grunts. But he hoped and prayed that it would be a seed that showed the worth of Christ.

At the party the first thing Will noticed was a strange sound coming from the parlor. When he entered he beheld Sean Rumpel playing the saw, and his tall, beautiful fiancé standing next to him in a dress that would have made Blaze gawk. In fact, Blaze *was* gawking at that very moment. Indiana and Mother and Father also had come, but they were huddling a bit awkwardly in the corner.

"Who's that?" whispered Cristina, pointing at Sean.

"*That,*" answered Will, "is a strange coincidence. I'll tell you all about it later."

Some people from church were there, and Pastor Ryan's wife had made enough deviled eggs and strawberry shortcake and ice cream to feed a small army. There was a little table in one corner piled with gifts, and Will made Cristina open all of them. Indiana had found some lovely shoes in the attic after Will had left, and these she had wrapped for Cristina, although Will was not sure why. Mother and Father gave a simple envelope with money and a letter that read:

Dear Will,
    We think you're mad for doing this, and we don't know what to think about this Cristina girl, but you're our son and we want you to have something to stay alive on at least in this fool's errand.
    Mother and Father

Sonny gave them the best gifts: a brand new blank leather book for Will to write in, and a complete drawing set for Cristina. Blaze gave Will some cuff links which he doubted he would ever use, and to Cristina he gave an autographed picture of himself in a frame. That gift excited her a little *too* much, thought Will. He would give Blaze a hard time over it later. Pastor Ryan surprised Will toward the end with an envelope of far more money than he would have ever expected from an underpaid minister.

"I think you're doing a good thing, Will," he said with a warm smile. "I should have told you this before, but...," he moved confidentially to Will's ear. "I believe you—about Cristina," he whispered.

"But I never told you!" said Will.

"I know. But you know how word gets around. A prophet is never without honor except in his home town. People think you're dippy. I've heard it all—you're a certifiable crackpot, kook, wacko, and on and on. But I believe you. I'm happy for you. Go somewhere to start fresh. It's the best thing you could do with this gift."

"I'm not certain I fully believe it myself," said Will.

Pastor Ryan smiled and raised his glass. "To Cristina then. And to the Lord who brings us miracles in miniature."

Will looked reverent and said, "So be it. To my daughter. And to her maker." And they both drank their sweet tea.

Chapter 17

Will and Cristina awoke the next morning before dawn and were about to head to the train station when the Johnsons came by. Sonny's wife had brought them more vittles for the journey: a box of doughnuts, a pat of butter, some extra peppery beef jerky, a loaf of bread, and some cold chicken sandwiches. Will was so astonished at the gesture that the only thing he could think to do was poke Cristina a few times in the ribs. She jumped and poked him back.

"Got both your telescopes?" asked Will.

"Yep. You?"

Will nodded and they shared a smile that only poets have imagined.

Once at the train station all went smoothly. With their luggage safely aboard and their seats found, they waved to Sonny's family outside the window amid the steam and hiss and echoes of grinding machinery. Were they sad? A little. It was light and momentary as is any sadness that finds itself in a fray of love and joy frantically trying to outdo one another. They sighed together and leaned back in their seats. It was a relief to be finished with planning and packing and preparing. The first long leg of the journey to Pueblo, Colorado stretched before them. All at once they got out their books and began to read. Every so often a lovely vista would come into view and turn their attention to the window.

"Goodbye, Babylon," whispered Will.

He asked Cristina what her book was about. It was one she had been given by Sonny's wife with a tangled plot woven through with risky ventures. As she explained, the train sped past a placid lake. The sun was setting and their gazes could not help but linger and watch the golden sky kiss the water. For them such painted skies sent frissons gasping through the soul, begging to be enveloped by one's whole being. They wondered together the same way.

"*Yehi or*," said Will.

"What?" asked Cristina.

"That's what God said when he made that light." What Will thought was, *And that's what he said when he made you.*

For supper they got out the cold chicken sandwiches from Mrs. Johnson and enjoyed every last crumb. Then they each had a doughnut.

"Duck, there's something about traveling that makes food taste tastier," said dad, licking his lips.

"Mhm," muttered Cristina with her mouth full of the last of her doughnut. When she swallowed she said, "Aunt Grace says mother used to make the best doughnuts in the world. But I was too young to remember tasting them."

Will grew solemn. "When did she die?"

"When I was three."

"I'm sorry. I haven't asked about her before now because it seemed a subject too sacred. I'm still having trouble truly believing that you really are…"

"You can ask me as much as you want about her now," Cristina reassured. "I love talking about mother."

"How did she meet me?"

"I don't know. If she ever told me I don't remember the story."

"Understandable. Did she have freckles?"

"Just a few on her nose and cheeks I think."

"Did she ever have the hiccups so bad that she drank water upside down?"

Cristina shook her head. "What kind of question is that, dad?"

"Ah, my girl, you want to understand the mind of a man—'tis a mysterious thing indeed," said Will. "Well? What of the hiccups now?"

"I don't think I remember that happening."

"Very well. Then answer me this, frog: did her hair make the angels jealous?"

"Of course," said Cristina.

"Did her eyes make the stars sing?"

"Absolutely."

"And what of her voice, Cris girl? What of her voice? Choose your words carefully now."

Cristina didn't hesitate. "It was mist and magic."

Dad clapped his hands and laughed. Cristina loved the full abandon of his laugh. Everything about it was wholesome.

"Great snakes! Where did you steal that from, you darling poet?"

"I didn't steal it from anywhere," said Cristina with a trifle of indignation.

"She's the beatenest little woman alive, I tell you!" said dad to the world outside the window. Just then a man came walking by with a stack of newspapers. Will turned to him and said, "She's a poet!"

The man looked over at the two of them, not knowing exactly what to say. With the same lanky height as Will he had on the uniform of a busboy.

"What's your name, sir?" asked Will.

"My name is Clarence, sir. Me is one a di help on di train. Sir, you want wan newspapah? "

"No thank you. I'd like you to meet my daughter, the parnassian. Now if I could only remember her name…"

"Cristina," chimed in Cristina. With a pretty smile she held out her hand to Clarence and they shook.

"Now where are you from, Clarence?" asked Will. "I've never heard that accent before."

"Jamaica, sir."

"Are you a pirate?"

"Sir? What you say?"

Cristina kicked dad under the table.

"Oh never mind. Welcome to the fair land of the free. What brings you to America?"

Clarence looked around a bit nervously. He was not used to being accosted with questions from the white folks like this. And he didn't want any trouble from the boss. He leaned toward them and said quietly, "Me on me way to Alaska to work and save some money."

"Really? We're going to Alaska too!" said Cristina.

"Yah mon!" said Clarence. "Me wanna get wan job on one of dem big boats. People say dem pay betta dan anyone, an dem want workas bad bad so dem no care if you black or white."

"What are you saving up for? A house?" asked Will.

Clarence looked around again. The coast was still clear. "To go to Hindia as a missionary – a bredren missionary."

"Jumpin' junipers, that's wonderful!" said Will. "Did you hear that, frog? He's a true son of Israel."

Cristina nodded happily. "Can you sit with us tomorrow, mister Clarence?" she asked.

"Me very sorry me can't do dat, missy, we no suppose to talk wit di white people dem on di train. So di boss say. Mi a work fo me ride on di train so me can't chance it."

"That's unfortunate," said dad. "We'll have to sneak over to where you stay when you're not working sometime. Then we'll talk more about India and Port Royal. I've always wanted to write an epic about Port Royal sinking into the sea."

"Yah mon!" said Clarence with a broad smile. And he went on his way.

"I like his accent," said Cristina. And dad nodded.

As the train sped along and Will went back to his book, Cristina grew drowsy and drifted off. He watched her for a long time in the light of the dying sun. Then put down his book, took out a pen and his new leather journal, and wrote.

> The world is shattered with fresh delight. How it is that He molds such miracles out of the dust breaks upon my consciousness like waves of confounding light and beauty. Her smile is eclipsing many things. Her tiny form has cast a shadow over my entire existence, the earth has shaken, the curtain has torn. I am rich with tangible, incarnate grace. Jesus' abundant life is on display in her face. There it is, alive in concrete expression. I see her and feel the weight of unworthiness. My heart flutters and shudders praise. She is a note of unearthly music. And God has sung it.

Will awakened the next morning to Cristina tapping his shoulder. "Dad, you've gotta see this! It's beautiful!" Will got up and peered out the window sleepily. They had reached Colorado. All the hues of spring that Texas had forfeited must have ended up in this place. Will had never seen Colorado before. There were actual mountains like those he had read about in storybooks. They rose above the earth with breathtaking power, overshadowing everyone and everything with proud silence. Little drifts of snow could be seen on their peaks and sapphire blossoms flamed out against their verdant fields. Turquoise and amethyst, lilac and rose met his eyes by turns.

The whole world was clothed with pine and wilderness. Young trees in early leaf spread out their hands to them in welcome.

"Shhhh," dad put his finger to his lips. "You hear that, Cris?"

Cristina nodded and kept her face to the glass. "The wind is calling to us," she said. And dad kissed her head.

She got out her new drawing book and began sketching.

"Are you going to draw one of these sylvan vistas?" asked dad.

"I'm going to try to draw mother. After all, beautiful scenery is only the backdrop for a beautiful woman."

"*I'm* supposed to say that! Stole the words right out of my mouth, she did!" Will shook his head.

"Naomi read that to me once out of a letter you wrote her about mother."

Will did not know what to say, but he could not stop smiling. "Maybe we should write a letter to this mysterious creature of the future. We could write it together and I can give it to her when I meet her."

"But would that be breaking the rules?" asked Cristina.

"By gad! The rules have already *been* broken! Little girls aren't supposed to fly through time and visit their hapless fathers-to-be! At this point a letter won't hurt anyone."

"Alright then. I'll write my part first and then you write yours. But you mustn't laugh at mine if you read it."

"On my honor, your majesty."

"You can just say, 'yes ma'am', dad."

"Yes ma'am."

Chapter 18

They set to work writing the letter for mother together, and it turned out to be rather frisking and frolicsome. Dad kept his promise and didn't laugh when he read Cristina's part. He only shook his head a lot and smiled. Then they talked about Marley, Cristina's best friend in the future. She missed her and was going to have to write her some letters in case she ever got to take them back to the future.

At about five o'clock they decided to sneak over to the cargo car and see Clarence. They snuck successfully, and it turned out to be a ramshackle old car with more colored people than they had expected. Everyone had their own little group where they laughed and talked together. But Clarence sat alone. He explained to them that he didn't fit in with the rest because he was the only one from Jamaica. Cristina and dad pulled out goodies from their pockets that they had brought to share with him: a doughnut wrapped carefully in a napkin, half of a butter sandwich, a big piece of jerky, and an plum. Clarence proved to have a keen appetite and polished everything off before they knew it. Then he told them about his home in Kingston, about the beauty of the warm island water, and about how he used to be able to walk to the beach from his house.

"You must have gone swimming every day!" said Cristina.

But Clarence explained that he did not know how to swim. Most people on the island never learned or were just too afraid of the water.

"So is there a beautiful lass waiting for you to return?" asked Will.

There was not. Clarence sadly told them that the last girl whom he had planned to marry showed her true colors when he had decided to go to India. She left him without giving it a second thought and broke his heart.

"It probably fo di bes," said Clarence. "Me probably a go die on di mission field after some years."

Will asked him why he had chosen India.

"Boy di trut is dat di woman dem in Hafrika and China would distract me too much. But not in Hindia at'all. And Hindia need missionary like any udda place, so a deh mi a go."

Dad tried valiantly not to laugh over this, and Cristina could see him squirming.

"What do you miss most about Jamaica?" she asked.

Clarence missed his aunty who had taught him how to cook. He also missed fresh sugar cane and coconut milk. And he missed the warm weather. "When me di go to Texas, everyone dey complain bout di heat while me di shivering unda a blanket."

When they arrived in Denver they bought tickets to Cheyenne and continued on their way north. From Cheyenne they had to take a train headed toward Salt Lake City along southern Wyoming. There were sprawling skies that left them gasping from the color and majesty. There were green greens and red reds and royal purples that made the world seem like a great palette in an artist's hand. Twice they sped through a deliciously dangerous storm, the rain pelting the windows until they seemed ready to shatter, the thunder making the depths of their souls lurch. Once lightning struck right outside their window and the crack and roar that followed caused more than a few people to scream.

"Did you feel that, Cristina? That feeling that the sound was going to unravel all the cells in your body? That's what it sounds like when God speaks. That's why they couldn't bear it at Sinai."

Then up they went through the southern part of Idaho, with its rivers that spoke poetry to their eyes, its lush plains that beckoned and beckoned, its strange rock formations and exotic trees and sunsets that awakened goodness in everyone. When they reached the northern edge of Oregon they were scarcely prepared for the beauty that lurked ahead of them. The pines and the sheer natural splendor of the landscape nearly made them hop off the train and forget all about Alaska. The air itself made them drunk with wonder. One breath of the pine scented purity, the faint mist of distant cascades, the odor of fertile earth, was like drinking crisp, golden wine.

"I feel like I've got joy in my lungs," said dad.

And he was not alone. The mountains made them question whether they had ever truly seen mountains before. They envied passionately the wild animals who could call such an Eden their home. Dad wanted Cristina to pinch him and Cristina had dad pinch her. So together they sat wide-eyed and well-pinched. Sometimes they forgot to eat because their cups were so full of a light they had never known. By the time they reached the other side of the cascade range and arrived in Portland they had forgotten that they had no money left for the remainder of the trip.

"What'll we do now?" asked Cristina as they stood with their telescopes on the platform.

"Well, let's start by counting what we've got left. Let's see…I've got God, and I'm standing next to the prettiest girl in North America, who just happens to be my daughter. There now, did someone say something about money? I'm still the richest man alive."

Just then a man sitting on a bench called, "Will! Will!" and waved for him to come over. Will hesitated for a moment. He did not know this man, nor did he understand how he knew his name. Reluctantly the two of them approached the stranger. With a large belly and a mustache that could shelter several baby birds, the man proved to be jolly enough. When he saw Will up close it dawned on him that he had been mistaken.

"Will? I'm sorry sir, but I must have mistaken you for someone else. I beg your pardon."

"No trouble," said Will. "But my name really *is* Will. A strange coincidence to be sure!"

"No doubt!" Then the man looked at them both intently. "Is there anything I can do for you? Please, ask me anything and I'll do my best."

Dad and Cristina looked at each other.

"Uh, I'm afraid I don't quite understand what you mean, sir," said Will.

"Well I'll be ding-busted if I didn't say it straight as a string!" said the man. "Do you need anything? Ask me for it if you do!"

So Cristina blurted out that they needed money to get to Alaska. The man smiled at her and said that she should have asked for something more challenging. Right there in front of them he pulled out his pocket book and gave them more than enough cash for their journey. They would even have some left over to buy food. With that he shook their hands, wished them luck, and hobbled off.

"It all happened so fast I didn't even get to pray about it," said dad a little dazedly. "So much for me having a biography like George Mueller. Ever since I met you, daughter o' mine, the world's been turned on its head."

Once they were on a train again dad asked, "Are you still sure you want to head to Alaska? We could always dig up a nice little house somewhere in Portland or Seattle."

"I'm sure," said Cristina.

"Do you really think it could be prettier in Alaska?"

"I read in a book once that it's the most magnificent of all lands."

"Those are mighty high words, duck. We shall see, we shall see."

Once they arrived at Seattle they boarded a small cargo steamer loaded with supplies and bound for Anchorage. The captain agreed to drop them off at Kenai along the way. The two of them had never been on such a vessel before and they watched everything with eager fascination. They thought they had lost Clarence, but almost at the last minute he appeared and asked the captain if he could come along as an extra hand. Will and Cristina vouched for him eagerly and Cristina gave the captain a look that made him think he would break her heart if he said no.

"Alright. Come along then," said the captain. And he went off shaking his head and muttering, "Southerners."

"We won't tell him you can't swim," whispered Cristina. "Your secret's safe with us." And dad winked at him.

As they began their journey past the small islands of the northern coast of Washington it felt as though they were weaving their way through a storm of beauty. Magnificent forests rose up clean and strong amidst the bluest water they had ever seen. There were little detached islets full of silent mystery and allure, and the distant cries of the gulls echoed with some lost secret. They were traveling to the end of the world where the light was sweeter and the colors full of ancient melody. Everything flourished in marvelous luxuriance, from the noble conifers to the creatures of land and sea. Sometimes they could see spiraea and wild rose, yellow mosses and lichens clinging to steep cliffs, and spots of oak, dogwood, and alder. The glacier sculpted mountains of the Olympic Range gleamed white against the horizon, and dad sighed.

"A Godless life is not even half a life," he said with the wind in his hair, standing on the deck under a clear blue sky. Cristina looked up at him. His eyes were squinting and she took his hand. She did not know exactly why he had said it, but she knew he was right. With the cool air rushing about her, her heart lifted up a silent praise to God. This was the first time she had transposed the joy and beauty of the world into praise to the One who had made it. And it would not be the last.

They stopped briefly at Victoria on Vancouver Island, with its quaint cottage homes and abundance of fresh honeysuckle and roses. There were cascades of flowers, flowers climbing, flowers flooding the woodland paths. Red dogwood berries shone out amongst lush greens, and the whole island seemed in a flush of exuberant existence.

On they went, and the air grew colder and sometimes fog rolled in. During such days they retired to their tiny cabin and napped, read, snacked, and talked about more things than they thought possible. They also spent time with Clarence when he was off duty.

One starlit night out on the deck the three travelers watched the moon hide behind a cloud and make it glow.

"So where your wife be, Mr. Millhouse? She a go join you lata?" asked Clarence.

Will simply stared off in the distance and said dreamily, "We'll be joining her. One day in heaven. She's the finest woman you could have met, Clarence. She had wisdom flowing in her veins. And a bit of the dawn too. Am I right, Cristina?"

"Right as you'll ever be, dad."

Will nodded and smiled. "Tell Clarence more about her, frog."

So Cristina did. She told about how she sang and danced in the kitchen when she thought no one was looking. How she loved libraries and bookstores and sometimes would forget to make dinner if she was reading something good. How she laughed with grace and played the piano with elegance. How she always lit up a room with her smile and always looked the prettiest at a party. About the time she burned a hole in dad's shirt with the iron and said a bad word in front of a minister. How she teased and loved Grandma Naomi, how she wept often in prayer, and how she adored the music of Bach.

Dad winced over the last part. "I can forgive her for adoring Bach because she swore in front of a minister," he said magnanimously.

"Didn't you ever fall in love with a lady like that, mister Clarence?" asked Cristina.

Right away he nodded. "Ya mon. She di named Maria. She di come from Cuba but her family di come to Jamaica to live when she di young, so she di speak Jamaican. Me never go forget di time me see her. She di work in di market and she look at me 'n smile. Me neva neva tink about a white girl before dat, but she di special. From di beginin me should a neva take to her cause me know di Cubans neva gonna let their daughter marry no Jamaican. But dey say dey were Christians so me di tink dat I might have a chance. Me called her 'my pearl', and she di love me so much. When we di just meet she di tell me that if she ever cook for me, me would fall in love wid her. She di right, but not only 'cause of her cookin."

After a moment's pause Cristina said, "Then what happened?"

"Her family say she not for talk to me no more. We di still pass secret notes to each other back and forth wid people we di know and trust. But den one day di whole family move back to Cuba and me find out only afta dem leave. Mi neva hear from her for a year. And den somebody me know di go to Cuba for business and find out dat she swear she no marry nobody but me, even though her fada beat her. So me di find a way for go to Cuba and finally find out where she di live. But by dat time she di sick with fever and di doctors couldn help no more. Her fada woudn let me come in for see her, but her mudda di desperate and she di tink dat if she di see me it would help her get betta. So she let me in one evenin when di fada di gone out to drink. When Maria di see me she smile and say she could get betta now. But dat neva di happen. Di next morning she died."

There was nothing to say, so they stood in silence for a moment. Dad reached over and patted Clarence's shoulder, and Cristina sidled up to him and put her arms about him tenderly.

"I'm so sorry," she said. "I'm so sorry." And a tear fell from each of her eyes.

When the days were clear and bright they could see wonderful bays and capes that curved along the water in pristine wildness. Every hour brought more charming newborn scenery that made the usual discomforts of a sea voyage fade to almost nothing. As the steamer glided along the coast the expansiveness of the scenery only deepened and broadened. There was no redundancy but only endless variation of tender art and fine, ethereal nature. Shining waves caressed and frolicked their way to azure headlands.

"You see that point there?" said dad. Cristina covered her eyes from the glare and peered off to the distant rock where dad was pointing. It was jutting out over a quiet inlet and a friendly meadow lay nearby.

"That's Poet's Paradise. There. How's that for a name?"

"I like it," said Cristina.

"And can you see that cascade?" He helped her up onto a pile of rope to see better. She saw it. Hemmed in by spires of spruces was the mouth of a bay carved into solid rock. At its northern edge a brawling river fell like a bride's veil down into the turquoise water. There were steep green velvety slopes and hemlocks that looked like they might be singing.

"What shall we call it?" asked dad.

Cristina thought for a moment. "How about Bridal Bay?"

"Well done!" Dad clapped his hands.

Later that evening dad fell asleep writing. Cristina peeked over at his journal and read:

> Our lives are punctuated by grand glory every minute. We find ourselves dreamily gazing at one masterpiece after another. Let all the earth worship and sing praises to You! For You have filled our eyes with beauty and ever fresh delight. But what is all this grandeur next to the girl standing by me, hair streaming on ocean gales?
>
> For I have a song in my heart. It is a fairy song. It is an old song, yet young and fresh with the dew of yesterday. It is timeless and invasively present. It is a hymn of heaven, a carol of cupids, a chorus of cherubim. It is a strain of ineffable verse, a ballad of cheerful eternity, a sonnet

sung by princes and kings. What is this melodic miracle? Or more precisely, *who* is this miraculous melody? She is a little woman. And she is my daughter.

During that voyage life seemed one endless adventure. When they entered the Wrangel Narrows they held their breath as the steamer crept through the boulders scattered dangerously all about the passage. They listened to the shouts of "Hard-a-port! Steady! Starboard!" as they steered carefully past buoys marking hidden reefs, admiring the captain's piloting skill to guide such a large craft through to safety. Emerging from the Narrows they caught a glimpse of the first noteworthy glacier looming six thousand feet upward. They stood like statues, agape, seeing its serpentine form winding over the mountain and finally disappearing behind the towering splendor of "Devil's Thumb" ironically pointing heavenward at a height of nine thousand feet.

Then before they knew it they arrived at Juneau and took on supplies. While they rested there they heard talk of the legendary city that appeared suspended in the air just in front of the Fairweather mountain range. A gruff old man with a mustache was talking earnestly about what he had seen.

"Professor Willoughby wasn't crazy, I tell you. I was at Glacier Bay and when I awoke one morning I got up and could scarcely believe my eyes! There it was, a city with cathedrals and massive buildings and all European-like. It was all in a halo of light. I could almost hear the bells of steeples in the churches but there wasn't a soul livin' there."

He paused and everyone waited eagerly for him to continue.

"Then, it started movin'. I tried to follow it as fast as I could, being such a glorious sight that I couldn't let go of easily. But it kept movin', and when I started runin' it all a sudden went up into the heavens like a vapor. But it was there, true as life. And me not havin' had a drop to drink that week!"

As they drew nearer the Kenai Peninsula they left their coastal route and cut across open ocean. One night they encountered a storm that left them breathless. Will met it gleefully and held Cristina who was rather frightened. The next day brought them waters so calm that the whole ocean became a giant mirror.

"That's what God uses to admire his own glory," said dad. And just then a whale broke the surface and made a splash that could have capsized a smaller boat.

Then dad changed the subject: "I saw an iguana in Mexico once that you remind me of. His name was Gomez."

"How on earth do I look like an iguana?!" Cristina was not feeling complimented.

"Haven't you ever seen one?"

"Only in drawings. They're ugly, dad."

"Ugly?! That's where you're wrong, my dear. Magnificent and adorable creatures they are. Even kissable."

"Sorry, dad, I'm not convinced. They're hideous. You can call me frog, but not Gomez."

"But—," sputtered dad.

"Nope," Cristina cut him off and shook her head. "I'm not kidding, dad."

"Well, a girl's gotta defend her self-respect, I suppose. But you'll see how cute they really are one day when we find a live one."

They talked about the mysteries and charms of the ocean with Clarence, and Clarence taught Cristina how to dance the Jamaican way. They watched birds of all kinds hover around the boat and sometimes land on its railings. Dad saw an albatross and took to calling Cristina "Albatross" after that. She looked at him quizzically and shook her head, trying to look indignant. But she couldn't help loving him all the more.

At long last they entered Cook Inlet and docked at the port of Kenai. They bade goodbye to Clarence who would be continuing on with the steamer and set out to explore a bit. Wandering through the town made them feel as though they had gone back in time fifty years. The roads were hardly more than pathways, and the area seemed to be so…wild. Yet with this wildness there was mingled a very cordial air of welcome. It was in the quaint log cabins and the barber's cheerful sign. It was in the smiling faces that greeted them as they strolled down the road and in the fat stone chimneys that were part of every home. And it was in the distant laughter of children that they heard.

"This is it, Cris girl. We've reached the end of the world and I couldn't be happier. There's a whole new life ahead of us now. And it's time to ask if anyone knows Peter Edmonton."

Chapter 19

Before they went traipsing about asking for Will's father they decided to stop in at a small restaurant that stood near the water, having famous appetites from all the excitement. A cheery, fair-haired girl greeted them and served them what they wanted. Hot coffee with pancakes and eggs was what they had, and they made quick work of finishing the last crumbs. The girl's name was Daphne Canning and she had a sweetness in her voice that was a little too sweet when she spoke to dad, Cristina thought. Daphne did not know anything about Peter Edmonton, so they paid their bill and went on their way.

"Peter Edmonton?" said an old ship captain named Zedekiah, stroking his bushy white beard meditatively. "Never heard of him. Any relation of yours?"

"He's my grandfather," said Cristina.

"I'll keep an ear out for him then. Lots of independent hunters and wandering gold-seekers in these parts. You never know who'll appear out of the clear blue. Welcome to the both of you. You'll not find a finer piece of scenery this side of the globe, that's for certain. If you've need of a place to lay your head for the night that big white building you see yonder is where you'll find a happy lot. The Baptist Mission. They should have plenty of room for you, and if they don't they'll make some. Ask for Paul—he's the missionary in charge. He'll make sure you're taken care of. And when you want the best salmon in town stop by my place one day. Just ask where Cap'n Zed's place is and anyone'll know. Don't be surprised if someone calls you 'Chechakos.' That's what they've taken to calling newcomers 'round these parts."

After inquiring of a few more strangers as to the whereabouts of Will's father, they decided to see if there was room for them at the mission. As they approached they saw a great white new frame building of about ten rooms, having two large halls, and a pleasant double parlor overlooking the bay, with a good view of incoming ships from the south. Quite close by stood an old block house or fort with an antiquated lock on the door and hundreds of bullet holes in the outer walls.

Before they could even knock, the door opened and they were greeted by a short smiling woman with wavy, peppery hair. She introduced herself as Aunt Kay, and ushered them in. Paul soon came to meet them. Small of stature with a balding head, he made up for his height and hair by warmness of smile and a gentle kindness that could be felt in his words and gestures. Delicious smells were drifting in from the kitchen, the floors were clean and bright, and children's voices could be heard about the halls.

"We're caring for a handful of youngsters who were either abandoned or orphaned," said Paul. Some are Eskimos, some were unwanted, and others were left without parents who died up north looking for gold."

"We shall look forward to meeting them," said Will.

"We shall!" said Cristina.

"I'd like to offer you one of our rooms," Paul continued, "but I'm afraid with all the children and a few other boarders we're full. But we do have a place in the attic that's clean and that might meet with your approbation."

Cristina got a thrill over how he said the last part. It sounded very elegant.

"Would you like to see it?" asked Paul.

They did. Up they went and found a cozy area with just enough light from two small windows. From the rafters hung curious articles of apparel made for the winter months, some of them being skins of spotted seal or wild reindeer. There were old mittens and mucklucks in numbers, many in need of mending. There were also other furs and canned goods of every sort. Although there were no beds Paul assured them that cots could be found for them, or they could use some soft furs for cushion on the floor if they preferred to sleep there.

Cristina and dad looked at each other and both instantly knew what the other was thinking.

"We'll take it!" they said nearly at the same time.

At about quarter to ten, when all in the mission had gone to bed, Will and Cristina slipped out onto the veranda. They were there to watch the lowering sun, sinking so slowly it seemed that God was savoring the moment. They sat and tried to stretch their hearts to absorb the sight. Cook Inlet stretched before them in dazzling quicksilver. Beyond the water snowy mountains rose up in mist and power. The sun was hovering just above their proud peaks, igniting color and casting flaming gold. Beautiful hues flowed above them in the broad expanse of the sky, and they were silent. The extreme distances, the majestic grandeur of the ranges, the untamed light were greater than anything they had ever seen before. And like many a traveler before them they grew weary with wonder and sought relief in sleep.

In the morning they met the mission's seven children: Alison, Elizah, Olive, Anernerk, Akiak, and four year old twins Tara and Tommy Diddle. There was much hustle and bustle around the breakfast table, and they all eagerly devoured the oatmeal and biscuits Aunt Kay had made.

"We must go and buy us a house soon, frog," said dad. "How much have we got left to spend?"

Cristina had counted their money the night before. It was about enough for a few more meals. "Not nearly enough to offer for a house," she said, looking a little forlorn.

"You look and sound like one of the disciples. Five loaves and two fish, my girl. That's all we need."

They told Paul and Aunt Kay about their quest, got some good advice on where to start, and set out into the blossoming world. Daisies and buttercups seemed to be popping up everywhere. There were blue bells and paint brush and lupine that splashed the fields with glory. Not very far to the north from where the Baptist mission stood, they entered a clearing and saw a house that looked abandoned.

"What do you think?" said dad.

"Not enough trees around it," said Cristina.

"And you can't see the ocean from the window," added dad, and Cristina agreed. "Well, I'm glad we got that settled. I like house-shopping with you, you young sock."

"*Young sock*? Since when am I a young sock?" Cristina exclaimed.

"Well, you're certainly not an *old* sock," said dad. And he picked her up smiling and swung her in a circle before she could protest.

"Now if we want a view of the ocean we'll have to hike up to higher ground," said dad.

Up to higher ground they went and they found it there waiting for them. It was higher ground, but there was no house.

"What if we built a house?" wondered Cristina aloud. "Isn't that what you used to do at your job, dad?"

"Not exactly. But I did learn an awful lot more about tools and wood and things than the average fellow."

"If we built a house ourselves then we could make it perfect. We could make sure it had magic about it. We've got all summer after all, and we wouldn't need to pay for it all at once."

"She reasons like an woman who knows her onions," said dad to a nearby squirrel. To Cristina he said, "But it'll be backbreaking work."

"We'll have friends to help us."

"But where will we stay in the meanwhile?"

"In the mission's attic, of course."

"But we haven't got any tools."

"We'll borrow them."

"But how will we pay for the materials?"

Cristina put her hands on her hips and looked at him with a tilted head and raised brow. Dad glanced back at the squirrel who was watching them. "She's got me in my own trap! And they never taught us in school how to argue with girls from the future.

"Alright, Cris girl, I won't deny you've beat me. You've got too much lawyer's blood in you—and there's no telling where you got that from."

Chapter 20

If Cristina had known exactly what was involved in building a house, she might not have pushed so enthusiastically for it. Her head soon swam with the amount of planning, preparation, and details that needed looking after. But dad made it all seem like a breeze and she admired him all the more. Oh how their days quickly filled with things to do! There were people to meet, conversations to be had, a blueprint to draw up, games to be played, letters to write, and chores to be done. All the while they kept asking if anyone knew Peter Edmonton. And without telling each other, both of them secretly kept an eye out for a fair woman named Meadow—mother. Cristina's attempts to draw mother were still not successful. In frustration she had thrown several of them in the fire already, saying they didn't come close to the magnificent reality. One day she decided to write a lengthy epistle to mother while dad was away making arrangements for lumber. By the time he got home he found her asleep, pencil still in hand, and some sheets filled with her clear, dainty cursive. Careful not to wake her, he took up the pages, tiptoed to the window, and read:

Dear mother,
    I love you. I wanted to set that straight before I wrote anything else, since this is the first letter I've ever written you. I love dad too. Isn't he a brick? I understand why you married him. Me and him get along real swell. We're here in Alaska now. Kenai is the town where we decided to live. You would say it is beautiful. There's not really anything that isn't beautiful here. Dad speaks poetry about it all the time. He writes psalms to God about it even. I bet you never saw flowers like the ones here. I don't know all there names yet but there are ever so many colors. There's white ones with yellow in the center, pink showy ones, and blue and violet ones where the bees love to go. Then there are

yellow ones along streems and delicate purple ones the butterflies like. There's red and cream and different shapes. And there's a pretty one Mrs. Little Mickey says is called an "Arctic Daisy." Doesn't that name make you happy? Mrs. Little Mickey is fine as floss, as dad says. She's not really little. The whole Little Mickey family is big and fat and they live very close to where our house will be. Elizah says Mrs. Little Mickey is the best cook in town. I think it's true. Her husband is a butcher and they have three sons and four dogs. One son is Gids. He's my age. Right now we're staying at the baptist mission with Mr. Paul and old aunt Kay. Their also very pleasant a generous. Dad says he'd merry aunt Kay if she was younger but she's too old so you mustn't worry. And I'm here to make sure he doesn't merry anyone else. I've heaps of friends already. Elizah is my best friend. She is an orphan that Mr. Paul found when she was a baby. Somebody didn't want her. She's an Eskimo and she's six. I think she wants to be like me. She follows me around and tries to do everything I do. She even wants to make her hair golden and she can talk up a storm and is real sweet and hugs me a lot. Dad says she's sensible for liking me so much. Captain Zed says dad's awfully biased when it comes to me. Is that a good thing, mother? Cap. Zedekiah is very old and has a white beard. He cooks us fresh salmon sometimes and tells corking stories about when he was at sea.

We live at the mission right now while we're building the house. There are other orphans there besides Elizah. Alison is a girl my age but she doesn't like me. I don't know why. But Tara and Tommy do. They're twins and catch frogs for me. They say frogs bring you good luck. Twins are jolly, don't you think, mother? I wish I had a twin. Olive Peachy is 12. Her parents died in the gold rush up in Nome. She's very very pretty and proud about it. She makes me feel insignifacent sometimes. There are two more Eskimo children at the mission who are orphans. Anernerk is five and her name means angel. Isn't that splendid? And there's a boy who's name is Akiak. I think that means brave in Eskimo. He's nine. Their both quiet because they don't speak English very well yet.

Guess what? We're building a house! Hopefully you'll be able to live in it too someday. I think it will be lovely. I'll be sure to make the kitchen extra handy for you. Even though we got here without much money God has helped us. We thought we would have to buy the land where the house will be, but it turned out that we only have to live on it for a certain amount of time and take care of it and it's ours. Dad is working hard and lots of people are helping us build. The Big Mickeys have donated some things because they own the general store. But the Big Mickeys aren't really big. They have rabbits, cats, and lots of chickens. They have four daughters. Faith is nine. Then there is Hope, Charity, and baby Dorothy. Dad says that I've got more faith, hope, and charity than all of them, so he doesn't need any more daughters. Dad says things like that. Faith likes dad lots. She's a tomboy and cries every sunday when her mother makes her wear a dress. But she comes and helps when dad and the men are working. She fetches them nails and hammers and saws when they want them.

Mr. Sam helps us with the house more than anyone. He's an Eskimo from far up in Nome. He rides a unicycle around town because he bought it from a miner who used to be in a circus and needed money. He taught himself to ride it and he's nifty on it now. Dad says he has stentorian risibles, which I think means he laughs loud. He really laughs about everything. And he's always talking about politics and interesting stories from the past. But he knows a good deal about building houses. Brook is his granddaughter and she's sixteen. She's very tall and seems self conshus about it.

The Billy Jims don't know a thing about building, but they bring food to us while we work. They have five children. They give us heaps of advice about living in Alaska. They say lots of people have died in Alaska because they didn't know enough. I wish they wouldn't tell so many sad stories about people dying. Once in while Titus Pepper comes to help. He's old and his wife died. One day we're going to go fishing together and he'll teach me. Dad says he's sensible too.

(This letter is longer than any I've ever written in my life!) We have another friend who helps us sometimes who's name is Cousin Noah. I don't know who's cousin he is but everyone calls him that. Noah's very white. He used to be a gold miner and people say he's filthy rich. But he doesn't act or dress like a rich man. Then there's Mr. Gomez who is from Mexico and always forgets that we don't understand Spanish. And there's George Ross who everyone calls the town grump. Mr. Sam says he's an atheist but when he's drunk he believes in God. That's when he comes and offers to help but dad doesn't let him. Then when he's sober he only stops by to criticize. He reminds dad of an old boss he had and we pray for him sometimes at night before bed. We also pray for a man named Young Jim. He doesn't seem very young anymore but he's a hunter. He brought us some fresh raindeer meat once and dad found out that he doesn't know Christ.

I don't think I've told you about Miss Knox yet. She never married because she acts and talks like a man. Her favorite thing is to go out for days to hunt. Then she sells the furs and the meat. She's killed bears and moose and foxes. I never knew there were so many kinds of foxes. She says the black fox has the most valuable fur.

Dr. Snodgrass is the town doctor and I like him. He gave us some furniture that he wasn't using. He's a kind man. Uncle Rockefeller is also a kind man but he loves to argue. He comes to the mission and stays up late arguing about theology with dad. He never stops smoking his pipe. But he brings me peppermints. Dad says he's sensible for doing that.

It's getting late and I'm very tired, mother. I love you. I can't wait for you to meet dad. Do you know that I love you? I do!

Love, Cristina

Will finished the letter with a sigh and a grin on his face, thinking that he must remember to make a chart for his daughter on the use of *their, there,* and *they're.*

"What a girl," he whispered.

Chapter 21

With the help of helpful and handy neighbors and a little of his own gumption, Will got on just fine with the construction of the house. The town folk called the area where they were building Aspen Aisle. This was because a clump of slender aspens had grown up together in a small level place that looked out over the bay, and there was a natural passageway through the midst of them that looked like an aisle had been cleared. They were spread out enough to leave room for a modest house without the need to cut down any of them near the edge of the ridge. After clearing a few juniper shrubs they had a perfect plot from which to see the water and also enjoy the trees. The entire grove would be their backyard and they would have plenty of water from a small brook that fed into a pond beyond the aspens. The trail wound its way up about a quarter mile from the dock, and their nearest neighbors just happened to be the Baptist Mission.

Just now the aspens were all in a flush of luxuriant green, shining in the long hours of sunlight like deep jade next to the blue water and sky. Lashings of magic were about the place, and everywhere Will and Cristina looked they found beauty to infuse them with energy to work. Yet they seldom felt that they were working. The cool air, the tender rustle of the breeze, the wildflowers always in sight all combined with the singular exhilaration of knowing that soon they would call such a place "home." And so the work slipped naturally and effortlessly into pleasure.

"You were right, duckling," said dad one day as he sawed away at a piece of wood.

"Was I?"

"Alaska *is* the fairest of all lands. No doubt about it now. But now I'll never stop wondering why anyone lives in Texas...."

"Or any other state for that matter," said Cristina.

"I suppose we'll find out when winter comes."

Many hands made light work and Cristina made sure she was part of all of it. When the men lifted heavy beams, she lifted too. When dad hammered, she hammered. If a shovel was free she would wield it with all of her strength if needed. The month of June came to a close with their house nearly finished.

"She's got spunk—a capital girl," remarked Cousin Noah. "Her mother must have been first class."

"A finer woman I never knew," said Will.

"I've been meaning to ask you something. What would you say to a trip up north to Anchorage in my boat—you and your daughter and me? Seeing as this house is nearly finished we need to fill it proper and paint it and get a few odds and ends for the winter that the Big Mickeys haven't got at their store. In Anchorage they've got more to choose from, and a bit cheaper too."

"Well, I should consult my daughter, the financier," said Will. He called her over from where she was busily sanding a countertop and asked her about the idea. She shook her head.

"I'm afraid we haven't the money for any of that right now, Mr. Cousin Noah," she said.

"But we're much obliged for the offer!" added Will.

"I'm afraid I wasn't exactly clear." Cousin Noah cleared his throat and smiled. "You see, it wouldn't cost you a dime. I'd foot the bill and we'd get you stocked up on whatever you need. This young lady ought to have a decent kitchen and pretty curtains as any woman has the right to. And a good, warm bed if I might say so."

Will was left a little speechless and Cristina had to pipe up for him. "Then we'd love to! Thank you!" she said, smiling up at him. And as she did so an ocean breeze fluttered her hair and made it glitter in the sun. Cousin Noah walked away grinning and wondering why he hadn't offered something like that before.

The voyage to Anchorage took place on another day of clear skies and winsome weather. Right away they noticed that Cousin Noah's yacht was more than a trifle nicer than the cargo steamer they had taken to Kenai. Northward they went with their host at the helm telling them stories about his mining days and pointing out different landmarks along the way. They saw the town of Nikiski and the mouth of the Swanson River. And he told them about how the Cook Inlet got its name.

"You see, years ago there was an explorer named Captain Cook. He was one of the most daring English navigators of his time, along with Bering. But he came to a rather ironical end. On his return voyage it is said that he was *cooked* and eaten by the natives on one of the *Sandwich* islands."

Dad laughed. "If I didn't know better I'd say that was a rather contrived piece of fiction."

"The truth is often more bizarre," said Cousin Noah. "But as you've probably learned by now, Alaska's not for the feeble of heart. It's a man's world. And to live in a place this beautiful has its sacrifices. You'll rarely find women folk up this far unless they've been dragged here by some husband who don't give her no choice. They say Alaska's ninety percent men, and I've no doubt there. And the few women 'round these parts who ain't married ain't a sight prettier than the fish we catch."

Anchorage turned out to be another picturesque place, only it was much bigger than Kenai. After they explored the area for a while, they headed to the mercantile where Cousin Noah said they could find just about anything they needed. But what they found waiting for them at the Star Mercantile was not what Will had expected. A young woman greeted them as they came in, introduced herself as Evangeline, and commenced to help them find everything they desired. She had low, straight brows and a complexion of nothing but lilies and cream, and Cristina noticed dad's attention drawn to those details.

There was a melancholy surprise every time one looked upon this woman. Her large, brooding eyes made one feel as though some previously unknown void of the heart was suddenly awakened. She had entrancing features and a delicate form to which clung a dress of lovely saffron. Dad was suddenly very quiet, which was *not* like dad. And so Cristina kicked him while Cousin Noah was asking Evangeline where they might find some good sharp kitchen knives.

"Her name's not *Meadow*!" she whispered.

Dad pretended not to understand what she was talking about, which made her even more angry. "Of course it's not Meadow. It's *Evangeline*. Isn't that a lovely name?" he whispered back.

"What are you two whispering about?" broke in Cousin Noah.

Evangeline was looking at Cristina with a cheerful kindness that melted her heart when she saw it.

"Oh, we were just trying to remember if miss Evangeline had given us her last name. It is *miss,* correct?" said dad.

When Cristina expected to see Evangeline blush prettily, she saw her expression change to a hard, pale one.

"Yes, it's miss. Miss *Schoenkopf.*"

"German!" said dad. "I've heard they're some of the most beautiful people in the world. I'm assuming you know what your name means?"

She nodded unsmilingly. "I do."

"Well it's fitting," said dad with his most charming smile. But when he looked straight into her eyes he did not encounter welcome or shyness, rather a closed darkness.

Just then Cristina dropped a hammer on dad's foot. Dad yelped and Cristina attempted some sort of apology for her clumsiness. But they both knew it wasn't an accident, and Cristina gave him a warning glare that sobered him for a bit.

While the two men were calculating how much salt and canned goods they should store for the winter, Evangeline's hand began wandering to Cristina's hair, but then stopped abruptly. Then she bent over and whispered in Cristina's ear. Cristina nodded a bit hesitantly and the older woman beckoned, looking at her with a reassuring smile, and the two of them hurried up into the storage attic.

"Here's where the best fabrics are. We never keep them down below because women come in so seldom. I've just been aching to see this made into some lovely curtains," said Evangeline, holding up a roll of pretty peach cloth. "It's simple and clean, and I love the color, don't you?"

Cristina had to admit that she did, but she tried to hold back any enthusiasm.

"This could be for your bedroom, and this red fabric will be perfect for your kitchen. It will combine nicely with all the other lovely colors in the fall outside your window and contrast with any wood furniture inside."

Evangeline kept bringing out other options for sheets and then asked if she would be needing any yarn for knitting.

Cristina admitted that she did not know how to knit or sew, but she intended to learn how as soon as she could.

"I'd be happy to show you. I'll be coming to Kenai soon to teach at the school. I'm only working here to earn a little money before I make my way down to start my real employment."

"Thank you, but Aunt Kay—a friend of mine—is already going to teach me," said Cristina.

"Well I'll be happy just to have an acquaintance when I arrive. It's comforting to know that there are people like you in Kenai. I can't wait to see your new house. You're awfully brave to move up here. Did you already have family or friends in Kenai?"

"Nope. It's just the two of us—dad and I." Cristina fought the impulse to confide all her hopes and fears to this woman. She knew instinctively that she could trust her, but she resented it at the moment. She wanted mother, and not this...this imposter.

"I rather suspect something about you two."

Cristina stared back at her a little blankly.

"You're Texans, aren't you?" said Evangeline.

Cristina sighed. "Yes," she answered a little forlornly. "But how did you know? You only just met us."

"I could hear it in your accents," she said, smiling brightly.

"Really?"

"Really. There's no mistaking it. And I think your eyes are lovely. They remind me of a poem I read once—'dew-lit eyes', the author described them."

"Thank you," said Cristina.

"Are you two going to visit the bookshop while you're in Anchorage? I've heard they've no library or bookshop in Kenai."

"I'll have to ask my dad. He'll probably want to go. He lives to read and reads to live, he says. And he said that if there aren't any libraries in Alaska then I should bury him in a glacier."

Evangeline laughed. *Oh no,* thought Cristina, *her laugh is lovely.* If she had used dad's words she might have said that this woman's laugh blossomed full and without any control save that of a sweet gracefulness that rang and sparkled from her soul. But then again, Cristina was not dad.

"I once knew a—someone—like that...." Evangeline peered out the small attic window and pensiveness darted over her face for an instant. Then she glanced back at Cristina and smirked. "And I'd be willing to bet you're the same way."

Cristina nodded and smiled weakly.

"Well when I come down to Kenai I'll have my modest library with me and you'd be most welcome to it."

Cousin Noah insisted they get everything that was even hinted at, including the cloth for curtains and sheets, and even some yarn and a little extra fabric for some dresses. He also insisted that they both select a pair of mukluks for the winter, even though Will and Cristina could not remember ever wearing anything more strange-looking or awkward on their feet. Evangeline helped them load their purchases onto a wagon that would take everything to the boat, and then she directed them to "The Reading Moose" secondhand bookshop. Being surrounded by books again and not having Evangeline around was a great consolation to Cristina, and she soon cheered up again. Each of them picked out a book, including Cousin Noah, and they spent the night in town at the cozy home of a friend of his. The next day they journeyed back to Kenai.

As Anchorage faded from sight, Cousin Noah lit his pipe and propped up his feet on the boat's wheel. "Did you cast your optics on that Evangeline girl at the mercantile?" he asked Will. "A right high steppin' cat's whiskers beautiful girl if you ask me."

Will raised his eyebrows and nodded, staring off at the silver water and snowy mountains.

"But mark my words: no woman like that wanders into Alaska for no reason. No sir. Those kind of women are here to escape ghosts of their old life. They might be peaches and roses on the surface, but underneath.... I'd stake a good steak that she's running from only God knows what. It's always that way up here. The women folk don't come here lookin' for love. They come here because love let them down. Or worse, they come here lookin' to break a man's heart because some worthless cuss broke theirs. That's about the size of it, son. I've seen it time and time again. Some of them even turn out to be murderers, runnin' from the law. And take our own Miss Knox for instance. Only the good Lord knows what specters she's got in her past. No sir, there's something fishy behind most of them. Take it from me, and don't go stirrin' up trouble with any of them. It ain't worth the botheration."

Will listened and knew Cousin Noah was right—about Evangeline at least. He had seen it in her nervous demeanor as they said goodbye. He had felt it in the slight edge of her voice as she told them where they might find a good eatery. Most of all, he had noticed it in her cold gaze and knit brow as she stood at the doorway watching them leave.

Chapter 22

They moved in the next week. The things they had gotten with Cousin Noah all fit splendidly with the little house. There was plenty of canned stuff in the pantry now, and the bedding was fresh and comfortable. Cristina felt that living in a palace could not be grander, and dad said that they would have trouble entering the kingdom of heaven now that they lived in such marvelous luxury. Cristina reveled in how comfortable the gingham dresses were that they had picked out in Anchorage, and she flitted about the house "like an arctic fairy," as dad put it, tidying, cleaning, and preparing her kitchen to be useful. Old Aunt Kay secretly slipped her a copy of *The Beginner's Cook Book* and told her that she would make a fine lady of the house. Elizah gave her a bit of money she had saved up along with her best egg laying chicken and a dozen eggs. And old Titus Pepper handed her an envelope with a bill and a note in it. When dad read the note he said he didn't know whether he should be jealous or happy that old Titus was a very sensible chap. Tara and Tommy, the Diddle twins, brought a pail with sundry frogs and toads for her, "to put in the garden," they said.

The house-warming party for them was arranged by missionary Paul, and even the people who didn't like newfangled folk in town came. People brought food and supplies until Will and Cristina had no idea where they were going to store it all. The Big Mickeys spoiled them with fresh loaves of bread, flour, bacon, baking powder, beans, dried fruit, dried vegetables, butter, sugar, condensed milk, tea, and coffee. The Little Mickeys brought them salt, pepper, matches, mustard, cooking utensils, and dishes. Cousin Noah had already bought them woolen blankets, a few oilskin bags, and various tools, among many other things. Mr. Sam gave Will a knife with an ivory handle and to Cristina he gave a hatchet. "You never know when a girl's gonna need one," he averred. Cristina especially loved a small polar bear Anernerk had carved out of whale bone for her, and Gids Little Mickey gave her a beautiful black fox skin he had hunted himself. He also included a heart shaped note that dad couldn't help teasing her about. Captain Zed brought them the practical gift of some mosquito netting, Uncle Rockefeller made sure they had some basic medicines on hand, and the Billy Jims scraped together enough money to buy them each a pair of rubber boots and snow glasses.

There were more pies and treats there than anyone could eat, and everyone milled about the yard, leaning against the aspens and chatting, looking out over the sparkling water, expressing approval and delight over the charming two-bedroom house. Missionary Paul gave a little speech that made Will's eyes get misty and Cristina squeezed his hand. And afterward Paul handed them a hand-carved cedar box with two eagle feathers in it—one for each of them. The feathers were beautiful. Included was a note that said, "Consider the birds. Exodus 19:4. With love, Paul." From Daphne Canning Will received a squirrel skin tobacco pouch which the Eskimos call *tee rum i ute*. And so it was Cristina's turn to tease him about that. George Ross brought nothing, and everyone was thankful that he had drunk enough to be in a mood where he believed in God and was quite cordial.

As the party went on Elizah and some of the other Eskimo children wanted to dance, along with Mr. Sam, so they set about doing so merrily. As Will and Cristina were soon to learn, dancing is the principle amusement of the Eskimo, and it takes very little to get them started. It usually involves much jumping and hopping about and is always a fine display of joy as they sing their own traditional tunes.

It soon grew late and the crowd of visitors began saying goodbye and heading home. By nine o' clock dad and Cristina were left alone on their small veranda, the sun still shining brightly over the inlet. The wind rustled gently in the aspens and dad's arm was about Cristina, and they were happy.

"We're going to have to spend the rest of our lives saying thank you—to these people and to God," said dad.

Cristina hugged him and looked up into his eyes. "Will you carry me over the threshold?" she asked.

"Only a fool could refuse you that," said dad, and he picked her up and went inside. Cristina has nearly trembling with delight. This...this was *home* now. She had a home with her very own father.

Dad set her down and there were tears in her eyes, but she brushed them away and they both frolicked through the rooms like children laughing and hollering, "We have a home!"

Then dad bowed and said, "All hail the blithe queen of Aspen Aisle."

"Nope, I'm just the princess," said Cristina. "The queen has yet to come."

"Ahem, of course. All hail the blithe *princess* of Aspen Aisle!"

"Oh dad, I think this house is glad to have us, don't you? It seems like it's been longing for this moment."

"My daughter is rather sentimental," said dad. But she knew he understood.

The front room had a comfy reindeer skin loveseat and a big window from which to watch the sun set over the mountains. There they sat as the night grew late. The walls were mostly bare still, but the curtains Evangeline had picked out added lovely color to the rooms.

Dad said, "I wish Evangeline could have come to our party." But Cristina did not hear him. She was already fast asleep on his shoulder. He carried her to bed, tucked her in, and kissed her forehead. Then he lingered there, unable to move because of the tangle of glory in his soul. He stood watching her sleep, praying fervent, grateful, silent prayers for her. "May the steadfast love of the Lord abide in this house," he whispered.

Finally lying down in his own bed he savored the feel of the mattress. It had been a strenuous day and it was pleasant to lie in this comfortable place, watching the moonlight flicker leafy shadows onto the walls and know that his daughter was near. 125 Sunshine Lane now felt like a lifetime away in some distant, nebulous dream. The crowd of noise and ugliness that once surrounded him had been replaced with the whisper of the wind in the trees, the far off call of the ocean, and rapturous landscapes of untold, persistent beauty. He took it all and wore it over his soul as a garment of praise. Not even his dream meadow did he miss. It had only been a shadow and foretaste of this place. He now lived in a land a thousand times more glorious than that meadow, with a glory that permeated the air. There were open fields where he could run right now if he had the notion, and instead of iron fences and locked gates he was surrounded by friendly trees and floral songs. And yet he kept coming back to the thrill of the thought that *she* was here. The staggering sweetness of God frisking in the form of his own daughter. He thought about her eyes that shone like droplets of happy twilight, melting moonlight kissing the rush of daylight. About the waves of wise and playful enchantment that seemed to wash her face. When he saw her amaranthine grace he now wondered if he had ever seen beauty before. And when he loved her he wondered if he had ever really known what love was.

The next morning Cristina awoke to find that dad had already gone out fishing with Captain Zed. Beside her bed she found a note with her name on it in his handsome script. Unfolding it, she read:

Dear Freckled Fish,
 Good morning! I haven't really got anything to say. I merely wanted to call you a freckled fish.
 With all my love,
 Dad

She smiled and shook her head. Never could she tell what he might do next. His jolly unpredictability was something she loved more each day. For there is something about joy and love that make us unpredictable. They cause life to erupt in a flurry of dancing and twirling every which way, and often even we have not the slightest idea what our leaping hearts might do next. Perhaps that is why we can never anticipate exactly what God will do or how He will do it. For He is the most joyful and loving of all. His love keeps us guessing, keeps us surprised and startled. We remain mystified by His laughter.

Cristina set about putting more finishing touches on the house, and then she opened up her *Beginner's Cookbook* and studied it diligently. She worked like a beaver and eventually filled the house with tantalizing aromas. The red table cloth was put out on their tiny cedar table, the silverware they had gotten in Anchorage was in place (although it was not really silver), and the range was hot. Dad had made sure they had plenty of firewood stocked up for at least the first week, and she applied all the tips she had heard from Mrs. Little Mickey and Aunt Kay.

Noon was approaching, lunch was steaming and ready, but there was still no sign of dad. He had not told her when he would be home but she had assumed that he wouldn't miss lunch. Another hour went by and she started to get frustrated. Everything was getting cold and she was tired. After another hour of waiting she began to worry. Then he finally arrived around three. He had some nice fish with him and was very apologetic for coming so late. Captain Zedekiah had kept him much longer than he had wanted and then they had had trouble with the sail on his small boat.

Cristina was quiet and received him politely and graciously, but inside her excitement had all fizzled out. It was their first full day in the new house and she had wanted it to be perfect. A late, cold lunch was not her idea of perfection.

"Cristinakin! You've gone and made us a veritable feast! You ought to warn me before walking into a house full of such delicious smells."

"Make sure you wash your hands, dad."

"Yes, ma'am."

Everything tasted delicious except for the biscuits. She realized she had used two tablespoons of baking powder instead of one. Dad didn't say anything but she knew he was just being polite when he finished his second one.

"When do you think Evangeline will move to Kenai?" asked dad. The casualness with which he said it seemed a little overdone to Cristina.

"She's *not mother*!" burst out Cristina before she realized her temper had snapped.

"Woah, hold on. I didn't say I was going to marry her."

"But you *like* her, don't you? Admit it!"

"Don't *you* like her?" said dad. This made Cristina even more angry because the truth was that she did.

"Of course I don't! You're not supposed to be interested in any other women!"

Dad got quiet. "I don't even know her. Just try to be patient with me."

"I knew it! You're in love with her!" Cristina stood up and slapped the table.

"Cristina, nobody can fall in love with someone that fast. That's ridiculous."

"*You* could!" Her face was red and she was starting to cry with stormy eyes.

"Please listen to me, Cristina." Dad looked worried. "This isn't worth getting in such a fuss about. It's just a woman who was kind and memorable somehow. That's all."

"Will you promise not to be friends with her then?"

Dad sighed and shook his head. "I don't understand why you're so upset. If God has a different woman for me then it will be impossible for me to marry Evangeline. I believe that, and you should too."

"Will you promise?"

"I'm sorry, duck. I can't promise that. Besides, this town is too small to avoid her. She'll be your teacher. And I think she needs a friend."

"Well if you're going to be *her* friend then I won't be *your* friend." And with that Cristina rushed to her room and slammed the door.

Will gave her some time to settle down. It was agonizing to listen to her crying inside all alone, but he knew that she didn't want to see him. He had to be patient. She must have cried for at least twenty minutes, and then he waited out the rest of the hour before he approached her door and knocked. Silence.

"Cristina? Can I come in?" She did not answer. Will opened the door slowly. Cristina was lying on her bed staring at the ceiling.

"I can't believe you let me cry so long without offering to comfort me," she said.

"Would you have let me?"

"No," she sniffled.

"I see." Dad came in and lay down next to her and stared up at the ceiling too. Then he said, "Hey frog?"

"Yeah?"

"I love you."

She had not expected that. And there was something in the way that he said it that sounded like he meant it very much. Turning, she put her arms about him and did not let go for a long time.

Chapter 23

"Jerusalem crickets! You haven't read through the whole Bible?" exclaimed dad.

He and Cristina were sitting on a rock that hovered over the bay on a lazy Saturday. Their feet dangled over the edge almost low enough to touch the water. The music of the foam-tipped wavelets had drawn them, and they watched the ripples on the silvery surface like the silken ruffles of some queenly gown. The beach beside them was smooth and glistening, and there was a basket of bread and cheese and olives within reach.

"Well I've read through a *lot* of it," said Cristina a little defensively.

"What's one of your favorite psalms then? And you can't pick twenty three."

"I...I don't know. I don't think I've read the psalms, although Grandma Naomi read plenty of them to me when I was...in the future."

"Well we've done enough polly-foxing about then! We've got to read the Bible before school begins. We'll do it together."

Cristina smiled. "Very well. But that'll be a lot of reading every day. We've only got a few months."

"Let it never be said of us that we lived like the lilies of the field—'they toiled not, neither did they spin.' We must toil while today is called today, Crislet, lest the heavens tremble to look upon us."

That was dad all over. Lofty...dreamy...demanding...even whimsical, and always with a sprinkle of silly fun or delightful nonsense. Cristina nudged him.

"I'm only eleven, you know."

"Ah but you've got an old soul. It's uncanny—that soul of yours," said dad.

"How can you tell?"

"Fathers can always tell if their daughter's soul is old. It's a well known and established fact," he said.

Cristina nudged him again.

"Oh Cristina, if you only knew how much I don't say to you of what I want to say. You'd be amazed. I can see your soul in your eyes. I saw it the first day we met. It was old, yes, but not with wrinkles and gray hair, rather with the fine age of a shining jewel that needs only polishing and the right light."

"What other sorts things do you want to say and don't?" she asked.

Dad looked off at the mountains in the distance and thought a moment. She thought she saw more moistness than usual in his eyes.

"Oh, you'd get too proud for your britches if you found out," he dodged.

"I will not."

"You will."

"I won't."

"Fine, you win," he said. He paused for a moment and collected his thoughts.

"I wish I could say to you that…just to be in your presence is like the porcelain of salvation…. That I am often afraid of my unworthiness to be called your father…. That I see in you the tranquil gaiety of redemption and it humbles me…. That your beauty to me is like truth in its seamless purity, showered with the laughter of sunrise. And all the words in the world couldn't make you understand how my heart loves you…how it seems to expand with more love every day until I'm afraid it will shatter the universe."

He shook his head and sighed. "It's all sappy and sentimental, and I think you get the point now. I couldn't make a habit of saying such things or you'd go live with someone else."

Cristina nudged him a third time. "Hey, don't talk about my father like that."

And the universe came very near to shattering.

They started reading through the Bible together the next day, and it was appropriate since it was Sunday. Getting up an hour earlier, they took turns reading a chapter each.

"Brace yourself, ducklet. In one sitting we're about to see the cosmos spoken into existence and the mother of all beautiful women. Not to mention the great tragedy of the human race," said dad.

Oh how dad read the Bible! Cristina thought. She could never seem to read it with the same life, gusto, and steady exhilaration. She made him read the first three chapters before she took a turn; she loved listening to his voice too much. It was rich and bold and tremulous in all the right places, with a steadfast ring of sincerity woven throughout. Anything could sound beautiful when he read it, and Cristina felt that if dad had no other qualities she would still adore him for his voice. But just as there were things that dad resisted telling Cristina, Cristina resisted telling dad exactly what she thought about this. However, she did say, "I like the way you read, dad." And that was enough to keep them both happy for another whole day.

Six chapters later they headed down to the Baptist Mission looking as smart as they could muster. There was still no actual church in the town but the Mission hosted a worship service every Lord's day for all who desired to attend. As they arrived Olive Peachy came down and rang a big brass bell. The front room soon began to fill and they discovered that the United States Marshal was passing through and had decided to join them for worship. A good many Eskimo came quickly and arranged themselves in the benches along the walls. Mr. Paul always had someone interpret into their language, which was usually a young Eskimo named Ivan. Ivan also was a fair singer and loved music of all kinds.

All together the small congregation was full of striking contrasts. The gold rush of years past had brought many distinct nationalities to Alaska—Swedes, Germans, Russians, Americans, Canadians were all represented in that one room, along with the native people. One moment you might catch a whiff of perfume and the next a strong odor of seal oil coming from an Eskimo. On the backs of the latter one could often see small children, and if a baby cried from hunger the mother would promptly feed it, regardless of the assembled company. For with an Eskimo mother a child's wishes are preeminent.

Mr. Paul took up an English song book and read one of the songs aloud, with Ivan interpreting it verse by verse. Then they would sing it together. After a few songs Mr. Paul read the Scripture for the day and prayed in English. Then he asked one of the Eskimos to pray in their language. After this came the sermon on the text, during which an African American widow named Mrs. Lawson offered an occasional hearty "Amen!" Then there was a short benediction and the meeting was over. But nearly everyone lingered for a long time enjoying the conversation, and the room and veranda resounded with much laughter. Cristina couldn't help noticing dad laughing with Mr. Paul. It was so easy to make dad laugh, and so delightful. Although he could be dignified at times he was never too dignified to laugh with all his heart. And just as she was turning back to Elizah he caught her eye and his eyes said something only eyes can say.

The next morning Cristina woke up late. Dad had snuck in during the night and made sure the sun was blocked out of her windows. There was a note by her bed from him.

Dear daughter,
    You are my favorite daughter.
Your favorite dad,
Dad

When she opened her door she found him whistling and flipping pancakes and frying eggs.

"What's this all about?" said Cristina. "It's *my* job to make breakfast! You snuck in and kept the light out, didn't you?" Her hands were on her hips and indignation was on her face.

"You looked like you were needing a little extra rest. And you can't make *all* the meals around here. People might accuse me of neglect. Why don't you read the Bible to me while I finish this, and then we'll greet the day deliciously."

Dad gave her some tactful tips on how to improve her reading aloud as she went along. "You'll be a master someday soon, Cris my girl. And blokes from all around will pay money just to hear you read the stock exchange. And I'm *not* biased...no matter what they say."

Cristina wasn't so sure.

"You've got a voice, Cristy. It makes me think of grassy lanes and lovable winds and groves of beech and spruce. And it's got the flavor of summer in it."

Cristina did not know what voices had to do with trees and grass, but she thought she understood the spirit of the idea. When she got to the ninth chapter of Genesis and read about the rainbow after the great flood, dad had his comments as usual.

"God turned his bow from pointing at us to pointing up—at himself. That's at least part of what it means when we see rainbows. But here's the question, froglet: how can God keep his bow turned away from us still, when we deserve the arrows of his wrath?"

Cristina thought carefully for a moment. "Because of...Jesus?"

Dad finished serving their plates and sat down. He nodded and smiled. "Now let's thank God for rainbows and flapjacks and his son."

After they prayed Cristina had a question. "Do you think God ever might pick up his bow again and use it?"

"You mean will we ever see an upside-down rainbow?"

"I guess so," said Cristina.

"If we do it won't be because he's sending a flood. God always keeps his promises. But it may be on that day when the enemies of the cross cry out to the mountains and rocks to fall on them, to hide them from the face and wrath of the Lamb." Dad looked troubled.

"However," he continued, "God has other weapons for the day of judgment. Jesus will use a double-edged sword from his mouth to strike down the unrepentant nations. That's the side of Jesus a lot of people try to ignore."

Will and Cristina loved their new home. Every day they seemed to learn something new about one another. Cristina found that dad sang much more than he used to around the house. Often she would hear him humming a hymn or singing "Yankee Doodle" or "When Johnny Comes Marching Home." Sometimes he would catch her in his arms before she knew it and dance with her as he sang "Sweet Marie." Whether it was in the woods or in the kitchen or on the sand by the water, dad was always ready to dance with her. And dad discovered that Cristina was not a natural singer by any means, but there was spirit and free joy in her singing, which he loved. Every day she seemed to feel more at liberty to join him in song and not hold back, until the folks down harbor said that they could hear them at times in the distance. "That's the sound of happiness,"

Aunt Kay would say to Paul, and then close the windows for the evening.

All the dancing wore off on Cristina to the point that dad once caught her stepping a lively jig alone in the kitchen while making a potato stew. He watched her for a while before she noticed, and he knew for certain that God was singing.

"It's not very orthodox to say it, duck, but I'm jolly glad we worship a God who dances," dad said once. "I'm not convinced he would make such a fuss about dancing in the Bible if it weren't one of his favorite things."

"I'm glad too," said Cristina.

"And if I *didn't* know my Bible, I'd say the thing that made him dance the most was you," said dad.

Will and Cristina also eventually realized that they both wanted a pet.

"We need a parrot, that's what," said dad.

"But what about a cat? There's heaps of cats at the Big Mickeys," said practical Cristina.

"Father always says that cats are good for nothin'. They don't love you like dogs, they can't protect you, and they can't talk like parrots."

"But they don't cry over spilled milk."

"I can't argue with you there, froglet. But I'm afraid a parrot wouldn't cry over it either."

"But we've already got a chicken, and a parrot will die in the cold, and where on earth would we find a parrot?"

So they got a dog and accepted a cat from the Big Mickeys on trial, "to see if he's good for anything," dad explained. They agreed to call the dog Parrot so that it would almost be as though dad had gotten his way. And the cat they called Cat until his trial was over.

"We've got a feminine dog but I can't decide if Parrot is a feminine name."

"It's too late to change it now, dad. She already answers to it."

"I'll need another job soon to feed all these gaping mouths," worried dad.

Another thing they both discovered about each other was that they were not overly fond of moose. In fact, they distrusted them for some reason.

"Well everyone says they're dangerous, so that's plenty reason for me," said Cristina.

"I don't know, Cris girl, there's something else about them too. They look conniving and scheming—that's what I think. Almost like they've been secretly reading other people's mail…and even keeping it for themselves…."

"I couldn't agree more," she nodded resolutely.

"That settles it then. No mooses allowed on *our* property. No sir, no way, no how."

"But isn't the plural *moose*, dad?"

"Well no one ever asked me what the plural should be. Besides, it's a lot more *fun* to say mooses. And the English language owes me that much at least for all the years I've spoken and written it so fondly."

After much deliberation Cristina finally named her chicken William, after dad.

When she told dad he pouted for a while. "I've had some low points in my life, frog, but this one might top them all—a chicken has been named after me."

"But dad, chickens are dandy and noble…and they help keep so many people alive…and—"

Dad lifted his hand. "There's no use trying to convince me of the merits of a chicken, ducklet. I'm not too thick-headed to know when I've been humbled. I am made from dust and now a chicken bears my name."

"But dad—"

"On the bright side I shall be all the more favored in God's sight. For he says that the man upon whom he will look is him that is poor and of a contrite spirit."

"Well God knows you must need it after all the nice things I think and say about you." Cristina's eyes sparkled.

"*Now* you're speaking the truth, you young sock." And he swung her down next to him on the sofa. "But the question is, how is God going to keep *you* humble?

That night Will stayed up late and wrote.

> Who is sufficient for these things? What soul could possibly bear the weight of glory—of being her father? It all seems utterly impossible and improbable that so much

splendor might be contained in so small a form. The stars should explode for joy. The mountains should tremble and shake in wonder. The oceans should cower in bewilderment.

The flowers of heaven have scarcely dreamt a more resplendent dream. How these words seem so powerless to make you taste the sunshine in her smile, her voice! To make you feel the various tints and glimmers from her eyes plunging your soul into a singing sea of joy! To make you hear the melody of the dawn in a tiny soul.

When I am presented with such a precocious incarnation of spring and poetry, it takes all of my self-restraint not to stand up with a jubilant shout and proclaim that the New Creation has been born in our midst. Oh how hard it is not to leap upon the rooftops, clapping and skipping, bellowing to the dull earth that unrelenting hope has spilled into the world and will soon flood the hearts of men. What better way to start a firestorm of bliss and hope than with the meek beauty of a mere maiden? Light and gladness have again harmonized within my spirit. The preposterous song that is this little woman will haunt me for years to come. So many times she has left me reeling, reeling, reeling with worship.

In the morning a steamer pushed into the sleepy Kenai harbor. The captain's voice called out, "We'll see to your luggage, Miss Schoenkopf."

Chapter 24

Try as they might, Will and Cristina could not get used to the majesty of their surroundings. Everywhere they turned they found misty blue and gray ridges, sun spangled hollows, the harmony of tree and sky, emerald rivers, lush meadows and juicy berries. Those berries they picked often. With small baskets in hand, they would frequently come home with two or three quarts each. Elizah would usually come to help, since she seemed always to know where the best bushes stood quivering and laden with ripe fruit. She also knew the kinds that were not suitable to eat and could make one sick.

"That girl's wiser than a sack full of owls," said dad. "She knows the forest better than most natives three times her age."

Elizah and Cristina also harvested beautiful wild flowers and filled the house with color and fragrance. Elizah always knew the best places to find these as well. They picked alpine forget-me-nots, lupine, wild geraniums, dandelions, irises, marsh marigolds, indian paintbrushes, asters, narcissus, and bluebells.

Once they ran across some lovely monkshood while traversing a meadow.

"See that purple flower?" said Elizah. "Don't ever touch it. It's poisonous enough to kill you if you eat it, and the poison can get into your skin just by holding it."

"But it's so beautiful!" said Cristina. "It seems such a shame not to have it in my bouquet."

"Some things should only be admired and never touched," said Elizah, feeling like quite the sage.

"Maybe I should give some to miss Evangeline," said Cristina.

"Who's that?"

"A woman who just arrived to be the new teacher here."

"Why would you want our new teacher to die?" Elizah looked very concerned.

"Because she's...she's too...kind!"

Elizah stared at Cristina who had flushed angrily.

Just then they heard footsteps. Looking up they saw Will approaching with a smile.

"Hello girls! Gathering flowers for me, I see. How thoughtful of you!"

Then he laid down in the grass and they gave him a bouquet to hold against his chest as though he were about to be buried. Elizah giggled and then put on a very solemn air as she began to imitate a minister at a funeral.

Afterwards when they were at home eating dinner, Cristina said, "I didn't like playing that you had died. I already lost you once and I don't want to pretend that it happened again."

"I should have thought of that. I'm sorry," said dad. After a pensive pause he continued.

"Daffodil, I'm glad that death is dead, though. You'll see that when we get to Hosea. 'O grave, I will be thy destruction.'"

"But how can death be dead?" asked Cristina.

"When it's swallowed up by life and victory. When Jesus conquered it by removing its sting—sin. When it's been overpowered by grace."

"This soup ain't got no kick comin'," said dad after another pause.

Cristina knew that he meant he could find no fault in it. She smiled and said, "*Thank you*" with perfect formality.

The next day they invited Titus Pepper over for dinner. Even after twenty years of being a widower he had not lost his charm. When Cristina greeted them at the front door he took off his hat with a wide grin.

"Ain't you a sight for sore eyes, miss. How do you do?" and he bowed.

To Will he nodded politely and said, "There's nothing like a pretty girl in a fresh dress to brighten your day, is there, Mr. Millhouse?"

"*I'll* say. But we mustn't let her know that we're talking about her or she'll puff up proud as a toad. And we couldn't have *that* now, could we?"

As usual Titus praised Cristina's cooking until the last bite was swallowed. She even had made a berry pie for dessert and nearly got lost in an effusion of praise from both of the men at the table.

"The beatenest woman alive," remarked Titus with half his mouth full. And dad said something about all the songbirds of his soul bursting into melody from the taste.

Before long Titus began a tale of the girl he had loved. "She cooked almost as well as you do," he said to Cristina with a wink. "But she had to learn secretly from the household cook, since she was the daughter of a grand household. Before she started learning she didn't know the foggiest even about making tea. But she learned fast."

"But how did you meet? Were you the son of a rich family?" asked Cristina.

Titus laughed and slapped his knee. "Me? From a rich family? Far from it, my dear. Far from it. You see, I was nothing but a lowly footman and the son of a lowly farmer, trying to make my way in life. I believe I was 19 and she was 18 when I began working there. I would only see her when I went to fetch something or to serve at each meal. There she would be, sitting like a pretty doll in her fancy toilettes. She had pretty black eyes and a low, sweet voice and her movements—you wouldn't be believin' how graceful they were."

"Sounds exotic," said dad. "Don't forget her hair now."

"Ah yes, her hair. It was dark."

Dad and Cristina waited but he had nothing more to say about her hair, so they exchanged a silent laugh with their eyes and went on listening.

"Now I knew that she was hopelessly above me in my station, and that I'd no right to even speak with her, so I decided that I at least wanted a token of her beauty to remember her by before she married some lucky rich blighter and left. So in the winter months I would hunt for stray strands of her hair on her coats and shawls. When she came in with others from an outing of some kind it was often my duty to see to their jackets and things. Once I took them to the closet, I carefully stored away in my pocket any strands of her hair that I could find. After a few months I had enough in my collection to constitute a proper lock."

As he paused to take another bite of pie, Will nudged Cristina under the table with his foot. She nudged back.

"You're a man after my own heart, Titus," said dad. "I'm only sorry I never did such a reasonable thing myself before. So what happened next?"

"Wait," said Cristina. "What was her name?"

"Juliet Howard. But one of the lady's maids discovered my secret and told her about it. I think she thought she'd get me into trouble and turned out of the house. But it wasn't so.

"One evening I found an envelope under my door, and when I opened it I found a fresh lock of dark hair. And it was all fragrant and glossy like too. There was a note from her that said that here was a gift to save me some trouble, and that she wasn't sorry to have found out."

Cristina clapped her hands and bounced in her chair.

"That's when we began exchanging letters in secret. She would leave one in her coat pocket, look at me meaningfully as she handed it to me to put away, and then I would leave one in the same pocket for her to find later.

"This went on for a year I s'pose, and we were in love. Madly. You oughta see some of those letters she wrote. Better than gold and sweeter than honey. I know that might sound irreverent because the Bible's s'posed to be that way, but I can't think of a better way to say it. Anyhow, I loved her by that time so much that my head was spinning too fast to be cautious or 'exercise sound judgment', as my ma used to say. Then a nosy servant found one of my letters and took it to his lordship—her father. And he just about switched the devil—pardon the expression—and fussed and yelled and nearly broke one of his prize Italian sculptures. He was mad as hops and I didn't know what would become of me and I took to prayin' like a windmill. But then you wouldn't believe how she stood up for me. You never saw a finer woman speak her mind like she did to her papa that day. Right when he was gonna throw me out. She said she was goin' with me if he did. She wasn't gonna let me go for anything, and she told him so.

"Well sure enough he was huffy for a while afterwards, but I was eventually accepted into the family and we were married proper."

Dad and Cristina were afraid to ask how she died, but he continued right along, taking on a sober tone.

"The good Lord gave us three happy years together. More than I ever deserved. Then tuberculosis got a hold of her somehow. And she died. But before she went she said she hadn't a single regret. She said she had lived a fuller life than most who live to be a hundred, because she had loved me."

After dinner, as they watched old Titus make his way down the hill in the twilight that would last until midnight, father and daughter savored a silence between them. Then dad spoke up.

"You know what, daffodil?"

"What, dad?"

"I'm blessed thankful you're not one of those brooding, troubled girls who is full of herself and doesn't want help."

"What made you think of that?"

"Haven't I warned you about trying to understand the mind of a man?"

"Oh dad." She bumped him, but he just smiled.

"I'm going to write mother tonight," he said.

"Really?"

"I'm stealing your idea. I might even mention you, since I suppose you're mentionable."

"That's a swell idea all around."

"Should I write a prayer for her in it too? Or would that be too forward."

"You're married, dad."

"Not yet, though, daughter."

"Yes, include the prayer."

"That's settled then. Now, since you are *far* too young to know anything about romance and such, you are strictly forbidden to eavesread any of it."

"Is that like eavesdropping, but with reading and not the dropping?"

"Yes, nobody likes droppings on their eaves. 'Tisn't proper."

But Cristina *did* eavesread the letter the next day while dad was out.

Dear woman of the myst,

Cristina has bewitched me into writing letters to you, although you are an idea I accept by faith—a slender strand of faith. Do you have the faintest notion what a daughter we have? I must not say too much good about her here because I am quite certain that she will find it and read it soon. She has got some nosiness in her from one of us. I can't imagine who it might be. So, since she will read this, I will only say that I love her. And that I find my soul brimming with delirious draughts of warmest life because of her. And that I am unworthy of her—unworthy even to untie her sandals.

My love—may I call you that?—we live in a land of fantasy. You will swoon and ache with joy to see it, to smell and taste and hear it. It is a land of majesty teeming with unspeakable beauty. A new Eden. I cannot wait for you to step into our small home and take part in the glory and memories within its humble walls. Aspen Aisle is its name. The name alone hearkens to the lore of kingdoms and Victorian romance. It is a fitting abode for a queen such as you.

You must know that Cristina is fiercely loyal and faithful to you. Alas, I may falter in my ebbing faith, but she cannot forsake you, nor let me do so. She still tries to draw a portrait of you every once in a while, but the attempt ends in the fire because it never does you proper justice, she says.

Where are you, my love? What has taken you so long to appear? I often feel like the fool, hoping against hope. And so I must pray, for I know not what else to do. O Lord, in whose hand is the life of every living thing and the breath of all mankind, with You are wisdom and might; You have counsel and understanding. Therefore, impart these things to her. Let her life be brighter than the noonday, and its darkness like the morning. May she feel secure, because there is hope. Let her lie down with none to make her afraid. Lead her with strength and sound wisdom. Let the eyes of her heart feast upon Your splendor. Let them brighten at the sight of Your justice, and with the vision of Your righteousness. When she prays to You, hear her, and make light to shine on her ways. Make her foot hold fast to Your steps; keep her in Your way and do not let her turn aside. Let her hold fast to Christ's righteousness and not let it go.

With sincerity and an embrace,
William

Chapter 25

Dear mother,

When will dad and I finally get to see you? Dad wrote you a letter two days ago and I read it while he was away. He knew I would because he didn't hide it well. I'm glad he wrote to you. I love you, mother.

I still like Elizah best of all my friends. Dad says he likes her to and that she's one of a kind. She comes over and helps me cook sometimes. She says that hunger is one of the best sauces for a dish. I agree. We all have famous appetites. There is always so much to be done every day that you can't help working up an appetite. Dad makes sure to haul water from the brook near the house in the morning. Now he's working on something that will bring it all the way to the house on its own so that we won't have to do that anymore. He's very handy when it comes to things like that. Then I see to the food and cooking, and dad makes sure I have plenty of supplies and firewood. And we're busy as beavers getting ready for the winter months. Someone's always telling us that something else must be got ready.

Elizah and I also decorate the mission with flowers on Saturday night. We collect them from all around because so many of them grow wild. I love flowers, mother. I talk to the ones I have in my house while I cook. They make pretty companions. Sometimes Elizah and me ride in the back of the Big Mickeys' truck. Sometimes we go all the way with them to a place called Soldotna to get supplies. Isn't that a rather ugly name?

I have not yet told you about Parrot. She is our new dog! She's ever so jolly and loveable and cheerful. She's brown and has a real simple elegant look. Dad says she likes him best of all, but I know she really likes me best because I give her lots of tasty scraps from the kitchen. Cat is our cat on trial. He still hasn't shown himself useful. Dad says he's got one more week to catch a mouse or keep away a moose or he's got to leave. But we'll keep Parrot for sure. She truly is a dandy dog. She's loyal and respectable and smart.

They say that Peter Little Mickey is keen on Brook who is Mr. Sam's daughter. He always wears the same black shirt to church and tries to sit next to her. He is very quiet. Daphne who works at the diner won't forgive Uncle Rockefeller because he called her missus Canning instead of miss. He can be absent minded sometimes. He still comes to argue with dad about predestination and other things. Dad always smiles and says something that puts him in a corner but he won't admit it if he's lost an argument. Then he acts all indignated. But he still brings peppermints. He now brings treats for Parrot too. He always complains that things cost like smoke, but I don't understand why smoke has anything to do with it. Dad says that if Christians didn't have predestination to argue about then they'd be too friendly towards each other and people wouldn't think they were sincere.

Aunt Kay has been teaching me to knit and I've already made a winter scarf for dad. Now she's helping me make him some warm stockings.

Now I have bad news. There is a new woman in town named Evangeline. Dad and me met her in Anchorage and she's kind and pretty. Oh mother, I'm so cut up and worried about her because I'm afraid dad is keen on her. We already had an awful spat about it. She will be my teacher. I don't know what to do.

Dad and I are reading through the Bible together. When I read it with him it's wonderful and I understand. We change all the thees and thous into normal yous. We are reading Numbers. Dad says he wants to ride Balaam's donkey with me in the new heavens and the new earth. You can ride with him too. Last Sunday missionary Paul had dad preach. I thought it was swell and Gids said he wished dad would preach more. Olive says that missionary Paul's preaching makes her bored as toast, but I don't think toast is boring. Dad and me always make it by frying slices of bread in butter and it's delicious. Sometimes we put wild honey on it that Mr. Sam brings us.

Young Jim came again for a visit. I cooked some fish that we caught. I'm still learning about all the fish here. There are ever so many different kinds. Young Jim says he might have seen dad's father once. He can't be sure, but the name sounds familiar to him. Dad's hoping we'll find him soon. Young Jim says he never had a father growing up and told me not to take it for granted. He doesn't know that I didn't always have a father so I cherish dad heaps.

Hope Big Mickey is collecting buttons. We all keep our eyes peeled for stray buttons along the road for her. I found one but they're not easy to find. I have a shell collection. I use them to decorate the house. One day dad and I painted flowers and trees on some of the big white ones. I think I must be the artist of the home. We put the shells on the window sills.

My friends and I hunt for driftwood some days because it makes good firewood. Faith Big Mickey and I are going to help set up the summer festival. Faith showed me all her pet rabbits and told me all their names. She names them after people she likes and names the chickens after people she doesn't like.

Yesterday I was walking to the pond by our house and I saw a big moose nearby. It scared me more than a snake. I ran straight back home. I should have taken Parrot with me. Moose just don't seem trustworthy.

I asked Aunt Kay to teach me to make jam from the berries we pick. She said that she would but I need to get the jars first. The Big Mickeys might sell some. Miss Evangeline is staying at the mission right now so I always see her when I visit Elizah. I don't like that. She's chummy with Elizah to and Elizah doesn't understand why I can't be nicer to her.

Captain Zed asked me to help him write a letter for his mother. His eyes aren't good for letters anymore he says. I don't think his letter was as good as what he might have said in person.

Oh mother, I love you, I love love love you. Please come soon.

With kisses from your daughter, Cristina.

"Dad!" said Cristina.

Dad jumped. He had snuck into her room while she slept, found the letter she had written to mother, and was reading it by the light of a small, dwindling candle. Now he was caught red-handed.

"Shhhh," said dad. "I'm at a really good part."

"You shameless snoop!" said Cristina. She hopped out of bed and tried to snatch the letter but he held it high.

"If you don't give it to me I'll…I'll…I'll put bugs in your soup!"

"More protein," said dad.

"Then I'll put honey in your sheets!"

"Then I'll have sweet dreams," laughed dad.

"Then I'll become a neopelagian like Uncle Rockefeller!"

Dad instantly sobered. "You wouldn't dare."

"I so would!"

"Then I give in. It appears I have no choice."

"Good!" she said, stamping her foot.

Dad handed over the letter ceremoniously, and as she took it and turned he caught her ribs with a tickle ambush. Up went the letter into the air and out came squeals. After the ruckus was all over the two of them laid on the bed and talked until midnight. Cristina asked him what he thought they would do for the winter. Then they discussed plans for reading and learning during all the hours they'd be shut in because of the snow. Then they wondered what they might do for Thanksgiving, and what about Christmas. It was decided that they should stay in Alaska for Christmas and invite dad's family to join them, but he knew they wouldn't accept.

"Talking to you is as easy as falling off a chunk," said dad.

"A chunk of what?"

"I don't know. I read it in a book once. But it sounded easy."

Cristina rolled her eyes and smiled. "Mr. Paul says you're a crazy coon."

"That I am, darling duck. I shall wear that label as a badge of honor."

Dad kissed her goodnight and went to his room. He was smiling, and a tear rolled down his cheek before he blew out the candle.

The next day Titus Pepper came and fetched Cristina for a fishing lesson. Dad let Elizah take his place since there was only so much room in the small boat. He stayed behind to work on the aqueduct from the brook to the house. After about an hour he heard a voice in the distance.

"Hello? Anyone there?"

Parrot barked and reached the visitor first. Heading back to the house, Will found Evangeline waiting on the front porch with Parrot hopping about her excitedly. She was laughing and petting her and saying, "Good boy! What's your name?"

"Her name's Parrot. Welcome!"

"Oh, hello. Hello, Mr. Millhouse. But her name is Parrot?"

"It's a long story."

Will offered his hand. Instead of looking at him she eyed the ground. She wore a light turquoise shawl about her shoulders for the morning chill. Her loose hair drifted softly when she moved.

"I was just passing through and thought I might say hello to Cristina. It's...it's a nice place for walking up here."

"I'm glad you stopped by. You like taking walks?"

She glanced up at him and nodded.

"I'm not sure when Cristina will be back, but you're welcome to stay for some tea."

She began to fidget as she replied, "No, no, that won't be necessary. Perhaps some other time."

As she stood there on the porch with the sun and wind Will tried to read what was in her face. But it was inscrutable. She turned to go.

"Wait," said Will. "Since you're here I wanted to ask you a couple things."

Avoiding his gaze, she shifted on her feet and said, "Now isn't a good time. I really should be going." And she began walking away.

"Do you think you'll be happy here?" called out Will.

She did not answer, but merely offered a cautious wave as she hurried around the bend in the path and was gone.

"Well I'll be switched!" muttered Will. "Noah *was* right about these Alaskan women. She sure seemed addle-pated about something."

Cristina did not return until Evangeline had long been gone. Will decided not to mention the visit to her. She had brought home some lovely fish to fry up for supper. Her face was sun kissed and she had plenty to share about what she had learned from Titus.

"I'm not sure I entirely like killing creatures of any kind—unless they're horrid ones like snakes," she said. "But fish seem to be less difficult for me to kill. But I'm not going to gut them. I'll cook them, but you have to clean them."

"A tender-hearted frog o' the mist," said dad. "It's a fair trade-off."

While dad cleaned the fish Cristina wrote a note on a scrap of paper and put it under the napkin where he sat at the table. No one has ever revealed what the contents of that note were, but when dad read it he looked at her with a radiant joy. And when he gave thanks for the food his prayer was substantially longer and more earnest than usual.

Then he looked at her again, shook his head, and said, "What a Cristina!"

The next day dad and Cristina visited the mission for dinner because Aunt Kay had invited them. When it came time to sit down at the table Evangeline was nowhere to be found.

"She went off on one of those long ramblings through the woods that she's got a predilection for," explained Paul. "She said she'd be back in time for dinner, but I'm not surprised she hasn't showed. The girl's got a mind of her own and often doesn't come home for hours. There's a troubled soul behind that fair face of hers—there's no denying it."

Will did not recall much of the meal that night, except that he was rather mystified by the absence of this woman who roamed the forest as they ate. After dinner, as Cristina scampered about with Elizah while he helped wash dishes in the kitchen, he decided to ask Aunt Kay about Evangeline.

"Do *you* know anything more about Evangeline than the rest of us? If she's bound to confide in anyone it would be you."

Aunt Kay shook her head. "Not much. All I know is what she told me on one occasion when she was helping me sweep the parlor. I asked her if there was a man in her life back home, even though I said it was none of my business if she didn't feel like answering. She said that there had been a man, but not anymore, no. She said that was part of the reason she moved up here. Needed to get away and 'breathe new air' she said. I didn't want to pry, but I couldn't help but ask what had happened. She said it was difficult to talk about, and she just needed more time. That's all I know. Oh, and she's from Kentucky."

"I see."

"The girl's got a frightened look about her—that's certain. She seems afraid of life...afraid of people. There's no telling how she'll be able to take on the school in such a state. May God help the poor thing. I don't know what that man did to her, but I've a notion that it was him who's to blame for the bitterness I hear in her laugh sometimes. When she's playing with the children it's not there, but sometimes when she's around me it comes out. Some women can't hide a broken heart if their life depended on it. They think they're doing a swell job of it when all along they might as well have it written on their forehead."

"So you think she's got a broken heart then?"

"I'd be inclined to say so, but what do I know? Leave it to a man to spoil a pretty little thing like her."

"But maybe he just died. That happens all the time."

"I don't know. The men don't die like they used to anymore. They're altogether too healthy. And modern medicine always finds a way to keep them alive."

Will smirked. "Is that such a bad thing?"

"Sometimes it is. I've seen my share of men who weren't worth a mouthful of ashes, and the world would be a much better place without them—if I had any sway with providence. They think they can just have booming times with a girl, thinking they're big-bugs and all, but at the end of the day they're full of nothing better than hogwash...blattering soul-butter and lies that don't amount to anything. They give me the fantods."

Aunt Kay paused, shaking her head. "I beg your pardon, William, I don't know what got into me. It's only that I've seen a great deal of evil in my day. And men have been no small part of it."

"I understand. And I'll do my utmost to make up for all the sapheads who have given the male race a bad name."

Aunt Kay embraced him as he stood at the sink and said, "Oh William, you already have. You're a fine young man. I can only imagine how blessed your wife must have been."

"No, the blessing was all mine to have had her. I still don't know why she married me."

On the way home Cristina said, "I saw Evangeline in the window while we were eating dinner."

"What?"

"She was trying to keep everyone from noticing. When she saw that I'd seen her she put her finger to her lips and snuck off. I don't know what it was all about. She's strange."

"Strange indeed!" said dad. "What an enigma of a woman." But just as his mind was poised to puzzle further over the matter, he remembered he had a daughter. A daughter! And he forgot all about Evangeline as he raced Cristina the last hundred yards homeward.

Chapter 26

"I like a patch of carefreeness every so often," Will said the next week.

"You're always carefree, dad," said Cristina as she worked hard at dusting the house. "There's no time for carefreeness when there's chores to be done."

There was now a rhythm to life at Aspen Aisle. Mondays meant that things must be mended, and maintained if they were near to needing mending. On Tuesdays Cristina dusted and swept. Wednesdays were for scrubbing the floor, and Thursdays took them to the General Store for odds and ends. Fridays were days to bathe the dog if she needed bathing. Saturdays they worked on their garden together and tidied up their yard, and Cristina baked extra for Sunday. Saturday afternoons were for gadding about however they took a fancy. Sundays were just for church and lazing about. Most weekdays dad worked at the saw mill with Mr. Sam.

"But we don't do enough fool things anymore," said dad. "We're much too established and conventional now."

"Dad, you'll never be conventional. Why don't you write more? Try to get something published. That might stir things up a bit."

Dad stretched himself out on the floor and looked up at the ceiling. "She wants me to write, says she. I'll have to ask Parrot what she thinks of this."

"She'll agree with me."

"Will she now?"

"She will."

"Very well. What shall I write, my amphibious muse?"

"Poetry. And maybe a story or two. But short ones. No novels yet. You're too young to write novels."

"How old do I have to be to write novels?"

"At least as old as Jesus when he started his ministry."

"Well that about knocks the spots out of anything I've ever heard from you."

"So what are you going to write poems about?"

Dad did not have to think long. "Well, Cris my girl, I think I'll write about the winsomeness of women and the wonder of God."

"But that's too overdone."

"Ah, but that's where you're wrong, daffodil. You can't exhaust those subjects. Witness the long tradition of history. The venerable Thomas Moore... 'if man of heaven e'er dreameth, 'tis when he thinks purely of thee, oh woman!'... 'Drink to her who long hath wak'd the poet's sigh, the girl who gave to song what gold could never buy.'... 'The light that lies in woman's eyes, has been my heart's undoing.'"

Cristina rolled her eyes, stepped over dad, and kept on dusting.

"Even the great Michael Angelo...let's see now, what did he say... 'For O how good, how beautiful must be the God that made so good a thing as thee'... and we mustn't forget Longfellow...'a smile of God thou art.'"

"See?" said Cristina. "This is why you're too young to write a novel. It'd be all too mushy and full of stuff children wouldn't want to read."

Dad smiled as though she had given him the highest compliment in the world.

"I know what I'll do. I'll write about *you.* Yes, I'll write the sappiest poem there ever was. Then I'll hunt up some magazine to publish it."

Cristina groaned.

"Thank you, Cristina Millhouse! I don't know why I didn't think of it sooner. I can feel the thrill of literary inspiration beginning to brew. There's nothing like the glory of words, frog. The haunting ache and rush that a single line can give you... 'Breaking the silence of the seas.' Wordsworth knew what he was about, didn't he? And Herbert... 'The soul in paraphrase.'"

"But what about the Bible's poetry?" said Cristina.

"Spoken like a true Millhouse," said dad. "We mustn't leave that out. Dante said it was the best. You must be thinking of Solomon's great song... 'Let him kiss me with the kisses of his mouth!'"

"Dad!"

Dad's laughter echoed through the house.

149

"Don't forget that I have a duster *and* the higher ground!" threatened Cristina.

Just then a friendly "Hello!" came from outside. It was Aunt Kay's voice. Dad got up from the floor and opened the door. Her cheerful countenance greeted both of them, and after customary pleasantries she invited the two of them to have supper at the mission that evening. To this they acquiesced eagerly. It had only been a week since they had shared a meal with their good friends there, but that seemed like forever.

"Oh, and by the by," said Aunt Kay as she was leaving, "Evangeline should actually be joining us this time. Perhaps you can finally get better acquainted." She smiled brightly and was off.

Cristina glared up at dad.

"That was thoughtful of her," he said.

Later in the day a large steamer came by and dropped off some mail. Their first letters arrived since they had notified some friends and family of their address. Blaze had written, much to Will's surprise, and so had Sonny and Pastor Ryan.

"It appears Blaze has finally gotten his job in Los Angeles. I suppose that's another reason I should believe you, oh oracle of the days to come," said Will.

Cristina smiled wide and said, "You bet your bibby bobkins."

"He also says, 'Please send Cristina all my love, and I'll autograph anything she likes any time. I'll try to send a photograph from the film set in the next letter.'"

"Swell!"

But Will sat there wondering if his mother and father would ever write him.

Later that evening the two of them arrived at the mission for supper and were ushered in by Paul. Aunt Kay was busy in the kitchen getting the last few things ready and Paul told them to make themselves comfortable. Elizah immediately pounced upon Cristina, delighted that she was there, and the two girls left Will to browse the books on the shelves in the parlor. He pulled down a decorative edition of Longfellow and started when it fell open in his hands to a poem entitled *Evangeline: A*

Tale of Acadie. Curious and frowning, he scanned the lines and flipped through pages absently.

> Fair was she to behold, that maiden of seventeen summers;
> Black were her eyes as the berry that grows on the thorn by the way-side,
> Black, yet how softly they gleamed beneath the brown shade of her tresses!
> …Shone on her face and encircled her form, when, after confession,
> Homeward serenely she walked with God's benediction upon her.
> When she passed, it seemed like the ceasing of exquisite music.
> …Happy was he who might touch her hand…

"Mr. Millhouse," came a faint voice from behind him.

Nearly jumping, Will clamped the book shut and turned around. It was Evangeline. She stood in front of him in a plain, gray dress, avoiding his eyes, and continued, "Aunt Kay sent me to let you know we'll be sitting down for dinner soon."

Will thanked her and said he would be along shortly. Then he asked her if she had read any Longfellow. What he witnessed was what appeared to be an inward battle between an impulse to turn and leave with a curt answer and a whispering desire to linger. After a moment, she answered: "I can't say I remember. I once read poetry, but it's lost its taste to me as of late."

Will nodded and followed with another query. "What about novels?"

She nodded and stole a glance up at him. Then she seemed to be turning to go, but stopped and said, "They tell me *you're* a writer, Mr. Millhouse."

"Well, I scribble and dabble when I've got a yen to. But my wise daughter says I'm too young to be writing novels. I don't know where she gets such ideas."

This almost made Evangeline smile. "We had best be getting to the table."

Gids and Elizah fought over who would get to sit on Cristina's left since she wouldn't give up sitting next to dad. Aunt Kay pronounced judgment in favor of Elizah, and Gids had to settle for sitting across from her, next to Evangeline who sat across from Will. They feasted on hot macaroni, cocoa, bread and butter, jam, cheese, and canned meat. All ate heartily. All except Evangeline, that is. She looked too sad to eat, Will thought. No matter how vivaciously he spoke, Will found himself at a loss to lighten the woman's mood. His whit and chaffing with others at table appeared to go unnoticed by her. But when Cristina spoke Evangeline's eyes were riveted on the small girl. She seemed mesmerized by her every movement. At one point in the conversation Cristina nudged dad and whispered in his ear, "Miss Evangeline sure stares at me a lot. But she looks so sad too."

"She's a strange one. Maybe it'll be up to you to find out more about her."

Cristina shook her head. That was the last thing she wanted to do.

Then Paul piped up and told one of his stories about a woman named Gladys who had gone to visit a new church one Sunday. The preacher himself nearly fell asleep in the pulpit from his seemingly endless, droning sermon. And plenty of the congregation dreamt their way through it.

"After the service Gladys walked up to a sleepy gentleman, reached out her hand, and said, 'Hello, I'm Gladys Dunn.' And he said, 'I couldn't agree more!'"

Then Will asked Evangeline if she knew how to keep a turkey in suspense.

"How?"

"I'll tell you tomorrow."

Gids said that he didn't want to wait until tomorrow, and Anernerk and Akiak agreed that it wasn't fair to keep them waiting. Evangeline took it like a good sport and mustered a faint smirk. Cristina rolled her eyes. Aunt Kay and Paul laughed.

Out of the blue Will raised his glass and said, "I propose a toast to our school's new teacher, Evangeline. May you enjoy a year of welcome and success."

Everyone cheered and raised their glass in felicitations. Everyone, that is, except Cristina.

"Well, wasn't that just a booming time?" asked dad on the way home.

Cristina neither looked at him nor said anything. Her silence fell heavily on the air. Her gait had in it the motions of protest and disappointment. And when Will finally caught a glimpse of her brow he saw traces of anger written therein.

"You're upset about Evangeline, aren't you?"

Cristina continued brooding.

"We need to make her feel welcome. You yourself saw how sad she is. Heaven knows what has happened to her."

"There are plenty of *other* people who could have made her feel welcome."

"Oh my precious girl, I *know* her name isn't Meadow. I know she doesn't match what you remember of mother. There's simply something about her…I can't think exactly how to describe it. We don't even get along so well… but…."

"How do you know you don't get along so well?" Cristina flashed back with an accusing tone.

"Because she's aloof and closed off to the world. She likes *you* but won't talk to me. I found that out when she came by the other day while you were out fishing."

"She came by when I was out fishing, and you didn't tell me?"

Dad hesitated and then nodded gravely.

"I didn't think it would help to tell you."

"Well you're right! It doesn't help! I can't believe it, dad!" Her voice broke and an angry tear or two fell.

They had reached the house and Cristina seemed to be whirling out of the reach of reason.

"I apologize for not mentioning it to you. I'm a silly old fool. I won't allow it again," said dad, crouching down and looking into her face. "There, there, sweet laughter of the sea, you can forgive me, can't you? Won't you? I'll try to forget about Evangeline if you try to forget about your old dad's weakness."

"But you *won't* forget her! *I* can't even forget her! We can't get rid of her now and nothing I say will change you! And now I'll never be born!" She pushed away his arm and ran to her bedroom and slammed the door.

When Will followed after her she said he should stay away. Nothing he said or did could help. "Just go!"

Will went. But for a long time he stood by her door with heaviness of heart, listening to the child's muffled sobs.

Sometimes he heard plaintive cries of, "Oh mother! Dear mother, where are you? Where are you? Where are you, mother? Oh God, why? Why did you even bring me here? I don't understand. I don't understand. I don't...."

Long after her crying had ceased and quiet overtook the house he sat on the floor with his back against the door thinking and praying. By turns he took up his journal and wrote:

> There is a storm raging in my daughter's heart. I cannot fully understand it. Yet she is my daughter, and my heart cannot rest when she has allowed anger to build boundaries between us. It seems as yesterday that I was celebrating the light that shone within me at the thought that I, William Millhouse, have a daughter of my own. A truly real flesh and blood daughter of Eve who calls me dad. Nothing stood in the way of absolute amity. Love was welling up unbidden, undeniable, unquenchable, unstoppable, unconditional. I was marveling at how You take the whispering color of butterflies and the voice of the violet and shine them from her silver, merry heart. And now? What am I to say? Why does this strange woman affect both of us so potently? I would venture that Cristina is more strongly affected by her than I. All the weakness of mortality is mine. I am only a man. Who am I to understand tiny prophetesses from the future who have been transported Phillip-like into the life of this poor muggins? Mystery and bliss confront me at every interval, and I do my best, but my best is not good enough. And now my feet stumble on the twilight mountains, and while I look for light You turn it into gloom and make it deep darkness. My heart breaks for her. I am doomed to a fatherhood of failure without You. Has she been sent to lead me, or so that I might lead her? Perhaps the answer is yes.

Chapter 27

July was quickly slipping into August. The day after their quarrel dad and Cristina clasped hands in joy once again. Then that week school began. The one-room schoolhouse the community had built was situated in the midst of a lovely grove of spruces not too far from the sea. For Cristina it took only ten minutes of brisk walking to arrive from Aspen Aisle. The small building was clean and had been kept in good repair, and it looked as though it might be cozy even when the blizzards began to blow. Inside one could see neat rows of desks and chairs, with a large desk at the front belonging to the teacher. Some artwork from the past year's class still hung on the east wall, and beside the large blackboard in the front hung a sizeable map of the world. Cristina would often find herself distracted by the map, and begin dreaming of far off exotic lands where she and dad might travel. She wondered what the Maldiva Islands would look like, and imagined the two of them exploring each one, dark as nuts under the tropical sun, skylarking about in emerald waters. But mother would have to be there too. Beautiful mother in a white dress and straw hat. They would drink coconuts every day and snatch delicious naps under the shade while lulled by the lapping sea. Then they would roam the coasts of the globe in their own schooner, living off the sea, free to follow their wildest fancies, owning little but possessing everything. They'd have their books to keep them company, and dad would preach the gospel to strange, swarthy peoples. And, of course, there would be close calls with pirates, terrifying storms, undiscovered tribes, bizarre sea creatures, and the rescuing of an occasional castaway. But then her reverie would eventually end with a nudge from Gids or a meaningful *ahem* from Miss Evangeline.

At first Will was theatrically sentimental about Cristina being away at school for so much time every day. Even though he spent most days at his job he still resented the thought that she was not at home waiting for him. The first day he had off he worked on his "Cristina" poem and then sulked for a good part of the afternoon until she came home. When she finally approached the house Parrot and dad raced toward her. Dad cut Parrot off so he could win. Snapping her up in his arms, he swung her around and left her more thoroughly hugged than she had been in a long time. Meanwhile, Cat lounged in the sun sleepily.

"I've been sadder than Job's turkey without you here, sprite," said dad as they walked inside.

"Job didn't have a turkey, dad."

"Well that's only an argument from silence. And even you would admit that if he'd had a turkey, it would've been ever so sad."

Cristina shook her head and took a cookie from the cookie jar on the counter.

"I worked on your poem today, Cristy. It may be an editor's worst nightmare, but I can at least say that I've pleased myself immensely."

"Can I see it yet?"

"Nope. And there's to be no surreptitiousness about it, understood?"

Cristina didn't know that word, but she got the gist of the idea.

"Now, tell me how this new teacher of yours is. This miss…what's her name?"

"Dad, you know what it is. Nice try."

"Evangeline, then. Do you call her miss Schoenkopf or miss Evangeline?"

"Miss Evangeline. She likes that better. But Mr. Billy Jim says it ain't proper."

"*Ain't* proper? Ain't you supposed to be learning proper English at that school?"

"It's the Big Mickeys' fault. They're from the south, you know. And besides, ain't ain't useful?"

"You've got me there, you nymph. And I s'pose I can let you say ain't if you let me say mooses. But mind you keep it in moderation, like a nice spice that gives a tasty dish an extra twist."

She nodded and they both took cookies and sat down on the veranda.

"So? How's Evangeline's teaching coming along? Is she as lachrymose as always?"

"Why don't you come and see for yourself?" Cristina did not want to have to admit that Evangeline excelled as a teacher and was liked by all the students exceedingly. This was a way to avoid telling the truth, but she immediately regretted the idea. For dad to see her teach would almost certainly cause her to rise in his esteem. But there, she had already said it. She was in a pickle.

"Brilliant idea. I'll sneak up one day and listen through the door."

And that's just what he did the next day. Evangeline shed her glumness at the door upon entering the school, and no one would have guessed she was the same heartsick girl of a few weeks ago. She apparently had no interest in keeping order, rather her entire energy was focused on winning attention. The order then followed. Dad heard a confident, lively voice, at once articulate and easy to understand. She said only what she meant to say, and nothing more. Each sentence was weighed and selected for maximum effect, and her style was not entirely orthodox. She would walk up and down the rows of desks, picking a student now and then to dialogue with regarding the lesson. Sometimes she would sit on the corner of someone's desk to explain something, and other times pull up a chair to chat face to face with a pupil so that all could learn from their conversation. She was energetic and exacting, yet relaxed; her standards were high, but humility gilded everything she did. Her thirst for excellence was palpably insatiable, and she modeled it for the children. Effortlessly, it seemed, she held them transfixed. And she knew each one inside and out—their particular strengths and weaknesses, their fears and loves, hopes and dreams. There was not a family of a student she had not visited to assess their home life and parents.

One day she walked into the room during a break only to hear Olive Peachy singing a silly rhyme she had made up about Evangeline being an old, frumpy spinster. Olive was mortified, for she truly did not think poorly of her teacher. The girls around her instantly stopped tittering and Evangeline stared at her for what seemed to Olive like a fortnight. Her eyes were eerily calm, but the girls expected a roar of denunciation, which is what they had learned to anticipate from their previous teacher, Miss Marshall. Evangeline tilted her head to the side and said, "Let me hear that again…just hum the tune, if you please."

Olive did so hesitantly and nervously.

"I don't know all that much about singing—I can't give you lessons. But you've got a voice, Olive. God's given you a fine voice. You'd better give up those extra arithmetic problems on the weekends and sing."

Whereupon Alice went home and complained to Aunt Kay that Evangeline wasn't fair and "played favorites" on Olive Peachy.

Since Evangeline was staying at the mission, she began to play the piano in the parlor and accompany Olive on the weekends. Elizah and Cristina would sometimes listen from around a corner or through a window, fascinated by Evangeline's elegant skill on the instrument. Cristina would never admit it to anyone, but the music that Evangeline produced seemed to call the very heart out of her. And she could not deny that sadness settled over her when the music ended.

Evangeline was a teacher who threw herself into each subject with vigor, like a woman desperately trying to drown with work the memory of a shattered dream. She taught Geometry tempestuously, going to great lengths to make everyone understand. If she had to lie on her desk to memorably illustrate what a horizontal line was, she wouldn't hesitate. Circles and angles excited her, and each student couldn't help but assimilate some of her contagious passion for using a quality compass or protractor. When she taught science, each student was a different tree or constellation or creature, and they soon remembered names and interesting facts without much trying to. One day the children might be detectives, solving mysteries of history. The next day they might be warriors in one of the great battles of the past, victims of the French Revolution, or pilgrims landing at Plymouth. Some days they indulged in such jollity that not a few parents were scandalized and felt sure that no one could really be learning and having such fun at once.

"Where's your lunch?" Evangeline asked Cristina one day. Cristina looked a little foolish.

"I got caught up in a book and lost track of time. So I didn't make any to bring."

"Here, you can have half of mine. I got caught up in a book too and forgot that I had already packed my lunch. So I prepared double. Isn't that rather convenient?"

Cristina hesitated. She did not want to take any charity from this woman. But she had to face the bold reality that her stomach was gurgling just then, and the ham sandwich held out to her along with a cup of fresh blackberries looked…well, delectable. Her spirit was resisting courageously, but her flesh was weak. And besides, she had been on a growth spurt lately. Maybe just this once….

Taking the offered sustenance, she said, "Thank you. I'll pay you back."

"You'll do no such thing! Just swallow your pride along with that sandwich. There's a good girl."

Cristina began to react in protest, but her mouth was already full of something so delicious that she forgot how to be indignant. Evangeline could make good food! How on earth had she managed to make such a simple thing so tasty?

"Just last week I forgot to eat dinner altogether because I was reading. I only realized it at about midnight when I finally closed the book. If you had a bit of money, would you buy books with it first, or food? It's a very old question."

"I'd buy food and then go to a library and borrow books for free."

"Good idea! But let's just say you can't borrow books from anywhere. Which would you prioritize?"

"Well I know that dad would say books right away, and he might buy food with what was left over." Then she inwardly cringed at her mistake in bringing dad into the picture. The last thing she wanted was to be part of helping Evangeline become better acquainted with her father.

"But what about *you*?"

"I think I'd buy books just like dad," Cristina finally admitted.

Evangeline sighed. "Me too," she said.

Then Cristina asked, "Why didn't you come in to have dinner that evening when I saw you watching through the window?"

"That's a good question." Evangeline thought for a moment.

"It's hard to explain without telling a long story. You see, I came here to get away from something back where I came from that hurt me very much. I don't do well around young men like…like your father. Nor do I always like to be at a table full of company—I need to be alone sometimes to…to pray and think. It's part of healing I suppose. Forgive me if that's all rather vague."

"What happened that hurt you so much?"

Evangeline hesitated. "There's no time to tell you the entire story, but I can say this: I was betrothed to a man about your father's age. But he changed his mind."

Chapter 28

September was upon them before they knew it. Color swept into the world around, diffusing warm light throughout the forests. As the aspens began to turn Will and Cristina spent many an hour outside in the chilling air reveling in the fiery flush of beauty. Sometimes they would read, sometimes they would just sit and silently sip from the resplendence.

"It's a golden death, best girl. Only God can make death beautiful," said dad one day.

Cristina thought she understood. She had never thought about autumn that way.

"It's terribly inefficient. Terribly inefficient, froglet. Trillions of leaves dying and shed each year. He could have made them all evergreen, but he didn't. The economy of God—it rarely fits our own. Beware, Cristy. God is often kind in ways that will offend your mind."

Cristina nestled up to dad to get warmer and sighed over the splendor before them. They were sitting by the pond, and some of the yellow, leafy fire mirrored in the water. The slender trunks were white and the grass was still green, and the wind rustled everything softly. The sun was lowering behind them, its rays setting the leaves ablaze, spilling kindled light into their eyes until their hearts ached with something between praise and pain. The rushing hues were glowing against a satiny sky of vivid blue. Cristina gazed up and knew that life was alive and that God was great.

And so the days went by and everyone began to scurry to be ready for the oncoming winter. To be caught in an Alaskan winter unprepared is to court certain disaster. All the while Parrot waxed fat and doggish, and dad said it was a pity that she wasn't more dogmatic. But Fritz got lazier and dad cursed his decision to keep him. Evangeline had called Cat Fritz, and she had suggested that they keep him even though he wasn't useful—just for being soft and cute. "May the sun not shine upon that day I let the charms of a woman cloud my judgment!" said dad.

Dad was rather good at cursing things. There was a time when word reached Kenai about a drunk in Seattle who had murdered his wife and forced his son to beg for money, which he then spent on drink. Sometimes he would beat his son so that more people might be moved with compassion at the sight of a bruised, bleeding beggar, and give more alms. Dad was incensed.

"May the LORD strike him with madness and blindness and confusion of mind so that he gropes at noonday as the blind grope in darkness, robbed continually, with no one to help him. May destruction overtake him swiftly, and wailing screams be his only companions. May night and the grave swallow him up, and the depths of the pit engulf him. May he be a horror to all the kingdoms of the earth, with his corpse as food for the birds of the air and the beasts of the earth, with no one to frighten them away. Let his blood be consumed by dogs and fire, and his ashes be spread among jackals."

To Cristina it sounded very much like the Bible, but she wasn't sure. She shuddered. It wasn't often that she heard dad utter such words with such a tone.

Then dad kissed the top of her head and held her close for a moment, and said, "Come quickly, Lord Jesus."

Before long, as if Autumn's lavish wardrobe were not too much already, the northern lights began to appear. The first sighting occurred when the two inhabitants of Aspen Aisle were fast asleep. Miss Knox had seen the aurora while out on a late night hunt and reported them the next day at the diner. When dad and Cristina got word of it they nearly lost their heads with excitement. They planned all day and settled on a spot in the glade near their house from which to watch and sleep under the stars. Quilts and blankets were hauled to the chosen site, along with snacks and plenty to drink. By nine o'clock they had their camp ready, dad had built a fire and made coffee, and the two of them sipped and waited expectantly as the sun began to sink.

When the stars finally appeared the two of them lay down under their blankets and sang together. Dad knew so many hymns by heart. There was something extra special about singing *Fairest Lord Jesus* out under a starry sky like this—something that one never quite felt inside a church.

> Fair is the sunshine.
> Fairer still the moonlight
> And all the twinkling starry host.
> Jesus shines brighter,
> Jesus shines purer
> Than all the angels heav'n can boast.

Then they sang "All Creatures of Our God and King" and "How Great Thou Art" and "Joyful, Joyful We Adore Thee" until they were just about all sung out. Then they talked. Dad told her stories of his college days—stories that made her giggle and stories that appalled her. She asked more about his family and he told her, and then she wanted to know if he had ever gone steady with a girl.

"I can't say I have, moonbeam," said dad.

"But didn't you ever want to? Wasn't there someone you *wanted* to go steady with?"

"Yes. But you must understand that your old dad was too shy back then. Painfully shy."

"You? *Shy*?" exclaimed Cristina.

"Yep. And introverted to boot. Quiet as a mouse."

"I don't believe it."

"Believe it. You can ask Sonny someday."

"Alright, I'll take it on faith. But who was the girl and what was she like?"

"Her name was Ruth. She was—"

"But, wait. What does Ruth mean?"

"Good question. It sounds like the Hebrew word for 'friendship'."

"I like that. Alright, go on."

"She was, well…I remember clearly the first time I saw her. She had a kind of beauty that was altogether too painful to look at. It carried something a little *too* sweet and piercing. With every glance I felt as though I were stealing from the very storehouses of starlight."

"That sounds nice," said Cristina.

"It *was* nice. Her skin actually gave off a faint light of its own. For a long time I was convinced that she was an angel trying to conceal herself within the homely confines of a mortal body."

"Oh dad. That's silly."

"Well it was you who asked for it."

"Okay. Go on."

"It was the first time I understood what it was like to feel joy and terror intermingled. Every time I ran into her or saw her I would be shot through with a terrifying happiness."

Cristina smiled. "I think I understand what you mean."

"Good. So I wrote so much about her that I had to get a separate journal just for descriptions and musings about her. If you read it you'd be embarrassed and look for another dad."

"I would not!"

"You say that now. Someday we'll put your loyalty to the test, frog." Dad smiled and surprised her with a flash of tickling. When her giggles subsided he resumed his reveries.

"Alas, Ruth! Now you've got me reliving so many beautiful memories. I even memorized a poem by Thomas Hood so that I would be able to recite it for her one day."

"I want to hear it."

"Sure?"

Cristina nodded. They continued gazing skyward so as not to miss the first sign of the aurora, but nothing had appeared. It was getting late, and Cristina was getting sleepy.

Dad cleared his throat. "We'll see if I remember it. 'Ruth' by Thomas Hood.

"She stood breast-high amid the corn,

Clasp'd by the golden light of morn,

Like the sweetheart of the sun,

Who many a glowing kiss had won."

"I like the idea of being the sweetheart of the sun," commented Cristina.

"That's because you already are, you young sock."

Cristina reached under the blanket and poked dad in the ribs.

"Mischievous sprite! Am I allowed to continue with the poem now?"

Cristina assented.

"On her cheek an autumn flush,

Deeply ripen'd; — such a blush

In the midst of brown was born,

Like red poppies grown with corn.

"Round her eyes her tresses fell,
Which were blackest none could tell,
But long lashes veil'd a light,
That had else been all too bright.

"And her hat, with shady brim,
Made her tressy forehead dim; —
Thus she stood amid the stooks,
Praising God with sweetest looks!

"Sure, I said, Heav'n did not mean,
Where I reap thou shouldst but glean,
Lay thy sheaf adown and come,
Share my harvest and my home."

"I like that. Did you ever get to recite it for her?"

"Nope. She never even found out that I was in love with her. I never told her."

"Dad!"

"I was shy, remember? And she was more popular and sociable. Who was I to approach such a woman? Needless to say, by the time I finally had the gumption to approach her, some other tomfool beat me to it. They got married. To be fair, the fellow was decent and honest. She wouldn't have married him if he wasn't remarkable somehow. He probably had more money than I did too. But there now, that hasn't changed. I'm still as poor as Job's turkey."

"I thought Job's turkey was *sad*, dad."

"Sad *and* poor, my dear. The wretched, pitiful bird."

"Oh dad, why didn't you tell her? You should have, even after she started seeing the other fellow."

"Hold the presses! What's all this coming from the girl who is fiercely loyal to mother?"

"I didn't say that you should have *married* her. But you should have told her how you felt."

"I see. Well, perhaps I don't understand women."

"No, you don't," agreed Cristina.

"What!" Dad hadn't quite been expecting such a candid remark. "Upon my word! You do beat all, you…you. Fine, I won't try to argue over it. But women don't understand me either."

"So tell me more about Ruth," said Cristina through a yawn.

"She made me worship God. I can remember a time when I ran into her unexpectedly and we spoke for a moment—ever so brief it was. And after that I walked home shouting praises and psalms so loud that I'm sure I frightened not a few unsuspecting souls along the way. 'Blessing and honor and glory and power forever!' And then I ended with nothing left but 'Holy, holy, holy.'

"I was often tempted to capitalize pronouns associated with her. Slightly blasphemous, I know. Like many a naïve poet before me, I waxed on and on in my journals about the insufficiency of words to describe her. The same old cliché phrases really. 'She has conquered the world of words, the lands of language, the empires of expression.' All that sort of rubbish. Like every other young writer I praised the power of her 'one glance' and how she unwittingly changed the world around her by treading upon it. I compared her to stars and prayed dramatic prayers and begged God earnestly to take away the torture of her loveliness. I mused upon the idea of one kiss from her—a kiss that I swore would surely stop my heart. All that sort of rot. One minute I bemoaned what providence had dealt me, and the next I exulted in the thought of marrying her. I was silly as all men are at that age. I thought the only reason she could seem so beautiful to me was because she was meant to be my wife.

"Don't ever marry a twenty-one-year-old man, Cristina. Trust your old dad and don't. You'll rue the day you did. They're nothing but jugheads and chumps, and dumber than boxes of hammers—the whole lot of them. Nobody ever went broke underestimating their ignorance, no sir. Take my word for it. I was one of them. I even had dreams about her. Prophetic dreams, I thought. It doesn't matter anymore. I remember feeling her cry on my shoulder in one of those dreams. I felt her warm tears soaking through my shirt. I'll never forget it. Tears are a gift. Don't ever resent tears, froglet. They're treasures. Ruth, Ruth. Did I tell you how well she spoke? Clear, articulate, better than a politician. I struggled with the idea of having idolized her. I loved her too much, I thought, for it to be right. Sometimes I feel that way about you. I knew I didn't deserve her. I wrote slews and stacks of things about being unworthy of a girl like her—the same old trumpery that's been written by every son of a gun who's got a pen and the gumption to scribble with it. Everything reminded me of her in one way or another. I got to hold her hand once during a meal while we said grace. I almost wrote a sequel to the book of Psalms after that. I gloried in the details about her—everything I could learn. She loved strawberries and had a dream once about getting arrested in Cuba. I fasted on account of her, and thought about her every day even after she was betrothed to the man she married. I wept over her too. She changed me, no doubt. I wouldn't have had it any other way. No regrets. God is wise. And now you're asleep, aren't you?"

The only answer was soft, peaceful breathing. He looked at his daughter's face in the moonlight.

"You've changed me more," he whispered.

Will finally gave in to slumber at two in the morning, still awaiting a glimpse of the northern lights. They slept cozily and dreamed happy dreams.

Chapter 29

"Dear mother," wrote Cristina one gusty day in October,

I'm in school now. My favorite subject is mathematics. I also like science. Dad doesn't know where I got a love for science. Do you love science, mother? Miss Evangeline is my teacher and I think even you would be impressed by her teaching. I don't like to admit it, but I think I like her a little more each day. She wears pretty dresses now which makes people like her even more. But I'll always like you best. I love you. I want to visit the island of Unalaska with dad, and he says we should try to go before winter. I hope you appear before then and can come with us. We just celebrated Canadian Thanksgiving but we're also going to celebrate the American one. Dad says there's no harm in being thankful twice a year. But it will be hard to have another Thanksgiving without you. I'll try to still be thankful regardless though.

The other day me and Elizah found a bottle on the beach with a note inside it. I couldn't read it because it was in another language. Dad said it was probably Rushian. We didn't know any Rushians in town. Dad said that if we found anyone being chased by a moose he would be Rushian and could read it to us. Dad doesn't always make sense. When he acts extra nutty I tell him you must have married him because you were desperate. But I'm only joking. When Elizah told miss Evangeline about the note in the bottle she said she could read it for us. We had forgotten that her mother is Rushian and taught her to read some. But the note wasn't intresting, just sad. A prisoner in Siberia wrote it as his last words, and talked about how he hated all sorts of people and that he was dying as an innocent man. I was hoping it would be a romantic note and Elizah wanted it to be about how to find buried gold. Me and dad used the same bottle and put a letter to you in it. So if you find it you will know where we are and how to find us. At first I was worried that it might end up with the wrong woman. Dad said that if God's not sovereign over little things like bottles and waves and currents then he's not worth believing in. I agree. But I think dad offends other people when he talks like that.

We tried to see the northern lights but we didn't see anything the first night. The second night we saw a little bit of green color in the sky, but it wasn't a lot. It's hard to stay awake long to watch. I like camping out with dad under the stars. Dad named the lights 'love luminaries' and I came up with 'glory shadows.' Dad says he likes my name better. We're going to try to stay up and watch again soon out in the meadow near our house. Speaking of meadows, I asked Evangeline what her middle name was, just in case. It wasn't Meadow. I don't know why I asked. It's hard to explain.

When they went out for the third time to watch for the "glory shadows" they both had a sixth sense that something splendid was going to happen. But Cristina's high spirited hopes suddenly turned frigid when they ran into Evangeline in their glade that night. She said she had looked all over and it seemed to be the best spot to see the whole sky without too many trees in the way.

"But I don't want to impose. You both stay here and I'll find another spot."

"No, that's not necessary at all. There's nothing imposing about it," laughed dad. "We'd be *glad* for you to join us! Right, Cristina?"

Cristina just looked at him and nodded weakly. She didn't have the heart to be rude. And she knew that dad would not tolerate it. He had already had to punish her once for it, and that punishment had hurt him so perceptibly that it gave her pause. The pain she had seen in his eyes had been more dreadful than the punishment itself.

Evangeline, having stood up, looked unsure of herself and the situation. For a moment Will thought she would insist on leaving. Then all of a sudden with a little sigh she nodded her head, said nothing, and returned to her place. Dad and Cristina settled down with their blankets close enough to talk to Evangeline, yet with space enough to whisper to one another without being overheard. Dad said that next summer they would make a little sky-watching booth with a glass ceiling and bed in it just for watching the lights. They told Evangeline of their plans for a voyage to Unalaska, and Evangeline told them about the time her steamer stopped at the isle for coal and supplies. After having seen only water for days the place had appeared to her eyes like some sweet stage for a fairytale. She described its rocky cliffs and snow-capped, towering peaks; the hillsides that looked like a painter's palette of colors; the winding, wind-winnowed valleys, the sparkling blue of its secluded waterfalls, and the white reindeer streaming across verdant slopes. She had especially liked watching pink star-fish and blue and black jelly-fish in the clear shore waters. Then she described the beautiful Orthodox Church that shone like a jewel with its bright white walls and red roofs and green spires against the blue of sea and sky. Cristina asked what an Orthodox church was and dad said that it was a place for those who didn't like orthodoxy. Evangeline smiled and said, "Even if that's true, I heard them singing a beautiful hymn in Russian, and it drew me to walk inside and listen. It was a hymn that my father would sing to me when I was growing up—but in German."

Cristina wanted desperately to hear her sing that hymn, but she dared not ask. But dad asked, as she anticipated. Evangeline declined, mumbling something about not being a very good singer, but dad insisted. She put up a good fight for a while, but dad would not drop the request.

"Alright, fine. But only if Cristina wants me to as well," she said.

Dad waited and seemed to hold his breath, looking at her quizzically while a small battle between truth and loyalty raged within her.

"I...I do," she finally croaked. Dad said it was swell of her and kissed her forehead and snuggled down to listen. A crisp, clear voice, neither showy nor expert rose into the chilled night. As it grew in confidence it grew in charm, and it carried an enchanting, vulnerable timbre like a lily floating down a sunny brook. All at once she had the frankness of a bird—full-throated chords falling quick and strong, melancholy, breaking in upon dreams, rising and cascading in golden trills.

Jesu, meiner Seelen Wonne,
Jesu, meine beste Lust,
Jesu, meine Freudensonne,
Jesu, dir ist ja bewußt,
wie ich dich so herzlich liebe
und mich ohne dich betrübe.
Drum o Jesu komm zu mir
und bleib bei mir für und für!

Jesu, mein Hort und Erretter,
Jesu, meine Zuversicht,
Jesu, starker Schlangentreter,
Jesu, meines Lebens Licht!
Wie verlanget meinem Herzen,
Jesulein, nach dir mit Schmerzen!
Komm, ach komm, ich warte dein,
komm, o liebstes Jesulein!

Wohl mir, daß ich Jesum habe,
o wie feste halt ich ihn,
daß er mir mein Herze labe,
wenn ich krank und traurig bin.
Jesum hab ich, der mich liebet
Und sich mir zu eigen gibet;
Ach drum laß ich Jesum nicht,
Wenn mir gleich mein Herze bricht.

Jesum nur will ich lieb haben,
denn er übertrifft das Gold,
und all' andre teure Gaben,
so kann mir der Sünden Sold
an der Seele gar nicht schaden,
weil sie von der Sünd entladen.
Wenn er gleich den Leib zernicht',
laß ich meinen Jesum nicht.

Jesus bleibet meine Freude,
Meines Herzens Trost und Saft,
Jesus wehret allem Leide,
Er ist meines Lebens Kraft,
Meiner Augen Lust und Sonne,

Meiner Seele Schatz und Wonne;
Darum laß ich Jesum nicht
Aus dem Herzen und Gesicht.

When she had finished dad applauded and Cristina joined him with significantly less enthusiasm and volume.

"And now for the translation, please! At least I'm hoping you have one. I never studied German. Don't tell my daughter. She thinks I know everything."

Cristina elbowed him and Evangeline began with her interpretation of the hymn:

Jesus, delight of my soul,
Jesus, my best pleasure,
Jesus, my sun of joy,
Jesus, it is well known to you
how I love you from my heart
and am distressed without you.
Therefore, O Jesus come to me
and stay with me forever and ever.

Jesus, my refuge and deliverer,
Jesus, my confidence,
Jesus, mighty trampler on the serpent,
Jesus, light of my life.
How my heart longs for you, dear Jesus, painfully!
Come, oh come, I wait for you.
Come, O dearest Jesus!

Happy am I, to have my Jesus,
oh how firmly I hold on to him
so that he may refresh my heart
when I am sick and sorrowful.
I have Jesus, who loves me
and gives himself to me.
Ah therefore I shall not abandon Jesus
even if my heart breaks.

Only Jesus I shall hold dear,
since he surpasses gold
and all other precious gifts,

therefore the wages of sin
do no harm to my soul
since it is free from sin.
If he destroys the body,
I shall not abandon my Jesus.

Jesus remains my joy,
my heart's consolation and sap,
Jesus protects me from all suffering,
he is the strength of my life,
the delight and sun of my eyes,
the treasure and bliss of my soul;
therefore I do not abandon Jesus
from my heart and face.

Just as she was finishing they saw the first hint of a 'glory shadow' forming like a silver bow spanning across the sky. Cristina had been the first to spot it. In silent awe they watched as it began to widen and brighten until it seemed that the sun itself were dawning. The pale white light soon was completely opaque in its archway, like a luminous structure of glowing steel. Then, gradually, its harder edges began to fade as it shifted and writhed slow and ghost-like in a shade of green. After an hour it moved lower on the horizon, hovering just above the snowy peaks. It was melting music of color that transported one to a realm of new magic. All three watchers lay there mesmerized, happy, warm, forgetting sleep. Who could think of closing their eyes when so much sifting beauty might be missed? They did get hungry, though. Evangeline shared some doughnuts that she had brought along, and dad coaxed Cristina with his eyes to share some of her cinnamon cookies with her teacher. And so they munched and drank in draughts of the sky's wonder elixir.

Once or twice dad stole a glance over at the woman who had sung to them. The words still burned in his mind. Sitting now under the haunting, subtle light she was poised to the fine point of mercy. Her hair and eyebrows were darker than the shadows. The light played on her upturned face giving it the glimmer of some more intense reality. She was all woman, the rich lore of womanhood curving and woven through her. When she breathed in, the sky seemed to grow brighter. The wind itself seemed to linger about her, wanting to be near her, lifting her tresses in wraithlike ripples. But then Cristina would catch him staring and nudge him hard. Yet even she had a difficult time keeping her gaze from straying to the sight of her teacher under the radiance. She found herself admiring her with her whole heart. And she had a sinking feeling that the entire aurora and sky and sheet of stars had been made as a backdrop for this woman. It did not seem fair, and she resented the thought. At one in the morning she fell asleep and dreamed that mother was coming for Christmas. Somehow they had been notified that mother—sweet mother!—was only a day's journey away. And her little heart swelled with hope as she slept.

"My daughter has entered slumberland," whispered dad to Evangeline. Her answer came so slowly that he thought maybe she was asleep as well.

"I'm almost there myself," Evangeline whispered.

"I'm sorry about what happened before you came here," said dad.

"Cristina told you?"

"We share everything."

"I didn't wish to burden her with the details."

"Will you burden me instead?"

A long silence ensued, punctuated only by the moon's breath and distant starsong.

"I haven't told anyone here yet. I don't know if it will do any good," she said softly.

"I think it will. A sad secret makes the heart sick."

"Whether it's a secret or not doesn't change the sadness…or the heartsickness."

"I suppose there's only one way to know for sure. But it doesn't have to be me. I know that it's no use to pry where I'm not wanted."

In her balmy, southern accent, Evangeline began. "When I lived in Kentucky a certain man moved into town. His name was Wesley Carter. It wasn't long before his name was on the lips of every young lady, garnering praise and all. He was handsome to be sure, but I thought nothing of him until he began calling at my home. He had noticed me at church, and after speaking with my aunt (I had lived with her since I was twelve when my parents died of the fever), he began coming whenever he could to sit and speak in our parlor or on the veranda. I was flattered of course, and every other eligible woman in the county was rather jealous because he was so rich. At least that was what they said. I was eighteen and rather too easily impressed. He turned out to be an investment banker who had done well for himself. He was twenty six and I soon became overawed by him. His ways—his charm and sophisticated chivalry that he brought from New York contrasted starkly with what I was used to. He was intelligent, of course, and impressed me with his knowledge and opinions of the latest world news, which he would discuss at length with my aunt."

"He sounds like every woman's dream-come-true," said Will.

"Fancy facades usually do. But I was eighteen, remember. What does anyone really know when they are eighteen? A girl hardly knows her own self at that age. She hasn't the faintest idea how to measure and understand a *man*. Oh, but she thinks she knows. I thought I knew. My family even thought they knew. Everyone said it was a perfect match—you know how it goes."

A sudden blossom of light made her pause as they both caught their breath and watched. Every mystery of time and space seemed to echo in the cold, eerie beauty hovering above them. A west wind blew, and Will felt adventurous as he usually did when a west wind blew. With it some crisp autumn scent struck their faces and they filled their lungs with it. It was the wholesome odor of dry leaves mixed with wafts from wood-burning chimneys.

"It would be a waste to sleep on such a night," whispered Will.

"You can almost...*feel* the radiance," Evangeline whispered back.

Will silently agreed, and after a few moments asked, "So what happened with Wesley?"

"I'm not boring you?"

"Not a trifle."

"Very well...Wes courted and spoiled me for almost a year. He proposed on my nineteenth birthday and I accepted—the wide-eyed, naïve little fool I was. We were to be married within a few months that summer, but his father died suddenly and he had to go away to attend to the family's estate for some time. This time away kept getting longer and longer. Once the family affairs were in order, he was off to Boston for some urgent matters of business. The wedding was put on hold indefinitely, and his letters became less and less frequent.

"All the while I aspired to the task of the faithful, blushing fiancé, waiting and praying tirelessly for him. Some days were dreadful to be sure, but for the most part I gloried in the sacrifice and looked upon it as my feminine duty of loyalty and patience. Even when I hadn't heard from him for two months I persisted in writing him almost daily. All the nonsense and folly of a lovestruck young idiot poured itself out upon those pages to him. Vain and endless repetitions of 'darling' and 'you have my whole heart' were stuffed into envelopes—always scented with a little of my perfume. I'm ashamed to admit it. I was so young…so young…so *stupid.*"

She laughed with sneering disbelief.

"Well, when he had been gone about nine months I began having pains on my right side. At first we thought it was appendicitis, but when the doctor ran tests it was worse than what anyone had thought. The doctor discovered it was a rare kind of cancer, and to this day I remember how he shook his head and looked at the floor as he spoke with my aunt in the next room. He didn't know how long I would have to live, but he didn't reckon it'd be more than a few years, depending on how well I minded his instructions and took care of myself."

Will sat up and looked at her, not knowing what to say or do. A certain alarmed concern was in his expression. Ignoring him, she continued.

"A month later Wes came back. My heart had only grown fonder as the saying goes, and after the hard news I clung to him more than ever. I had wept for him and pined for him and exulted in the thought of his return. And he was finally there in my arms. But soon I realized that it wasn't the same Wes I'd thought I knew. He had grown distant and cold—something I could feel even though he still bought me extravagant gifts.

"Then the day came when I worked up the courage to tell him the sad truth about what was happening to me. At first he appeared extremely concerned and petted me like the small, forlorn creature that I was. But the next day when I asked him about our wedding, he began to fidget and his answers became evasive. He knew that he was the last great happiness that I could enjoy on this earth—a happiness that might even have had the power to save my life. He *knew* that. He had received all my letters. No woman had ever been more devoted to him than I was in that moment.

"Suddenly he didn't think it the best idea for us to marry after all. He painted it all in the light of 'my best interest' and that he wanted me to 'concentrate on my health' without the added 'stress of running a home.' Oh, it sounded noble and self-sacrificial on his part. But that didn't change how it was tearing my very heart out. I watched my dreams collapse—my last stab at happiness during the few years I had left. He finally convinced me to forget about the wedding. A month later I found out the real reason why. He went back to Boston and married a girl he had fallen in love with while we were betrothed."

A tear ran down Will's cheek.

"How long do you think you may have left now?" he whispered hesitantly.

"Only God knows. The strange thing is that my health and energy improved drastically right before I moved to Alaska. The doctor was hopeful that I may be on the mend. But he also said to be careful, since these kinds of things often relapse without warning. I could have another few years, or I could have another few months. It's just very uncertain."

Then she added. "Please don't tell anyone. You know how it'll make talk, and no one will treat me the same. Promise me you won't? And promise me you'll treat me like a normal woman, and not as a victim to be pitied?"

Will promised.

Long after Will had fallen fast asleep, Evangeline, feeling her heart a bit lighter for the first time in many days, began to tiptoe out of the glade towards the mission. Glancing down at Cristina sleeping, her heart filled with love and she knelt down and kissed her forehead. "God, bless her," she said. Then she crept away, whispering, "Jesus, my sun of joy."

Before they knew it, dad and Cristina turned the calendar to November. They still managed to watch more of the aurora displays, but their time was increasingly occupied with preparing for the approaching winter. They also did not get to visit Unalaska as they had hoped, so they said it would be a journey for the Spring. They got a new, pretty ingrain rug to cover some of the important floor space, and Cristina painted a few Scripture texts on the walls which dad had picked out. Over one window she had in white lettering, "Let him who walketh in darkness and hath no light trust in the name of the LORD, and stay upon his God."

As chilling winds began to sigh and moan outside more and more, inside the Millhouse home there was always plenty of firelight playing on the walls, soft beds with plenty of blankets, and tasty food. They loved the hominess of home. How the coffee steamed in their own little kitchen! How the hot bread smelt and the warm soups tantalized the two of them! Everything they could possibly want was stacked in the greatest profusion in the cellar and pantry: oatmeal, corn, flour, canned and dried fruits and vegetables, onions, potatoes, and some dried and smoked meats. One could also find plenty of French sardines, clams, oysters, and fine cocoa and cream. An abundance of firewood was at hand to keep them through the days of fierce cold and frost to come.

Both dad and Cristina appreciated the sweetness of well-earned rest and comfort after labor. They had toiled a great deal, and now it was nearly time to hunker down in their home and wait out the snow. They had acquired furs for outside garments, as well as some drill parkies for mild weather and to keep out water. Heavy mittens were ready, and Cristina made sure she had flannel waists and dresses.

When the last Thursday in November came they headed down to the Baptist Mission toting their contributions to the dinner. Cristina had made a pumpkin pie and dad had baked some of his delicious, crusty bread. Elizah was ecstatic to have them join, and she took their coats at the door with an air of importance. Evangeline had helped Aunt Kay for hours with the preparations, and now came out to greet them in a blue and white, polka-dotted apron, spots of flour still on her arms, and face glistening with hints of perspiration. Her hair was braided tightly, except for a few tendrils that had escaped in all the kneading and mixing and washing. The twins, Tara and Tommy, ran to hug Will about the knees, and they wanted Cristina to come see what they had helped make in the kitchen. Alison, Anernerk, and Akiak called out cheery hellos as they got the table ready, and Olive was watching Miss Knox play the piano.

Will noticed that there were two extra places set and asked Paul who they were for.

"We have a couple boarders passing through from Anchorage. One is a lawyer I believe—a Mr. Lardner. And there's a woman who is a dancer. I've forgotten her name I'm afraid," he said.

Just then the nameless woman descended the stairs and took her place quietly and stiffly at the table. Mr. Larder soon followed. Paul introduced them to Will and everyone else took their seats around a beautiful feast. Paul prayed, and before long everyone was either quietly savouring or mmm-ing to the clink of silver on porcelain.

"Miss Knox, I hadn't the foggiest idea that you played the piano," said Aunt Kay.

"I've been playin' since I was a wee tike of six. My momma taught me well. Heavens to Betsy! Ain't this turkey something else?"

"Your surname wouldn't happen to have any relation to *the* John Knox, would it?" asked Will.

"You betcha. You're lookin' at a direct descendant of the famous reformer whom they called the 'father of the puritans.' My family's mighty proud of it—always has been."

"Who's John Knox?" asked the dancer.

Miss Knox explained that he was "only *the most famous Scotsman in history*" and told a little about what he had done, and how Mary Queen of Scots had feared his prayers more than an army of ten thousand men.

Then Miss Knox asked the dancer if she liked hunting and the woman said no, she was a dancer. Mr. Lardner spoke up and said with an upturned nose, "Most people aim at nothing in life and hit it with amazing accuracy."

Will's eyes flared a little. "Mr. Lardner, would you care to enlighten us on what a *truly* worthwhile aim is?"

"Certainly," said Mr. Lardner, stabbing a few carrots with his fork. "A worthwhile aim is one that gives you prestige and respect—one that pays well. I've always considered myself blessed to be above the common lot who rarely make a difference in the world. That is the problem with the world—too many…*average* people. Pardon if I speak plainly. I mean no offense, of course." And he mustered a grin to all at the table, kept his back straight, and ate a spoonful of peas.

"I'm sure you don't," Will shot back. Then he turned and said with saccharine tones, "Children, would you like to hear a little story?" They did.

"Once upon a time there was a man who was given a mouth. It cost him nothing to use because he always opened it at someone else's expense. The end."

"That's not a very good story, Mr. Millhouse," complained Tara.

"I don't understand," added Alison.

Miss Knox then chimed in to change the subject. "That reminds me of a feller who once tried to court me. He'd use all them corkin' big words they teach ya at university and I didn't understand much a' what he said at all."

"You had a beau, Miss Knox?" exclaimed Elizah incredulously.

"You might say so I s'pose…almost. There was never much hope for the poor feller. He'd get busy soft-soddering me whenever he came round to the point where he oughta've been bumped! And so contrary too! He could start a bicker with a haystack. He wouldn't take no for an answer neither. He'd sing me songs whenever he'd snuck a chance, and he'd a voice so bad that it'd make you wanna tear your ears off and give 'em back to God."

Evangeline and the dancer laughed.

"Olive is fine singer," said Evangeline. "She's been progressing very well. Say, how about we have her sing something for us after dinner. Olive?" Most everyone agreed that it would be lovely, and Olive was happy to.

Then Aunt Kay, in an enormous burst of goodwill, asked Mr. Lardner how he had been enjoying Alaska. This seemed to open a floodgate of patronizing criticism. Alaska was, to Mr. Lardner, a savage land of uncivilized people who made no decent contribution to society. He hated the long summers and cold winters, hated the "beasts and critters everywhere", hated the primitive towns, and not a few other things. If Miss Knox had not interrupted him he would have gone on. She took to explaining to the dancer how the natives spent the winter by digging their homes underground and living in cramped spaces for months. Mr. Lardner added his two cents by saying that if they chose to burrow in the earth like animals then he was justified in calling them "dirty savages." Miss Knox countered that they were nothing of the sort, but rather a noble race in every respect. But Mr. Lardner only smiled tolerantly and said that their constant stink of seal oil did not conjure up the word "noble" in his mind. Then Will said that he would like to meet more Eskimos and learn about them. He admired their tenacity to live in such a wilderness of challenges to survival. Mr. Lardner said that perhaps their tenacity was merely stupidity for settling in such a place. So Paul very patiently reminded Mr. Lardner that there were children present and that it was *Thanksgiving* dinner, not a time for caustic opinions. There were some awkward silences, the dancer looked uncomfortable, and Anernerk and Akiak looked a little downcast. Evangeline appeared to be biting her tongue with a vengeance, and Cristina thought the color that had risen to her face made her look especially dazzling in the warm light.

In spite of Mr. Lardner, the food was scrumptious, and Alison reminded everyone to save room for dessert. The twins shared their food, not interested in the conversation at all. Everything Tommy didn't like, his twin sister did, and vice versa. So they cleaned their plates enough to please Aunt Kay who praised them for it.

Will watched Evangeline and marveled over how much she ate. Her appetite seemed to be improving. When Elizah finished her second helping Will asked her if she felt as full as she looked. She smiled and said that she did, and Cristina nudged him and whispered, "That's rude, dad!" Dad had asked her that many times already at home, and the joke was getting old.

Then Paul spoke up. "Well, here at the mission, as many of you know, we have a tradition for Thanksgiving meals. Before dessert we take turns around the table naming two things we are thankful for to God. Would you care to start, Miss Knox?"

Miss Knox surprised everyone when she said that she thanked God for flowers.

"You like *flowers*?" blurted out Olive.

"Well now, missy, just 'cause I'm a hunter don't mean I can't like flowers like any other woman."

Then it was Tara's turn and she thanked God she had a twin, and Tommy did the same. They also shyly thanked God for Cristina, calling her "Mistina" as they usually did. The dancer was thankful for her family back home and for the mission's kind hospitality. Akiak mentioned Aunt Kay and slingshots, while Anernerk was thankful for Uncle Paul and pumpkin pie. Olive thanked God for such a good teacher and Evangeline smiled meekly. Cristina leaned her head on Will's shoulder and said she was thankful for such a great dad, and for Elizah her best friend. And Will said he was thankful for his daughter—"the most beautiful little woman" he'd ever known. While most people did not notice the watery glimmer in his eyes as he said it, Evangeline did. Will was also thankful for books, and Paul said that he had stolen that one from him. Then Paul said very sincerely that he was thankful for the bread of life and the bread of strife. Aunt Kay cried a little when she said that she thanked God for all her wonderful children that she was so proud of, and she also named the sea and the mountains, even though that was three. Alison mumbled something about her cat and couldn't think of a second thing. Elizah was thankful that she would see her parents one day in heaven, and that God had made summer. Evangeline was thankful for her students and for fresh berries and fall colors and hymns and the beauty of Jesus and—until Elizah cried foul and said she'd gone over her limit. And then everyone began inserting extra things as they thought of them. Miss Knox was also thankful for the northern lights and music, and many had something they were thankful for about God to add—his love, his faithfulness, his word, his patience, his sovereignty.

Last it came to Mr. Lardner. Without any hesitation he said, "I'm thankful that I'm not a woman."

"*Damn.*"

It was Evangeline's voice. It had slipped out with more volume than she had intended. Now all heads turned to her. Paul and the dancer raised their eyebrows. Aunt Kay turned a bit white about the lips. Olive covered Tommy's ears instinctively, who in turn covered his twin's ears, and Elizah's eyes widened into saucers. Will tried desperately not to laugh and swiftly lifted a napkin to his lips to conceal his smile. Cristina's mouth fell open. Alison, who had been getting sleepy from eating so much, jolted awake.

Mr. Lardner laughed and said, "That's the most sensible thing anyone's said all evening. I bid everyone a good night." And with that he went to his room.

Chapter 30

"Well now, duck, how do you like the spunk in that teacher of yours? *Somebody* had to say that after that old reptile kept reptiling on. You wouldn't have thought it at first, but she's got sand!" said dad on the way back from the mission.

"I can't believe she swore in front of missionary Paul," said Cristina, feeling weary after a full day and full belly.

"Never you mind Paul! It's all those innocent children you should be worried about! Scandalous." Then dad chuckled. "I like a woman who can wield a wry word now and then. In my mind she's all the more a brick for it....but don't you be getting any ideas. I'll not be having my daughter utter such things around the house. I'm allowed to be inconsistent because I'm a man—and a young one at that."

Cristina sighed. "Mom must've been crazy to marry you."

"No doubts there, you young scamp. Plain dippy. There ought to be a law against women like her doing such blame reckless things. There's still time to stop her, you know."

But then Cristina was suddenly crying. They were nearly home and dad stopped and put his arms about her.

"What is it, starlight? It's not Evangeline, is it? I'm sorry, I should have held my tongue—"

"It's not her. It's just...mother. I didn't want her to miss...Thanksgiving with us. I even told her so...in the letter. Where is she, dad? Why does God take so long to answer our prayers?"

Dad simply scooped her up and carried her in the house, holding her tight. Setting her on the sofa, he lit a lantern, and rushed to his room. He emerged in an instant with a small, blue vial in his hand. Cristina was still sobbing as he sat down beside her.

"Don't mind me," he said. "I'm just going to put your tears in this bottle."

Cristina didn't know what to think. She knew her father was eccentric (if she had only known that word to describe him), but this…this was something from another planet. With dad collecting her tears she suddenly didn't feel as sorrowful anymore. It was all so far-fetched as to be somewhat funny. Smiling and sniffling a little, she croaked, "Dad, you're so silly."

"Am I now? Then you'll have to tell God and David that they're silly too."

"Why?"

"We haven't gotten there yet, but in Psalm 56 David prays, 'Thou tellest my'…. No, that English is too old fashioned. 'You know my wanderings: *put my tears into your bottle*: are they not in your book?'"

"Huh."

"And I have plenty of other reasons."

"Like what?"

"Haven't I always averred that a woman's tears are beautiful treasures? By gad, they ought to have been one of the sacrifices offered up to the Lord in the temple. What a pity that so many of them are wasted away, unappreciated, even despised every day. Who could not prize what emerges from the heart of beauty? From the recesses of the soul of creation's crown? They have caressed a woman's very eyes, and who could not love them for that alone? Are there many things more full of splendor than a woman's eyes? Surely the world is mad if it answers anything but NO. Blatherskite! And what could be more precious than the heart of a woman? It moves those tears to break forth from her eyes, each one bearing the secret magic of what she feels. What use is there in moving mountains if you can move a woman's heart? Is there anything more precious to be moved? And to *see* and *hear* and *touch* the liquid diamonds that issue from that movement—what glory! Down with the fools who believe the lie that these tears must be stemmed or be stopped! Flapdoodle! It is a tide of glory. Perhaps someday the world will be turned right side up and men will once again understand what is valuable and how to treat it as such."

"That sounds like a sermon." She was no longer crying. Dad had managed to arrest only three tears.

He sighed. "It must be that pumpkin pie getting to my head."

"Where did you get that bottle anyway? It's pretty."

"Sonny brought it back to me from Egypt. He found it at a trinket shop when visiting the pyramids. It used to have perfume in it I think."

"But what are you going to do with the tears once it's full?"

"I don't know. I might just keep them as a reminder of you. Or I might pour them out as a drink offering to God one day. Or if I fall deathly ill I'll take a sip of it and it'll heal me."

"Oh dad," was all she said, and she put her arms around him and rested her head on his chest. And there in the silence there was love. It wasn't long before Cristina fell asleep, and dad watched the lantern light dim, knowing he was most blessed among men.

Chapter 31

The following is what Will wrote in his journal during the first week of December:

Tuesday, December 1, 19__

Winter in Alaska pushes the boundaries of what I have known even in my imagination. Yesterday it was ten degrees below zero, and the snow continues to transform the landscape. Cristina and I tried our hands at a reindeer roast today with gravy and mashed potatoes. It turned out to be rather toothsome and we relished it. Often we both wonder how things are with the rest of the country and friends back home, but there are so few ships to bring the mail this time of year, and news is rare. We are beginning to adapt to our new way of life cooped up inside all day because of the severe cold. We have grand times, but one of us usually gets antsy for a walk in the woods every other day, or any bit of outdoor exercise. Snow must be shoveled regularly. When the wind dies down we sometimes bundle up for a romp around our cold, shivering aspen grove, and occasionally slide about on our pond. Neither Cristina nor I know how to ice skate, but Evangeline and Elizah promise to teach us.

On a clear day the sun rises at nine and sets at about five, and many days the clouds can make it seem like the sun never truly rose at all. We make the best of it, reading a powerful lot and keeping a merry fire going. And even though school is out I take to teaching Cristina a thing or two now and then.

Wednesday, December 2, 19__

I've yet to mention that Clarence is here now. He arrived the day after Thanksgiving. The fishing is mostly over for now, so he waited in Nome City for a while to get a boat down here to ride out the winter. The mission had a room for him to stay, and we go to visit him often enough. All the children love listening to him talk. It's the first time they have ever met a Jamaican, and he's been warmly welcomed by everyone there. So he and Evangeline and I spend not a few hours around the fire, sipping hot drinks and gabbing while Cristina and Elizah go about whatever mischief they devise.

Cristina thinks mother is going to be appearing in time for Christmas. She has faith that God will make her our Christmas present. I still have my doubts now and then about whether any of this is real. Do I truly have a daughter from the future? It feels entirely normal now, yet always entirely too good to be true. I wonder, if it is true, how long it will last. Surely she cannot stay forever. If what this little prophetess says is true, I do not have many years left to live. Only on nights like these, with the wind howling, do I dare to think about the implications of such knowledge. Cristina is dozing by the fire with a book in her lap. I cannot think of losing her. It is a thought as cold and bitter as the frozen, dark wilderness outside. It fills me with desperate longing to redeem every minute that remains. Praise be to the Lord of heaven and earth, who fashions dancing poems of light like her.

Beauty's Beckoning
"Come follow," Beauty's beckoning;
"O, with wonder you'll sing!
Rapt marvel shall enfold your heart,
Exquisite, from my art.
You must my masterpiece behold,
Lovely as e'er was told.
Ethereal—the music drawn,
Extravagant the dawn,
Mixed carefully with floral grace,
United in her face.
Rich mysteries were woven through,
Resplendent with what's true.
Adorned with joy more than them all,
Yes, beautifully small."

Thursday, December 3, 19__

Miss Knox stopped by the mission today while we were visiting Clarence. She met him and acted almost shy—the first time I have seen such behavior in that woman. Then Evangeline offered to fetch her coffee and asked how she liked it. "Strong and black," she said, "like I like my men." She smiled and all of us were not a little flabbergasted. For her meaning was unmistakable, and Clarence laughed nervously. Previously no one would have thought Miss Knox had got any preferences in men, especially in *that* way. Evangeline and I hooted over it so much after Miss Knox left that we nearly frightened poor Aunt Kay, who came running downstairs to find out what the commotion was about.

Friday, December 4, 19__

Evangeline braved the cold to pay us a visit today just to tell us all about another call from Miss Knox. She came in the midmorning and was wearing a dress that no one had seen on her before. It smelled faintly of moth balls, so it must have been stored away for a special occasion. Her usual costume never wavers from trousers, except on Sundays, and even then she has always worn the same brown dress. But the one she had put on today was peach and cream and *stylish*. Evangeline was even more aghast when she saw evidence of *rouge* on her cheeks. Evangeline said that she looked pretty, and with a little more help she might just blossom further. Miss Knox wanted to see Clarence, and when he emerged she asked him if he had ever gone snow hunting and whether he'd like to come along and see if they couldn't shoot a fox or two for a warm hat and gloves for him. He accepted, a little more eagerly than Evangeline expected, and they agreed to take along Akiak as well. I suppose the whole town will be buzzing with the gossip tomorrow.

Saturday, December 5, 19__

Cristina says that she thinks Evangeline is in love with me. I asked her why she thinks so and she says that it's just "something women know." I'm not convinced. She says that I ought to tell Evangeline the truth about my future and how Cristina got here before she gets her hopes up about me and I break her heart. If not for my supposed future muddying the waters, along with Cristina's fierce loyalty, I might have considered Evangeline months ago. What with her skin made from snow and dawn and spring wind. There is a stunning, pristine, maiden joy in her eyes (now I am sounding like the same fool who wrote about Ruth years ago, confound it) and when she smiles the universe seems to become young and meaningful again. Her dimples are maddening. Her mouth has such curious motions when she speaks—movements that make one feel that life is new. And her voice! In it is something of faery lands and graceful cascades and breezes caressing mountain grass. If only my daughter could understand that all these things are not so simple. I haven't the slightest idea if Evangeline would believe the truth. And I remain unconvinced that what Cristina said about her attitude towards me is verifiable.

Sunday, December 6, 19__

I think I shall use the *Beauty's Beckoning* poem as part of Cristina's Christmas present. Currently I am working on another longer one to accompany it. No buying gifts this year, since money is tight and must last through winter. Cristina keeps the blue tear vial by her bed now so that if she ever takes a notion to cry she can add to it. She likes the idea, and I couldn't be happier.

A week later they invited Captain Zedekiah over for one of Cristina's signature stews. Bundled up around the fire afterwards, he told them stories from his past life.

"When I was a youngster my parents died and my aunt took me in. Even though she had a chuckle-headed face, she really weren't nothin' but an old beast and I resented her somethin' powerful. She whipped me for nothin' without respite 'til I couldn't stand for it no more. I lit out and ran to the harbor. I'd always had a fascination for ships and pirates and the high seas, and I figured this was my only chance. I was only in my teens, and I boarded the first vessel that would take me bound for a foreign land.

"Soon enough my lips were black from the curses I learned, and my heart was blacker still. I lived a hard and godless life like the lot around me. Years went by. Fortune in my case was always a fickle dame, and I had my share of poor luck. But I stuck it out long enough to become a captain. I wandered and traded and tried to make an honest livin', and I began to grow wealthy. After some time I crossed the Bering Straight and found this fair country ripe for tradin'. We'd load up on wool, tobacco, and flour in San Fran, and then trade for skins in Alaska—polar bear, black and white fox, sea otter, beaver—and then we'd go back and sell 'em for more money than you could whistle at.

"Well, I found the nice little town of Golovin Bay and decided to make it my home, since I was a itchin' for a change and a rest. And there was this woman, you see. An Eskimo woman. She was called Qannik, which means snowflake. And she was as beautiful and graceful as a snowflake too. Bright and intelligent as well. Good swimmer, and she could trap and hunt better 'an any man I ever saw. She could shoot a gun in a blindin' snow storm and rarely miss her mark. If I ever saw a fearless child of nature, she was one of 'em. On land or sea she was free and steady and good-hearted. Can't nobody blame me for takin' a likin' to her. It couldn't be helped.

"The greatest miracle was that she somehow thought somethin' of me. Just by knowin' her I became a better man. And I married her. We had a love that them poets write about I reckon. You might say it was the kind that runs high and free on the crags of bliss like those wild mountain goats, sure-footed as could be, yet always skimmin' the heavens, breathin' the purest air, leapin' without a second thought and not afraid. She taught me how to live for others, and to walk aright. She was a fine woman.

"One day we decided to make a journey to St. Michael together. We thought the weather would hold up, but we were wrong. There were four trusty natives with us and three dog-teams. Hardy Eskimo breed dogs that were well-nigh impervious to the cold. Most of us knew the country perfectly, Qannik more 'an anyone. And we had a good start on a lovely day. All was fair and we reached Shaktolik to stay for the night.

"But the next day on our way to Unalaklik a storm swept up out of nowhere. We thought we were just about to find the town, so we pressed on. To resist an Alaskan snow storm usually means death. The temperature was droppin' like a stone, and the dogs trotted along bravely enough, but we weren't findin' Unalaklik. Everything soon became blinding. The gale was tiring the dogs and coverin' their faces with frost. Then the wind became a fury that made the dogs stop and curl up shiverin'. This is when one of the Eskimos cried out behind us "Muk-a-muk!" Qannik and I looked back to see an ice crack widening across our trail. We saw with a terrible dread that dark, cold water lay in that chasm, and there weren't no crossing it now. We were driftin' out to sea on a cake of ice. From the northeast hurricane winds were blowin', carrying us straight out to the open ocean.

"Qannik kept her head and immediately began diggin' a hole for a hut to get out of the wind. I set to helpin' her and when it was big enough we spread a sled canvas cover over it, tied fast the sleigh outside, and crawled underneath. All the merchandise and supplies we'd been carryin' had been aboard them sleds of the natives, so we had very little to subsist on. We melted snow for water and boiled a little for the bit of coffee that we had with us. Then the dogs joined us inside and we all slept in a huddle until dawn the next day. Everyone was famished and we didn't know what would become of us, until a big, fat seal—must've weighed nearly three hundred pounds—came to the edge of the ice cake and Qannik shot it. Now we had food and fuel, and them dogs didn't have to eat us nor we them. There ain't much that burns so well as seal oil.

"The storm hadn't died down completely, and it lasted another few days 'fore the sun came out. We could finally see the mainland many miles away. Two weeks passed and my wife shot another seal and some birds. The dogs looked bleak, and we weren't gettin' any nearer to the shore. Then one night I awoke to Qannik's hand on my shoulder. She said that the wind had begun to blow steadily from the southwest, and if it kept on blowin' we might be able to reach the shore ice and make our way home. We set to watchin' anxiously for long, weary hours, waitin' to see if the wind would hold out. After a few days we could tell that we were closer, but the wind changed and carried us out to sea once again.

"It was then that I understood with a vengeance what the good book says: 'the wind bloweth where it listeth.' It was a treacherous wind, takin' us from hope to dread and back again over and over. If not for my wife I would've gone mad. The thermometer was probably often at forty below, so there couldn't be no thought of swimmin'. Up until that point I'd never felt any use for prayer, but I set to prayin' as if I'd been born for it. Nobody knew where to look for us, and it was too dangerous for boats. Then one morning we woke up and saw that the wind had blown us all night closer 'an ever before. We were 'bout a dozen feet away from a piece of ice that ran all the way to the mainland, but the wind stopped and we sat there despairing.

"Then Qannik, she said it was now or never. She was going to make the jump for it with a rope and pull us in. I wanted to do it myself but we both knew that I weren't as light as her for jumpin'. I begged her to reconsider but she already had that stubborn light in her eyes that made me know it weren't no use trying to talk her out of it. I didn't like the risk. The water was blacker and colder than ever between us and safety. She removed her furs, and rolled them up, and threw them across the chasm. Then she took a line of rope and tied it round her waist, and had to run soon lest she perish from the cold without those furs. But I'll always remember the kiss she gave me before the jump. She was a brave woman, and that kiss was full of bravery and passion and hope.

"Running the whole length of the ice cake, she leapt and sailed like a seagull. I caught my breath. I'd never seen her fly so far. But it wasn't far enough. She grasped the ice bank but her legs landed in the water. I threw her a large hunting knife and she, with more strength than a woman ever had, crawled up onto the ice. Then I threw her a rifle and she chopped a hole and made it into an anchor with the rope fastened to it. Then I set to pullin' carefully until the ice cake slowly closed the gap and touched the shore ice.

"But there was still no time for rejoicin'. We needed to get off the shore ice lest another fracture take us out to sea again. Qannik was shivering somethin' terrible. Her wet leggings had turned to ice and there was no time nor clothing to make a change, and we were yet hours from the mainland. The dogs ran fast and cheerful to be free, but I worried all the way about my wife. Her muckluks were frozen too, and we finally reached an abandoned igloo and tried to melt off her frozen clothing with a good fire and get warm. She suffered silently and my heart was desperate for her sake. The dark fear of frostbite kept me up nearly all night caring for her and tryin' to make her comfortable. We both found it hard to sleep, and in the morning the sky was a clear blue pool. We thought this was a sign in our favor, and that we could reach home. But before long another storm blew in almost worse than the first. The snow whirled and we lost sight of the trails. We had to stop. We were hungry and exhausted, and we couldn't bear the thought of a night on the mountain with the cruel blizzard. Qannik tried to keep walking around in circles to keep her legs from getting worse. I walked with her, and for hours we did so with our eyes closed and finally grew drowsy.

"She fell asleep and I grew frantic. I wept and started hallucinatin' and couldn't tell what was real and what wasn't. I tried to wake my wife but she only moaned a little and remained unconscious. I'll always remember her face then, with her flushed cheeks and peaceful eyes. I knew I wasn't going to stay awake through the night. There's no tellin' how I stayed awake past midnight. But I did, and I finally fell asleep in the wee sma's with a prayer on my lips and sorrow in my heart.

"A few hours later some Eskimos found us. They made quick work of getting us to a safe, warm place. The journey there floats in my memory like a strange dream. I felt nothing and could hardly see or hear. Then when I came at last to my senses I could only fret over my dear Qannik whose life had to be saved. But although we saved her, she lost her legs. And with her legs she lost her heart—that heart so wild and free. She was never strong again, and although I nursed her faithfully for a year, she died. I had thought my love for her would be enough, but it wasn't. The loss of those limbs was too heavy for her. And the loss of her was too heavy for me. But somehow I keep on livin'. I don't understand it. I don't understand those ruthless storms. I wish I knew why providence.... But there. It's been done."

Chapter 32

"Buniq!" called dad. (He had taken to calling Cristina that when he found out it meant "sweet daughter" in Eskimo.) "Merry Christmas Adam! And tomorrow it'll be Christmas Eve! So, I have three gifts for you. One for today, one tomorrow, and the last on Christmas day. They're all rubbishy poems but they're from my heart. And I've got other things for you too."

"What more do you have?" asked curious Cristina.

"It's a surprise."

"What *sort* of surprise?"

"Not telling," said dad.

"Can't you give me just a small hint?"

"Hmmm. Let's see. It's got nothing to do with George Washington. There, that's your hint."

"Fine. Then I won't tell you what my surprises are either."

Dad, smiling, gave her a yellow envelope. She opened it and unfolded a piece of paper with his handwriting on it. They were sitting by the fire now, and sunshine was streaming through the windows for the first time in days. There were cold blue skies to be tasted outside.

"Go ahead and read it aloud," said dad. "It's about you."

Cristina cleared her throat and read:

The Song of Three Sisters
Love's lilting, fragrant voice is calling,
"Instruction, join in your voice and sing!
Lady Wisdom, my rosy sister,
Lift up with ours your part and glister!
Yes, mingle your ageless harmonies—
Rippling, immortal like golden seas—
Effuse these with us as I now lead
New strains for our hymn. And we will need
Ebullient, effervescent tones,
Enrapturing as those Beauty owns—
Waltzing with light from the womb of Dawn,

Incandescently reborn. As swan
Lifts up its dying song joyfully,
Likewise must our music matchless be;
Inspiring all with grace unfading,
Abiding floral sweetness spilling
Majesty, innocence, purity.
Sing, O sing this elfin lass with me!"

"I'm not sure I understand it," she admitted, "but it has pretty lines in it. I like the idea of a 'fragrant voice'…and 'waltzing with light' is lovely."

"After studying it a bit you'll get the marrow out of it," said dad.

The next day he gave her his poem "Beauty's Beckoning" and planned to give her his longer masterpiece on Christmas morning. But by the afternoon of Christmas Eve Cristina was beginning to feel feverish. She was also developing a racking cough and had to lie down. After getting her comfortable, dad bundled up and ventured out into the snow to find Dr. Snodgrass. It was a cloudy day and darkness was closing in fast by the time he had walked the mile to the doctor's house. But when he knocked he discovered that no one was at home. The neighbors informed him that the doctor had gone to Anchorage for the holidays with his family. If he needed someone he might find a nurse or doctor in Soldotna. Although the roads were impassable by motor vehicle, he could take a sleigh there and reach the town in an hour or so.

Will went back home dejected, cold, and worried. He found Cristina even more feverish and miserable. He cooled her brow and gave her the little medicine they had to try to reduce her cough. Then he hurried to the mission. Paul offered his sleigh and team to send for someone in Soldotna, and Evangeline said that she would stay and care for Cristina while he was away. Rushing the horses as fast as they would go, Will sped away. It was already dark and the lanterns on the sleigh were scarcely bright enough to see much. Fortunately, the road was well established and marked. The steeds did their best in the deep snow, but it was at least two hours before he reached the nearest house in the city. Therein he inquired about the doctor and they directed him to a nurse who lived only a few minutes down the road. He followed their instructions and came to a quaint house with warm lights. By the time he pounded on the door he looked rather frightening with so much frost about his face, covered in snow powder, and a dire look in his eyes.

A man opened the door. Will explained quickly. The man told Will to wait and soon a woman came, dressed and ready for the cold. She carried a small carpet bag with her and Will could scarcely make out her face hidden in the shadows of her shawl. Rushing into the sleigh without introductions, they made haste back towards Kenai. On the way they exchanged few words. It was not the time nor the weather for conversation, and Will's thoughts were wholly caught up with concern and prayers for his daughter. The faithful steeds could not go fast enough, the dark wind permeated everything, and the minutes dragged. Cristina's weak cough, flushed face, and racing pulse loomed before Will for the length of the journey.

Upon arriving they rushed in, Will heedlessly tracking in snow that puddled on the floor in his hurry to see how she was. Evangeline emerged from the room, looking relieved that they had come. The nurse went right to work, doing everything she knew. Soon Cristina's cough lessened and she was able to sleep. As the nurse had suspected it was pneumonia. They would have to take painstaking care of her and pray that the fever would break. Only then would she perhaps begin to come out of the danger zone. Evangeline said that Cristina had not ceased to ask about her father until he arrived. She had become slightly delirious from the fever and had said strange things. Will asked what sort of things and Evangeline said it was all just nonsense she couldn't really remember.

The nurse then said that she could do nothing more and that all that was left was to wait. Evangeline offered her a place to sleep for the night at the mission, and in the morning Paul could take her home. Will thanked Evangeline profusely, and then, in a rush of gratitude, embraced the nurse as he told her how indebted he was to her. It was only after they had been gone for hours that Will realized what a graceful, delicate woman she had been. The few glances he remembered of her in the moonlight and firelight had betrayed a fascinating femininity in her face. But this was only an evanescent thought, soon to vanish at the sound of Cristina's painful cough.

Chapter 33

In the days that followed Cristina gradually regained strength. The new year came and went. Many gestures of kindness came their way, and Will wondered at the number of people who cared about his daughter. Elizah faithfully watched as long as Aunt Kay would let her, sometimes falling asleep at Cristina's bedside holding her hand. Each day Will could count on a card or note from someone who wished her the best recovery. Gids sent two, one of them bearing a heart he had drawn. The Billy Jims brought a veritable parade of hot, delicious meals, no matter how bitter or windy the weather. There were baked sweets from the Big Mickeys, and the Little Mickeys brought a bottle of awful smelling, purple ointment a peddler had sold them that was "guaranteed to cure anything." Dad decided to save it for Parrot if she ever got sick.

When Dr. Snodgrass finally returned from Anchorage he came to see how Cristina was recovering.

"You owe this little girl's life to that nurse in Soldotna," he said to Will. "If I had been here I couldn't have done any better. I'm s'posing you've thanked her properly?"

"I'm ashamed to say that I haven't," admitted Will. "I don't even know her name, now that I come to think of it."

Not long after, Will made his way down to Soldotna to show gratitude where gratitude was due. Cristina was not yet strong enough for the trek through the cold, so he made the short journey alone, this time with a blue sky overhead and a gift by his side. The entire town appeared so differently under the dayshine. He shuddered to remember his first impression of the place in the shadowy, menacing cold. Finding the house, Will knocked on the door and waited. The same man opened the door as the first time, and Will introduced himself and explained his visit. The man smiled warmly.

"My name is Roger and you're very welcome. But I'm afraid she's not here at the moment. You can find her on the lake down the road ice skating. It's what she does to escape from the world sometimes. And on a day like today I don't blame her! You can thank her yourself when you find her. She'll be the only one on that lake."

As Will was leaving he suddenly turned back around and called out, "What did you say her name was?"

"What's in a name? She can tell you herself," Roger called back. Smiling, he shut the door.

Will shook his head. *What a strange thing to say*, he thought as he made his way in the direction the man had pointed him. The lake was not hard to find. A small clearing on the side of the road opened up to a view of it that looked like the entrance to a silver palace. A bright red knapsack marked the spot where the nurse had left her belongings before venturing out upon the ice. All was silent around except for the steady crunch of snow under his feet as he approached.

Then he saw her. All in white, with an orange scarf about her neck, she floated across the frozen, gleaming surface, and once in a while twirled like tenderness. Even from the distance he could see that a childish smile broke from the calm of her face every time she held out her arms to the heavens in a gliding arabesque. There was a girlish playfulness in her skating, and her hair streamed behind her in a cascade of gold. There was something wholly irresistible in the scene—it was a cup of quiet joy to be sipped and not drunk hastily. Her every motion seemed poetry itself—smooth, fresh, lively, sweet. And twice when she nearly lost her balance she laughed with free gleefulness.

Will had stepped behind a bush to behold all of this. For a while he could not bring himself to disturb the pristine vista before him. He watched breathless, mesmerized. How could he bring himself to disturb what he saw? Getting out a scrap of paper, he scratched out a note and left it with the gift by her knapsack. Then he crept away and headed back to Kenai with a smile on his face.

"I went to find a nurse and I discovered a fairy," said dad when he got back.

Cristina sat bundled up on the sofa looking much improved from the day before. "What?"

"I found a fairy, froglet! You won't believe me even if I tame down the reality of it."

Cristina looked at him a little blankly as he scooped her up in her blankety cocoon, and sat down with her. "We'll call her The Lake Fairy. There. Isn't it just busting with mystery and romance? By the way, have I ever told you that you're my favorite daughter? You're my favorite lots of things. Good as wheat—that's what you are!"

"Dad, you're getting sidetracked. Now what's this fairy all about? She sounds wonderful."

"Wonderful doesn't have enough wonder in it, duck. There's only *one* wonder in wonderful. Oh, these old, worn words—what use are they anymore?"

Cristina shook her head and coughed. "Dad. Try to slow down and tell me what this is all about."

Dad told her. And as he did the young child's heart began to swell with hope that perhaps it might be…just maybe…no, she didn't dare. But then the hope would begin to sprout and push its way up again. Could it be…the answer to her many prayers?

"But what's her *name*?" Cristina blurted out.

"Well that's the strange part. Her husband told me that I would find out myself when I found her, and—"

"She has a *husband*?" exclaimed Cristina.

"Why sure! Why else would she be living with that man, Roger?"

Cristina thought for a moment. "He could be her brother!" She nodded reassuringly to herself.

"Well, whatever it is, I don't have her name. I snuck away and she never knew I was there."

Cristina groaned. "Oh dad, we need to know her name!"

"Are you all worked up about this because you think it might be Meadow?"

"Of course!"

Dad kissed her forehead and grinned. "You're a romantic young sock, aren't you? Where on earth you inherited that from is beyond me."

"We have to find out her name."

"Maybe she'll write us a thank you note for the gift and sign it."

"But the gift is a thank-you itself," reminded Cristina. "She won't thank you for a thank-you."

"Point taken."

Then dad said, "Very well, if it'll make you happy, I'll set out for Soldotna as soon as we have another day of good weather and I can borrow the sleigh again."

Chapter 34

Good weather did not return to Kenai for some time, and Cristina pouted over this burdensome providence. If she had been stronger she would have walked to Soldotna herself so that her wonderings might be put to rest. But it snowed like it meant it, and soon there were impassible places on the road to Soldotna. They would have to wait longer to find out who the Lake Fairy was.

"Patience, ducklet. I think that was the name of Job's turkey. They'll clear that pass in no time. And then we'll be able to rush in and sweep that lovely creature off her feet."

"I get to kiss her first," said Cristina.

"Is that so! Who ever heard of such a barmy family! In both senses of the word."

Cristina didn't know what barmy meant, so dad made her look it up.

"All that barmyness is from you anyway, dad," she said, putting down the dictionary.

"Oh, we'll see about that when we meet this Meadow woman. She sounds like she's got her own healthy dose of it in her blood. After all, she marries *me*, remember?" And dad tickled his daughter before she could put up her defenses. She then tried to run in the midst of a fit of laughter, but he caught her easily and swung her back to the sofa.

"You'll have to be faster than that if you want to kiss her first, hopper!" said dad.

Just then a hurried knock sounded on the door. It was Aunt Kay. Evangeline was not well and she kept refusing to have them fetch the doctor.

"She's gotten so bad that I've put my foot down. Will you run to the doctor for me? I'm afraid Paul isn't as nimble in his old age as he used to be for trudging through this snow."

Will hesitated to leave Cristina but she gave him a look and a nod that assured him she would be just fine, and helped him put on his mukluks. The snow was still falling and the sun was just setting. Throwing on the last of his protection for the cold, he kissed his daughter goodbye and told Aunt Kay he would see her soon at the mission.

Thankfully, the doctor was home this time, and he made himself ready quickly. On the way to the mission Will told him what little he knew of Evangeline's condition. The doctor listened intently and shook his head now and then.

"A broken heart and broken body in this kind of climate doesn't stand much of a chance," were his words.

When they arrived at the mission the doctor set to work doing what he could, but he admitted that there was not very much he had to offer. Things were in the hands of providence now, and Evangeline meekly submitted to his attention, although he sensed her dismay at having caused so much trouble. Knowing that she wished to keep her condition as confidential as possible, the doctor gave his frank recommendations to Evangeline and Will in private. Alaska was no place for her in winter. But he was afraid that trying to travel in such harsh conditions was even more risky. She should wait out the snow and keep a strict regimen of rest. Then she should think seriously about returning to a climate with less extremes.

After giving her something to help her sleep through the night the doctor went home. Will watched her in her bed. There she was, drawn and pale, with her eyes closed, breathing shallowly and coughing little coughs now and then. He whispered goodnight and turned to leave, but she said, "Wait."

It was so faint that he nearly missed it. Crouching down beside her bed, he said, "Yes? I'm here."

"I need Cri—" She coughed and a spasm of pain rippled across her face.

"Cristina?" asked Will.

"Yes."

"You need Cristina?"

She nodded.

"Now?"

She nodded again.

"What for? Do you have the strength to explain? It's alright if you don't. I don't want to—"

"I can. A little. You see, when she's near me there's something…I can't explain. She makes me feel strong and well.

Just the sound of…her voice sometimes. It will help. May she spend…the night with me?"

Will brought Cristina. Cristina was a bit confused and resisted at first, but dad told her firmly that it was time to lay her prejudices aside. Life and death were hanging in the balance. Before leaving her with Evangeline he pulled the tear vial out of his pocket and handed it to her. There wasn't very much in it.

"If we weren't so happy together this would be full by now," he said. "I want you to make her drink every last drop before she goes to sleep."

Cristina stared. "But—"

"Shhhh." Dad bent down and put a finger to her lips. "None of that," he said softly, soberly.

She nodded.

"Good girl. I love you, starshine."

"I love you too, dad."

They went upstairs together. Dad prayed for Evangeline and then went back down to the parlor. There Aunt Kay had prepared a snug bed on the floor for him by the fireplace. And it wasn't long before he fell asleep, overcome by exhaustion.

Will awoke to Clarence singing in the kitchen. Before long the Jamaican came in spryly and offered Will a cup of hot coffee. Sitting near Will, Clarence suddenly said, "Mi tink mi a gonna marry Clarissa."

"Who's Clarissa?"

"Clarissa Knox! Or Mis Knox as you'd be calling her."

"Pardon me. Who knew she had a first name?"

"Yah mon. Clarissa Campbell. Sound good, no true?"

"I suppose so. But is she truly another woman like Maria—from Cuba? That was her name, right?"

Clarence hung and shook his head. "Yeh, dat a her name. Maria is a one of a kind girl, no odda girl like she 'pon the earth. No use in a waitin' fo one."

"I'm sorry to hear that. Could it be that your faith is too small?"

"No. Me always know me fate in life fo suffer. Me and Clarissa a go make wan good team. She say she will follow me go a Hindia. And she can't wait fo hunt di foreign animal there. She a wan strong woman—fit fo di mission field. She love me too. We get along alright. What more me want?"

"Well I suppose you've had a good effect on her. I'll admit she's become much more charming around you."

"When me did fall inna love wid Maria me follow me heart … an look where dat lead me. It did a wan disasta. Me have to be practical dis ya time yah. It no realistic to tink me a go find wan wife like Maria who a go go Hindia wid me. People here in America speak nuff of romance, but a no so it go where me come from. Romance is no di reason we marry. Romance is di reason people make problem."

"Very well. Who am I to stop you? You're a wiser man than I. Miss Knox is certainly a decent woman who knows what she believes. She's mature. Can she cook?"

"Not like me. Me cook betta," admitted Clarence. "But yah mon, she can cook. She like it too."

"Then I wish you all the best."

"Tank you."

Just then Cristina came down the stairs. She obviously was tired from having slept rather uncomfortably on the floor next to Evangeline all night, since the cot was too small for both of them to share. Dad wanted to know how the patient was and Cristina said that she seemed to sleep fairly peacefully through the night. Yes, she had given Evangeline all of what was in the tear vial. No, she didn't look as pale as she did last night. She was awake now, and Cristina wondered if dad could take a turn watching her while she helped Elizah with her chores. Will agreed.

"Good morning!" Evangeline greeted him with a tone of cheerfulness as he entered and sat down.

"Good morning. You look a sight better than you did last night. You gave us all quite a scare. Are you feeling as better as you sound?"

"Quite, thanks to you. Having Cristina here did help as I suspected."

"Well, we'll never know exactly what helped—the prayers, the Cristina, or the tears you drank. Or perhaps a combination of the three. My money is on the tears."

Evangeline smiled. It was good to see her smile. He hadn't seen that smile in a long time. It was wholesome and honest.

"Cristina explained about the tears before I drank them. All I can say is that I'm truly grateful to you for giving up such a treasure. I don't know how I'll ever repay you. It's one of the grandest gestures anyone has ever made towards me. *Thank you.*"

"Don't mention it. It's what anyone would have done. I hope it wasn't too salty."

"No, I think the salt might be part of the magic of the elixir."

"Good. Cristina thinks I'm nuts for it, but I'm happy to prove her wrong. Thanks for being the trial patient."

"Anytime." Evangeline sighed. "I hope it doesn't bother you—what I told you about Cristina last night. I hope it's not too strange."

"Why on earth should it be? It's *sensible*, that's what. What I can't understand is how there aren't more people like you. *That's* the strange part of it all."

"That's a mercy. I marvel over her. She's got something in her face. The first time I saw it there was this…this unbidden affection that welled up to overflowing in my breast. It was the most singular thing. I can't recall it ever happening before."

"The two of us have more in common than I thought."

"Well that's silly. It's not remarkable that a father is overwhelmed with affection towards his children."

"Isn't it? I disagree. Love is always a miracle. Love is always a tearing through the fabric of reality. We try to take credit for it but it's always the result of grace. There's nothing natural about real love."

"You sound like Shakespeare now. I understand. I sometimes envy you the position you have as Cristina's father. More than a few times I've dreamt about what it might be like to spend all day with her. I don't know how you survive the weight of glory of being loved by her."

"It's loving her that's hardest to bear. It's like running up one of those snowy peaks across the inlet without stopping—exhausting but exhilarating; sometimes terrifying. Terrifying because of the responsibility before God. Because you know how unworthy you are of such joy."

"What was it like when she was born?" asked Evangeline.

Will thought for a moment, struggling to invent a story but feeling it would not be the right thing to do. Finally he answered, "I wasn't there."

"I'm sorry to hear that. What kept you away?"

"Time."

"What do you mean? Surely you didn't miss out on her birth by being late. Or is she adopted?

"No, neither."

"Then what?"

Will saw that he wasn't going to get out of this predicament easily. He couldn't lie outright to this sick and troubled woman. Not now, not after last night.

"I'm going to tell you something that you must promise to keep a secret. I've kept your secret from everyone but the doctor (and Cristina of course), so I'll expect the same courtesy from you. But you'll find it hard to believe. I still struggle to believe it myself."

"Very well," said Evangeline soberly. "I'll swear on the Bible if you want."

"That won't be necessary."

"I'm ready then."

Will slowly explained to her the real reason he was not present at Cristina's birth…yet. He told her about his life before meeting her, how her appearance turned his world upside down, and how Cristina had discovered that he was her father. Evangeline listened quietly, a little wide-eyed and incredulous, which hardly could be avoided. When Will finished he paused to let it sink in.

"So do you think I'm dippy?"

"No," she said. "It's hard to take it all in. I hope you'll forgive me if I take some time to absorb the shock of it."

"Certainly."

"I suppose that this means that Cristina has always known who her mother will be, and has been looking for her."

Will nodded.

"And that the two of you have been hoping to run across her any day."

"You might say so, yes."

"What is her name?"

Will hesitated. Evangeline had grown very quiet. Her words seemed forced now.

"Meadow."

Evangeline closed her eyes and turned her head just in time to conceal the trickle of a tear from her right eye. Then she said, "Thank you for telling me. I hope you find her soon. She'll be a very…blessed woman."

"Cristina thinks that the nurse that came to help when she was sick might have been her mother. We're going to go to Soldotna just as soon as the weather brightens and they clear the passes, to find out her name."

"She seemed very sweet."

"Yes, she did. We call her the Lake Fairy." And Will told her why.

"Oh my, it sounds like there'll be a wedding soon in Kenai. How on earth will you go about courting her if her name is Meadow?"

"Well I'm sure I'll rush in foolishly and frighten the living daylights out of her, and the only thing that will keep her from running away for good will be an intervention of Providence."

Evangeline smiled weakly. Then she coughed a bit and said, "I think I ought to rest a spell. Thank you for everything. I owe you my life, I'm certain. You should go home and rest yourself. Please give Cristina my profound gratitude."

Will left. Evangeline listened to his footsteps on the stairs, listened to their goodbyes at the doorway, listened to the door finally close. Then she gave way to silent, heaving sobs.

Chapter 35

That day was a long one for Evangeline. She lay on her cot and contemplated her life for hours. All the old pain Wes had caused her came flooding back. She had come to Alaska thinking she would escape the past and heal, but instead she found her heart nursing a fresh wound—the wound of having the wrong name. Cursing the day of her birth, cursing her name, she wondered why she should go on. Why did her body continue on living so maddeningly when her heart had nothing left? She thought back to the time not so long ago when she had cared for the feverish Cristina as they awaited Will's return with help. Cristina had looked at her and cried out, "Mother! Oh mother!" in her delirium, and had clung to her. How her heart had soared and nearly broken with those simple words. Secretly she had hoped that one day those words would not be the words of a mind afflicted, but of a clear soul full of fondness. Not since those fateful days with Wes had she dared even to let hope's foot in the door, but that night it had sprung through a window and came flying to her hearth like a fair-eyed friend. And for a moment she had trusted that hope, only to be betrayed by more disappointment than she could bear. Now she faced sadness at every turn. She was shut in so that she could not escape the broken pieces of her life's vagrant dreams. Her eyes grew dim, and she whispered tearfully, "How long? Will you forget me?"

The doctor's orders to stay put until warmer weather came were not to be borne. She had to leave Alaska or die trying. Her folly would laugh at her each time she saw Will or Cristina. Soon she would be forced to watch and hear about a certain Meadow coming into their lives. It would be the talk of the town for ages, and she would sink down into despair. This was not how she wished to spend her last evanescent moments on earth. She had had her northern adventure, and she had reaped tragedy for the bargain.

With a sudden inspiration of clarity and resolve, she knew what she must do no matter what anyone else said to the contrary. She would wait until her strength returned and then act at once.

Over the next few days Evangeline's strength did improve, but Aunt Kay noticed that all the softness that she had gained over the past few months had turned back into hardened listlessness. She had a determined look in her eye, and seemed more closed off than ever. Aunt Kay worried and Paul prayed, until one day there was word that a rare steamer had come to port on its way to San Francisco. That news seemed to bring a change over Evangeline. She was curious about the ship and asked many questions. The next day she snuck out of the house and no one found out exactly where she had been. "Just out for some fresh air," was all she said when asked.

When dawn came a day later, she asked Elizah to do her the kindness of sending for Cristina. As she waited she packed and tidied the last of her belongings. On her desk sat a stack of envelopes with certain names on them. Beside the stack was one special envelope labeled "Millhouse." This she gave to Cristina along with Will's tear vial when she arrived.

"You forgot this after giving it to me to drink," said Evangeline. "I'm returning it, but it's full this time."

Cristina looked a bit taken aback. "You mean you…"

"Yes, those are my tears."

Evangeline sat down and held Cristina's hand. "I wanted to say goodbye to you in person because…well because I love you. I fell in love with you the first day I met you, and even though I don't know how to explain it I need you to know it. I can't stay here anymore. I know that me leaving will cause a stir, and everyone will want to make me wait until the cold weather passes, but I can't wait. I need to let you and your father focus on finding your mother, and I don't think I'm strong enough to bear watching another woman claim you both as her own. I know I'm a little fool for saying so. I know. I've been silly and presumptuous. I let hope kindle when I should have stomped it out before it had a chance. Heaven knows how dearly I've paid for it. I don't mean to pour all this out on you. Forgive me. I only wanted to see you one last time. I don't know how much longer I'll have to live. But meeting you has made these remaining moments of my life beautiful. Thank you. I don't expect you to feel the same way about me. Not at all. Nor do I pretend to know you that well, but the little I *have* known has been precious—the hours in the classroom seeing your kindness and gentleness, seeing your intelligence and moments of forgetfulness, your flaws and strengths, your zeal, your eagerness, your love for books and creatures and Elizah."

There were tears on Evangeline's pale cheeks now. To Cristina she was a picture of a frail and pitiable woman. And what is a child to say in the face of such sorrow? Cristina said nothing. Yet her heart was moved with compassion. This was her teacher after all. She had not been able to resist a growing fondness for her, and she stepped forward to embrace Evangeline.

"Where will you go?" Cristina finally asked.

"Kentucky."

"Okay."

Evangeline looked into her eyes and caressed her hair. Then she took the fair little face in her hands and kissed her forehead. She embraced her again, and Cristina wondered at her sudden strength.

"Me and dad will miss you."

"Thank you. Those are generous words."

Then Evangeline was gone. With a few hurried goodbyes on the way out of the mission, bags in hand, she made her way to the port. Cristina stood in the parlor looking at the bottle of tears and the card in her hands. It was all so sudden. She could scarcely believe it was possible that Evangeline might vanish from her life so swiftly. Was not this what she had wanted for a long time now? Would this not solve the 'problem of Evangeline'? Yet now that she was gone Cristina felt nothing but a nagging emptiness. She wandered home in a daze of unexpected loss. When she arrived at the house she gave dad the letter and the bottle. Tearing the envelope open, he read:

Dear Will and Cristina,

By the time you read this I will be on my way to San Francisco. Will, please forgive me for not saying goodbye in person. It was not that I did not want to; rather it was because I wanted it too much. I have played the fool twice now. First I thought Wes was the right man for me, and I was wrong. Then I entertained the notion that I might be the right woman for you, and I was wrong again. It is all entirely my own fault for hoping, for recklessly running to this wild land for refuge. I did not expect to meet either of you. One has so little control over one's actual life. Who can know what will happen around the corner? I am sorry to lose the friendship of you both. Love does strange things to a person. Although I leave with a heavy heart, please understand that I will never regret having known you.

For a long time I have imagined and hoped that people like you existed in this cynical world, and now I have living proof. Thank you for *being*. Thank you for your kindness and compassion towards me. Thank you for providing a flash of joy in this grim season of my life. That is all to say, I am grateful for the light of Christ in you, for your love, and for bearing my cross with me. I stand unworthy of any of it. When I came to Kenai I must admit that my trust in God was shaken, trembling, failing. Knowing you has been part of restoring my soul.

You may count on my prayers for you always. Godspeed to you, and may the LORD keep you under the shadow of His wings. I wish you all the best happiness in this world and in the world to come.

Sincerely,
Evangeline

Chapter 36

Will and Cristina took a couple days to recover from the shock of Evangeline's departure. It struck through Will's heart like an icy Alaskan wind. That delicate girl had grown to love him? Cristina had been right after all, confound it! She would never let him forget it now. But there was nothing to be done but wait and pray. There was not likely to be another steamer for a long time, and he had not been given the chance to talk her out of it. But he understood. It *was* easier this way.

Yet both Will and Cristina felt a lingering uneasiness about the whole affair. They tried to forget it by keeping themselves in their usual routine, burying themselves in books, writing more letters, some to mother, some to friends back home, shoveling snow for hours, fighting to keep the house from becoming a block of ice. For a while they entertained the hope of returning soon to Soldotna, but they were forced to give that up as the weather grew worse. Their patience would be tested as they awaited a lull in the extreme cold so that the roads might be navigable once more.

Meanwhile dad went back to scribbling in his journal.

Wednesday, January 15, 19__
    Last night it was so cold that we had to take out our raincoats, steamer rugs, an apron or two, and other miscellaneous cloths and wraps to keep warm. We piled them on one bed and snuggled down underneath. When I am tempted to complain I stop and end in praise—for such moments with my daughter are precious. Who knows how fleeting and few they will be? There we were laughing at each other and at the storm outside. I snored, of course, and Cristina had no pity in bumping me until I stopped. Then later I woke up and bumped her and accused her of snoring (a false accusation, but she deserved it). Now she says that she fears that mother will never get a decent

night's sleep when she marries me. The poor woman. If she only knew what trials await her.

This morning we got word that old widow Mrs. Lawson ran out of firewood. The mission, Mr. Sam, the Big and Little Mickeys, Uncle Rockefeller, and even George Ross, and I donated some of our own so that she can make it through to spring. It will be a close shave for us, though. They say it has been ten years since such a frigid winter came through Kenai.

Then smash! Dad had an idea one day. "I'm going to paint your portrait!" he said.

"But you can't draw and we haven't got any paint."

"With words, with my pen! You'll sit down and pose and I'll describe you like an artist. Then it'll be like having a perfect photograph of you to…remember you."

"Do I have to stay very still like they do for photographs?"

"Nope. But I bet a picayune this'll be just the thing we need to add some spice to our routine. I'll even let you read a bit while I sketch."

Dad got out his notebook and Cristina, catching the spirit of the notion, went to her room, slipped on her blue summer dress, and then hurried to sit close to the fire.

"By jing, Cristina Millhouse, you are a dandy. Dressed to beat the band sure as God made the little apples."

Cristina laughed in spite of herself. "You can't talk like that every time a girl puts on a dress, dad. They'll think you're nuts."

"And they'd be ever so right, wouldn't they, frog?"

She giggled and nodded.

"That's it. Just the smile we need for a proper memory. I'm going to start with just one of your eyes. If I run out of things to say about it, then perhaps I'll move onto your nose or your mouth. We'll likely need several of these sittings."

"But do I get to read what you write afterwards?"

"Do I have a choice?"

"No," she said.

And dad shook his head and started.

Her eye is like a sunburst of inconceivable joy. Her eye is the crown jewel of a face all strewn with treasure. Her eye is like the soft love of a maiden's soul. It is the blooming heart of a flowery face. Her eye kisses the heart of those who see it, tenderly, with the grace of a lily. It calms the stormy soul, frees joy, and gives the spirit wings with but a glance. It beckons and invites the weary to come and find rest and refreshment, as a white-dressed virgin might offer water to a weary traveler. It heals by simply being, by simply beaming beauty and sweetness. It is the nectar of light, a window into a fathomless well of untold wonder. It is a dazzling pool of mystery. It is a beacon of heaven's delight.

Although her face is not smiling markedly, there is a faint smile on her lips, making the dimple visible in the corner of her mouth….

"Alright, I'm ready to hear what you have so far," Cristina said.

Dad acquiesced without a fuss and read aloud.

"But dad! You didn't even mention what *color* my eyes are! There's no way anyone could guess what I actually look like from those descriptions."

Dad laughed. "The girl's got a literary critic's mind, and the tongue to go with it."

"Besides," she continued, "most of that doesn't even make sense. How can an eye kiss anyone anyway? And what is the nectar of light? Light doesn't have nectar."

"Neither do daisies laugh, but just now you look like their laughter," said dad with twinkling eyes.

"See? You did it again. No one can *see* laughter, so how can someone look like it?"

"I suppose that shall remain a mystery until someone older and wiser can explain it to us."

Cristina gave an exasperated sigh and flopped onto the sofa. "You're hopeless. We'll try this again tomorrow, but you've got to try harder to make good sense. Not everything in life can be poetry, dad."

"Can't it?"

"Nope."

"That's what I get for reading Ecclesiastes with you. You're too young to be such a jaded philosopher. Children are supposed to see the world as one big candy coated rhyme."

"But it ain't."
"You mean it *isn't*?"
"That too."

"Well it's times like these that I'm reminded of the hapless snail in Psalm 58. He 'melteth' away. And the only time he got mentioned in the whole Bible was for a curse."

And with that, dad tackled his daughter on the couch. She never knew it was coming. These had come to be called "tickletackles" in their household, and Cristina squealed with surprise.

The next week dad wrote a letter to mother.

Thursday, January 23, 19__
Dear Meadow,

Our daughter says that not all of life can be poetry. What do you think? Perhaps there are simply different kinds of poetry. But I have to admit that there are the prosaic prose seasons of life, as well as the poetic prose seasons. Lately my life has seemed entrenched in a season of verse. Although I am not a gifted poet, I understand the enchantment of real poetry. I hope you will bear with my wandering musings. Our daughter makes me almost unrecognizable to myself each day. And who can I ramble on and on to about her besides you? Cristina will make you prouder than Jehu when you meet her. I cannot wait to watch you light up when you meet her, to see your own blossoming delight in her. She misses you so much. We both hope and pray that you are not much longer in coming to us.

Yesterday C and I played knights and maidens. Being cooped up for days with a howling Alaskan blizzard outside will make you do all sorts of things to pass the time. I can see her vividly and clearly still. There she was, swirling about now and again, like some ballerina from the heart of a violet. Scattering starshine, streaming from her hair; her apron elegant and fine, pulling at all the universe in its pretty spiral. While watching her you feel very sure that at any moment a lyric of light might spill out of her. Or that a cherubim's song might be born and flash into the room, flaming in honor of her. Or that a sunlit garden might suddenly materialize. She is a mythical creature through and through, yet as familiar as my own breath. So many times I experience moments when the days go by and I awake, thinking that my memory of her cannot be what I have thought and written. Surely her presence is not that strong, reaching, purling with unspeakable grace, wild with gentle kindness. But then I see her again, and I marvel. And then I must go on acting conventional, as though the flaming mist and magic before me is common. So I go through the motions, sometimes as though in a trance, wondering all the while why more people are not on their knees worshipping her creator, why there is not the sound of weeping, as people feel their unworthiness to behold such a little woman. It is often like the people of Israel trying to act nonchalant about the first appearance of a pillar of fire leading them by night. The burning presence of Yahweh. It is hard to be casual about such a presence.

I am writing purple prose now, as is the fashion to call it. Do I apologize? No. I grow weary of apologies. What I write is from the heart and I will not lie and say that I exaggerate. When all is said and done it only feels like understatement. Down with the fools who want the world cold and grey! Down with the cynics who scoff at cloudbursts! Down with those who are dull and bored with peppermint sticks! Down with the philosophers who cannot stomach a God who rends the heavens with His voice!

Oh, Meadow, the weight of fatherhood is too much for me to hold alone. Won't you come and bear the glory with me?

Chapter 37

Dad awoke one mid-February morning to a flop on his bed and an eager voice saying, "Wake up, dad! It's the day they're supposed to finish clearing the road! And the sun's out! You should see it!"

Dad groaned and rolled over. He was not an early riser like his daughter. Besides, the morning chill beyond his bed was a strong reason to sleep just a little bit longer. Meanwhile Cristina began rocking and poking him.

"So rude!" he croaked.

"C'mon dad!"

He squinted open his eyes and caught a glimpse of the bright face hovering above him. Then he clamped them shut again and said, "It's too cold. Too early."

Cristina tried another tactic. "I'll make my famous flapjacks if you get up."

"That's a start," he mumbled, "but not enough."

"Hmmm...I'll have fresh hot coffee waiting for you."

"I only drink coffee to make you trust me."

"I'll love you forever," she coaxed.

"You can't help loving me anyway."

"I'll take one of your turns sweeping the house."

"That incentive's mild as goose-milk. Might as well offer me a bar of soap."

"How 'bout I write you a letter and give you three kisses?"

Dad opened his eyes. "How many pages? At least four fat ones?"

"Yes sir, a nice corpulent letter. And I might even throw in another kiss if you make it snappy."

Dad sprang out of bed faster than Cristina had ever seen. In a few quick steps she ran into his arms and kissed his scruffy cheek. Then she kissed his other cheek and his forehead. And dad hugged her so hard she was sure every bone in her body was going to be broken.

"I'll save the fourth kiss for later, and I'll make flapjacks out of the goodness of my heart anyway."

"You would," said dad.

After a hearty breakfast dad and Cristina borrowed the sleigh from Paul and were off. They hooted and hollered as they glided down a sparkling road of white splendor. The sun shone with more alert energy than it had in a long time, and Cristina said it must be happy to look down on the world again after such a long time. Dad said it was a day of clear brilliance. They passed glistening hills and one fairy pattern after the other in the snow. There were little hollows and tunnels now and then that made them wonder what creatures might be hibernating therein. Sometimes they would drive past clearings on either side of the road that opened up into unbroken silver pastures.

All manner of footprints could be seen dotting the landscape. The exquisite outlines of snow-crusted trees held them captivated—trees that were at once gracious and dignified and serene. Fine evergreens furnished the velvety canvas with color, and the junipers and beeches cast ragged shadows. Once in a while they would stop and simply listen to the expansive silence around them. It was a silence one could touch and smell. They felt like the only two people left in a great world blanketed with icy jewels.

Cristina broke the silence. "I can't stop thinking about Miss Evangeline. I feel so sorry for treating her like I did. I shouldn't have been so beastly."

"I suppose you felt you had to be jealous of imposters on mother's behalf. I can understand that."

"But it wasn't right…. I was so unkind to her when she was loving me so much the whole time. I knew she was. But I was so wicked and afraid."

"Did you get to apologize to her before she left?"

"No." Cristina hung her head.

"Perhaps you should write…never mind, she didn't leave us with an address. We'll have to ask Aunt Kay if she left one with her."

"I wonder how she is," said Cristina.

"I imagine pretty sadful."

"I wish she hadn't had to leave—"

"Under such circumstances," filled in dad, nodding his head.

"Will you forgive me for getting so angry with you about her?"

"I already have."

Cristina cuddled up against dad and kissed his cheek.

"That's number four," she said.

"It's highly risky business to be kissing a man while he's driving. He's bound to lose his head and run straight into a tree."

Cristina kissed him again.

Dad shook his head and they both were silent and happy for a time.

"Do you remember the spelling contest at the end of school?" asked Cristina.

"How could I forget it?"

"I can't believe Miss Evangeline challenged anyone from the audience to compete with her for the spelling bee finale. I'm glad now that you took the challenge."

"That woman can spell enough to spite Samuel Johnson himself. But I *let* her win."

"No you didn't!"

"How do you know?"

"Because I could *see* it in your face. I know you, dad."

"Blue cats! Has my pride no refuge from thy gaze? Fine. She beat me fair and square. But how was I supposed to know how to spell boutonniere? The blasted French and their orthography! I blame them."

"I'll miss her voice too," said Cristina.

"Is that so? Because I will too."

"I didn't want to admit it, but the way she sang that hymn that one night made me tingle all over and ache in my heart. It was so beautiful."

"I'll miss getting to help her whenever something went wrong at the school. She really was quite helpless when it came to problems with the well and the stove heater getting clogged. She was always so thankful when I fixed things."

The two travelers lingered in memories for a while, and then dad asked, "What do you suppose we ought to do if the Lake Fairy turns out to have the right name?"

"You mean Meadow?"

"Shhhh, it's too sacred a name to be spoken hastily."

"Oh, dad. I don't know. We can make all the plans we want, but we'll probably end up forgetting everything because we'll be so happy."

"We could always kidnap her until she comes around, and then Paul could marry us."

"Or we could just propose today and hope God makes her say yes."

"You could do the proposing. You're much more persuasive than I am," said dad.

"No, you have to do it, even though I *am* more persuasive."

"And she'll see my glorious complexion, throw all caution to the wind, and rush into my arms, crying, 'I will!'"

"And then we won't bother about a big wedding because that takes too much time."

"I couldn't agree more, Cristinaest of Cristinas. But what of the honeymoon?"

"I'll allow you one day alone, but that's it."

"I'll take it. And then we'll start right off at being a family."

"And we'll show her so much affection that she'll have to make rules so that she can sleep and get things done around the house," said Cristina.

"Yes, but we'll treat her like a princess too, and we won't let her lift a finger to work much."

"Good point, dad. And you'll write at least one poem a day about her."

"I wouldn't be able to help it. And you'll obey her perfectly."

"Of course! And you won't be able to keep a job because you'll always skip work to see more of her, so we'll be terribly poor but terribly happy."

Dad laughed. "My daughter knows my going out and my coming in!" he said to the sky. "And *you'll* be so distracted by her beauty and loving and admiring her that you'll fail all your studies. So you'll be terribly doltish but terribly happy."

"I will not!"

"And we'll both fill up many tear vials because we'll be weeping for joy and thankfulness so much."

"And then we'll use those tears to wash her feet," added Cristina.

"Brilliant. And we'll never get sick because we'll be so happy."

"And we'll make her sing to us every evening!"

"And we'll read heaps of books together and go on long walks in the woods and eat such good food that we'll all get fat. But we won't care because we'll be so happy," said dad.

"And Parrot will love her all the time."

"And when she goes outside all the creatures of the forest will crowd about her and push and shove to be closest to her. And Parrot will have to clear the way for her to walk," said dad.

"I couldn't have said it better myself," said Cristina.

"Oh, and we'll be so tempted to idolize her that we'll have to repent every week."

Cristina thought about that for a moment. "But it'll be such pure love that it couldn't possibly be idolatry, and she'll inspire us to worship her creator all the more."

"Out of the mouths of babes," said dad. "But I'll kiss her so much that it'll gross you out."

"No it won't. I'll just admire your *sensibility*."

"Good. But will we have time for any other friends? It sounds like all our waking moments will be occupied with loving this woman how she ought to be loved."

"Yes. We'll be so happy that we'll have heaps of happiness to share with others. It'll spill out of us on everyone else. Besides, we'll want to show her off to everyone. It'd be selfish not to."

Dad's arm that had been around her this whole time squeezed her hard.

"I like dreaming with you," he said.

Chapter 38

When the two travelers finally arrived in Soldotna Cristina could hardly contain her excitement.

"I have a feeling something very important is going to happen," she blurted out, eyes shining.

After asking dad how she looked, and after dad asking her how he looked, they stepped up to the door of the Lake Fairy's house, feeling as nervous as anyone does standing at the threshold of untold promise and discovery. Will knocked three times on the door and then whispered to Cristina, "No tackling her with kisses on the first visit, ok?"

She nodded and smiled.

This time it was not Roger who opened the door but the nurse herself. She wore a dress of warm crimson, and her cheeks were still flushed from ice skating not long ago. The breath of both dad and Cristina almost went from them at the first wave of loveliness that shone from her countenance. There was a wild, mystic beauty before them: the hair of spun gold that hung behind her in two heavy, lustrous braids, the oval face marked with lines of youth, the smooth, slender throat, the blue of her eyes that held ponds of twilight and hints of ocean calm and lilac thoughts, the delicate, black eyebrows, the sylphlike arms with perfect shape and texture, the elegant, graceful hands with rosy-nailed fingers.

Before they had time to stumble over their words, they were welcomed warmly and whisked into the house.

"It's such a pleasure to see you again!" said the Lake Fairy. "You look like a different person now that you're well again," she said to Cristina. "I'm so glad I could be of some help."

"We really are so grateful to you," said Will. "I wanted Cristina to be able to come and thank you herself. Please pardon us for taking so long to come. I'm sure you know about the snow and the road...."

"Oh yes, I understand completely. Believe me, your gratitude has already been much more than any other patient has ever shown me."

Just then Roger came in from outside and greeted them. Then he turned to the Lake Fairy and said, "Hey sis, why don't we have them stay for tea?"

At this Cristina nudged dad and whispered, "I *told* you she was his sister."

"Splendid idea! You'll stay, won't you?" said the sister.

"We'd love to!" they both cried.

As the Lake Fairy was heading to the kitchen Cristina said, "But excuse me, miss. We never did get your name."

"Oh yes, pardon me. I'm Agnes. Agnes Porter at your service." She smiled brilliantly and disappeared into the kitchen.

Luckily Roger was not watching either of their faces after they heard her name. He would have seen a pair of crestfallen expressions along with a good bit of shock.

When Agnes emerged carrying steaming cups of tea, she said, "I do hope you don't mind us not offering you any coffee. We don't keep it since we've never quite gotten used to the taste."

Then Cristina said, "Do you like Bach, Miss Agnes?"

"Oh, not especially, but I *do* so enjoy Mozart. Why do you ask?"

"I…just thought you looked like someone who might like Bach." Cristina looked a little sheepish.

Agnes laughed good-naturedly. But although her laugh was pleasant enough, dad and Cristina were both beginning to notice a certain grating shrillness in her voice.

"What sort of books do the two of you like to read?" asked Will.

"Well, my sister's not exactly the reader in our family," at which Agnes nodded a bit guiltily, "but I have a tremendously high regard for the work of Jane Austen…."

That was when Will stopped paying attention. Jane Austen?! Who on earth loved Jane Austen? Will knew not how to identify much longer with such a being. Cristina looked at him forlornly, her eyes saying, "We should just go." But they were there now. They owed this woman a debt of gratitude, and the least they could do was show some manners. "We have to be polite and stay longer," dad flashed back to her with his eyes.

"How has school been for you, Cristina? I've heard talk that there's a brilliant new teacher this year. Do tell," said Agnes.

"Uh...she's a peach, I guess. She must be the best teacher Kenai's ever had. I heard Mrs. Little Mickey talk all about the teachers they've had in the past, and she's not like any of them."

"To call her 'brilliant' is actually an understatement," chimed in Will. "I've witnessed her teaching myself and it's second to none. She's fragile and grave on the outside sometimes, but underneath she's got inextinguishable fires of devotion and enthusiasm and energy and absolutely limitless humility."

Agnes clapped her hands. "My! That's quite a glowing description! It makes me want to go back to school myself."

"What's her name?" asked Roger.

"Evangeline Aileen Schoenkopf," said Cristina.

"Oh, Aileen is a beautiful name. Our grandmother's name. Means 'of the green meadow'," said Roger.

"That *is* lovely," said Agnes. "Some people get all the beautiful names. Now, Cristina, how are you feeling these days? You look strong, so I'm guessing you're back up to full steam."

"Pardon me? I'm sorry. What did you say?" said Cristina. "Oh, yes. Yes. I...I'm just fine now, thank you, ma'am. Thanks to you." She forced a smile.

"How long do you two plan to be in Alaska? Have you moved here for good?" asked Roger.

"We...uh...I...Cristina and I don't really know. Life is...uncertain for us these days. The Lord keeps us on our toes. But we've built our own house and like it just fine here. There's no place as beautiful as Alaska. That's certain."

"Oh dad, I just remembered that we need to be back soon for your *appointment*!"

"Ah yes, I almost forgot. Please forgive us for having to rush off. Thank you so much for the tea and for saving my daughter's life. If you ever need anything please let us know. May God bless you."

And with that they were out the door and back on the sleigh. Dad and Cristina looked at each other for a long time, but neither of them said anything.

Chapter 39

"Cristina," dad said at last. There was something in his voice that made her know he was very serious. "I think there may be something you haven't been telling me."

Cristina sat beside him in a pronounced stupor, eyes wide, barely conscious of the world around her. "I don't understand how this could have happened," she said barely above a whisper.

"Is it possible that your memory of what mother looked like has faded?"

Cristina shook her head. "I didn't want to admit it. It seemed so shameful to forget what your own mother looks like. When I ended up in the field where you found me everything was so fresh in my mind. But then things began to fade very quickly. And then when I began trying to draw her it was too far gone, and I didn't know anymore." Cristina was crying now.

"She died when I was so young. Oh dad, I'm so sorry. I'm so sorry! I thought it would be easy to find her if she had the right name. I was afraid of miss Evangeline because I liked her so much and she didn't have the right name." She dissolved into sobs and dad put his arm about her.

"There, there, lily. I know what it's like to be blinded by my own pride and pigheadedness. I trusted you, and I'll trust you again."

"But you shouldn't forgive me, especially for how hard it was on miss Evangeline!"

"Grudges are too ungainly and heavy for me to hold onto. I've not got the time nor the energy for it I once had. I'm sorry. I'm gonna have to let it go. God knew this was going to happen, my girl, and he planned for it to happen, and he meant for it to happen. Besides, to paraphrase a very judicious person, 'What's the use of being a Christian if you can't trust that our wise God is working this for our good?'"

"But why did he have to make it so complicated? I thought that if we knew the future it would make everything so…so simple."

"He loves shattering expectations. Confounding the wise. He tells us the future and then we're just as surprised when it happens as if he hadn't told us anything at all."

"But how will we find her?"

"Oh, Aunt Kay will have the address. Never fear."

"What will we say to everyone when we leave?"

But dad didn't answer. Cristina looked up and saw tears glistening on his cheeks. They held each other in silence for the rest of their journey home.

They stopped by the mission and Aunt Kay did have an address, but when they entered the doorway of their home nothing felt the same. Normally they would have been overjoyed with the hominess and a deep sense of belonging. But not today. They wandered about listlessly, not knowing exactly what they should do with themselves. Dad finally got some soup together for supper, but the soup didn't taste as good as it usually did. They huddled around the fire afterwards, trying to get warm, but it seemed colder than usual.

"Well, we must look on the bright side: we have her address. It was lucky she left it with Aunt Kay out of common courtesy. But…."

There was no need to say it. They both knew too well that the chances of a steamer coming soon were too low to get their hopes up. Unless a miracle happened they could be trapped in Kenai for at least a month.

So they waited. Will soberly went back to his writing and spent many hours helping Paul at the mission with miscellaneous mending. Cristina, with renewed resolve and new perspective, set to writing a journal of letters for her mother. They told everyone that they would be leaving soon in order "to visit family", and they kept their suitcases packed and ready in case a boat came along. It was hard living like that day after day—always hoping you might be leaving and never able to. They could make few plans, and they were not even sure that they would be able to attend the wedding of Clarence and Clarissa. The days slowly began to grow longer, and they eagerly listened to every shred of maritime hearsay. Dad kept on being dad and Cristina kept on being Cristina, but a bit of worry often lined their faces. They kept on loving each other, but more often the love was fierce, as a drowning man grasps for anything that floats. Both of them wondered how much more time they would be granted together. It was something they never spoke to each other about, but they understood. And when they held hands as they walked, they both consciously savored it as though it might be the last time. When Cristina smiled, Will seared that smile violently upon his memory. When dad laughed, Cristina thrust the dear sound into her heart and tried to chain it there forever.

But soon they discovered that it is not easy to bottle and store up grace and love. For they are like air that is breathed in and out, and by them we live.

Hope and pray as they might, the steamer did not come, and the weeks dragged by. They even fasted, which was something Cristina had never done. But they continued learning a lesson in patience.

Clarence and Clarissa's wedding came and went. It was a simple affair that took place at the mission. Lots of Eskimo friends attended, and the parlor got rather crowded and the smell of seal oil permeated everything. Even the wedding cake tasted a little like that pungent odor in the air, but nobody cared because of the joy of the occasion. The Billy Jims refused to come because they didn't think it was decent for their children 'to see a white marrying a black.' Titus Pepper came but tried to protest when the opportunity for objections came. He said that it wasn't right for a Presbyterian to be marrying a Jamaican, but Paul shut him up fast with some Bible verses and a quick, stern look. Missionary Paul preached a beautiful sermon that made most of the women cry. Even Miss Knox's eyes misted a bit, but later she would never admit it. She would only allow that her eyes "were sweating."

Cousin Noah surprised everyone by bringing chocolate bars from Anchorage for all the guests, and the Little Mickeys made the cake. Then the Eskimos got to dancing as they usually do at parties. Mr. Gomez sang in Spanish and Uncle Rockefeller and Captain Zed clapped. Clarence and Cristina danced together because Clarissa wouldn't. She was embarrassed and said that no proper Presbyterian like herself would be caught dead doing such a thing. It was the first time anyone had seen Miss Knox embarrassed, and Mr. Sam teased her. Paul laughed and didn't fret over the dancing even though it made Aunt Kay very nervous and uncomfortable to have such forms of gaiety in a Baptist mission. She told Paul that next time he would be allowing them to bring their own "beverages" (she meant alcoholic drinks, but it was too difficult for her to say it outright; it would be unseemly for a lady like herself to utter).

Meanwhile Will wrote in his journal:

> We grow weary of waiting. We are learning things about ourselves and about forbearance. Helplessness engulfs us, and yet is such not the essence of being poor in spirit? A thousand different feelings overtake us about our time here, about Evangeline, about saying farewell to our friends. No matter how we hunt for answers, for clear guidance, we find none. I am face to face with my own cynicism, lamenting how much I resent extreme dependency. Yet dependency is the heartbeat of abundant life. I need rest from the weariness of doubt, the wandering of my heart over wastelands of fear and anxiety. My faith meanders during times like this. The cold creeps down to the soul with its chill. I am inadequate. Who can father such a child as Cristina? How much longer will You leave her with me, O Lord? But I know Your answer stands as with all such questions: trust me.

On a Tuesday, a steamer finally slid into the sleepy Kenai harbor. Word spread fast, and Will and Cristina were the first to secure passage aboard. They bade goodbye to the dear friends, but assured everyone that they would be back soon before anyone felt their absence. Much advice and small tokens "for the journey" were heaped upon them, and they scarcely could fit all that they accumulated into their telescopes. A small crowd gathered at the water's edge and waved to them as they cast off. Small pieces of ice still were washing up and down upon the sands with a clicking sound and the ocean was smooth as glass.

Once aboard, Will and Cristina realized why they were the only people in Kenai who were traveling by that particular steamer. It was called the "Elk", and was not the most suitable boat for passengers looking for a comfortable and pleasant ride.

The cabin they had been given was cold and foul, and the rations offered them turned out to be meager and often stale. "Prices are high," said James the cook. "And what's a man like me to do when he ain't supplied proper? No taters, no chicken, no fruit, no fresh meat. Makes settin' up fine meals mighty hard. It's the truth, I tell you!"

The "Elk" was an old vessel, almost as old as the captain, Stanley, who was nearly through with the steamer business. Will and Cristina found themselves longing for fresh air as they set off on the smooth waters. But fresh air meant braving the cold. Their cabin had only one lamp that swung over a table, hardly giving any light because of how stained with soot the glass was. Dirty dishes were scattered over an oilcloth on the table, and the air combined the smell of coal-oil, fish, and tobacco. There was no heat nor fire, nor was there a place to be found for it. Some dingy curtains hung loosely on wires about two portholes, and their berths were the only clean things in the place, which made them thankful. And in spite of the conspicuously indecent state of their cabin, they were content. For they were on their way at last, bound for mother.

That night they had a fitful sleep and heard men running about, along with a few shouts. The long, deep-toned whistle of the steamer sounded, and then finally they were able to resume their dreams. In the morning they discovered what had caused the commotion. Two men had been rescued from an open boat that had been blown out to sea. The men were nearly frozen, and had been battling with a bad leak in their dory. They were set right again with some hot drinks, food, and dry clothes. But they both smoked like volcanoes, and Will and Cristina could hardly bear entering the cabin where they were to say hello.

Since there was no fire onboard to warm themselves by, dad and Cristina were forced to open their trunks and put on more layers than they had imagined possible.

"Try to suppress your risibles," said dad as Cristina looked at him and giggled uncontrollably. "You look a sight yourself!"

But when dad tried to tickle her she exulted in being tickle proof from all the layers. "This simply will not do," said dad. "We need to get to San Francisco soon."

Chapter 40

One night Will found himself tampering with Cristina's "Meadow Journal", as he liked to call it. She had fallen asleep early while he read the Bible to her, and sea travel seemed to make her more tired than usual. He read:

Dear mother,

You don't need to have any douts about dad. If anyone tells you that he's too crazy for you, don't listen. He *is* crazy, but it's the right kind. Do you understand? But he's the very best father in the world. I want to write a biografy of him. Did you know that he once fought a painter? It's a long story. I'll tell it to you sometime. If I don't get to write his biografy then you should. He's got lots of journals you could read. And he's ever so handsome, mother. You have to see it. I hope you do. Maybe he's not handsome like Blaze Thunder, but he is handsome. Don't listen to anyone who says diffrent. And he's such a good man. He does good things all the time. He helps people. When you marry him you'll see. I've lived with him for a long time now, so I know. He'll be the very best husband. He'll clean up after himself and even do it without you asking. He'll help you with all sorts of things. He loves to help. He'll even do the nasty things you dont want to do, like cleaning up rat droppings. And he never gets angry! Only when someone does something very wicked, or when someone talks bad about God. But normally he's very patient. You'll never find a better husband mother, I promise. He's the loveliest person you ever saw. He can be very absentminded about some things, but you must forgive him, alright mother? You must love him for all his nuttyness like I do. He's very warshed. That's a word we made up. It's a long story, but it's the best word to describe how nutty he is. And you musnt be to hard on him because he's very sensitive and proud. Yes, he's proud, but I think you must be too, so you can help each other not be so much. Make sure not to try to make him eat too much or he'll get frustrated. And if you scratch his back he'll love you forever. He's a dreadful snorer, but if you coax him to sleep on his side then you'll be swell. And make sure not to put too much salt in his soup. He'll finish it politely of course but he won't ask for a second helping. And dad always asks for a second helping of soup if he thinks its good.

Oh mother, he's a fine man. You can tell him all kinds of things and he'll understand. He listens like a good friend. And he's gentle too. He loves to talk, and you'll make him ever so happy if you talk to him all night. And if you write him nice things he'll love you even more. But mother, you must be prepared to be loved so much that it might make you dizzy and frightened. He loves like a thunderstorm. I read that in a book once and I thought of him straight away. But it's all right because you'll get used to it, won't you mother? And thunderstorms make beautiful things grow.

Oh, and dont forget to pray for him, mother. I know he prays for you a lot. He says all the time that he's not fit to be a proper father or husband, so you must pray for him. And make sure you read your Bible ever so much because I know he admires women who do that and he'll kiss you lots if you do. And if you sing to him he'll kiss you even more. I hope you like kisses, mother because if you don't then you need to learn to like them even more than pie and ice cream.

What else? Oh yes, you've got to know that dad is very generous. He loves to give ever so much. He says that if giving was a spiritual gift he'd give it away. I have heaps of things that he has purchesed or made for me. You have to tell him not to buy you so many things because he could easily spend all the money he has and then you'd be poor. So just be thankful for things he gives you but try to encourage him to give you things that don't cost money—like letters, fruit, poems (he's a swell poet, mother), flowers he picked himself, cleaning things around the house—those kinds of things. He won't be able to live without giving you things all the time, trust me.

When he asks you to marry him dont try to play hard to get like miss Canning does with the men. I don't know what he'll do if you don't accept the first time he asks you, but you shouldn't risk it; it wouldn't be wise. Not that I think you would ever do something like that, mother—I'm just trying to be helpful.

When they arrived in San Francisco they nearly ran off the boat for joy. It was their first time to see that grand city, and they had close to a whole day to be tourists. They found a place to secure their belongings and set off to wander the streets and marvel. The weather was mild enough to wear only one or two layers now, and dad was grateful to have access to his daughter's ribs whenever she was saucy.

"I haven't thanked you for all the detailed advice you've written to mother about me," said dad as they ambled among scads of people. "It's good advice. I'm sure she'll appreciate it."

"You're welcome." Cristina smiled and felt grown up and wise.

"The worst of the journey is over. No more cold, fishy cabins. Should we ride the trolley?"

Cristina thought they should. As they went higher up they marveled at the beauty of the sight before them. It was a clear day and the ocean sparkled and glistened. The ships that dotted the scene looked like toys, and the sheer modernity of everything dazed them a bit. Soon they had to return for their things and make their way to the train station. They bought their tickets and sat down on a bench to wait and rest. Cristina got out some bread and cheese they had bought at a local shop, and they made a good meal of it.

"Serve yourself a cup of light," said dad.

"Dad, I don't feel good."

"Is it your stomach? Something you ate?"

"No. I don't know what it is. It's just strange—." And she suddenly clung to him, burying her face in his chest.

Dad held her, but he felt something now too. It was as though she were becoming lighter—or was all the gravity around her changing? He felt disoriented for a moment, and then heard her say a passionate, "I love you." Then in one horrifying moment she faded as a lantern might dim and expire, and was gone. He was suddenly grasping air, and crying out,

"Cristina! Cristina! No! God, no!" He looked about madly, stood up and sat down again several times, and then stood like a statue until convulsive weeping doubled him over. A few people looked at him askance, but no one stopped to ask if he needed help. The steam from the trains poured all around, and the roaring engines drowned out most of his sorrowful sounds. How long he cried he never knew, but for hours afterward he sat on that lonely bench, completely unaware of his surrounddings, barely conscious of anything passing before his blank stare. His train was called and left, but he never realized nor cared.

Chapter 41

The memory of the time that followed Cristina's disappearance was little more than a blur of stinging bitterness in Will's mind for years to come. It is the account of him stumbling through the wasteland of his own heart, sinking in tears, gasping for sanity. Such searing pain stifled hope, and his faith fluttered frantically to stay alive like a butterfly in a hurricane.

Objections could not help but rise up in his mind with hot gall, replaying themselves over and over. Tragedy's grim outline seemed to lurk in every corner of his life. For days he tripped aimlessly through the city of San Francisco, clinging to the chance that Cristina might appear somewhere. But he knew deep down that she had been taken away for good, and he suppressed that knowledge as long as he could. He hardly ate, and for two nights he slept in the open air on park benches, not caring what became of him. On the third day an old widow saw him and took pity on him, thinking he was a homeless tramp. She gave him a square meal and made sure he had a hot bath. He was quiet and only repeated "thank you" now and then. When she asked him questions he simply closed his eyes and shook his head. She did not even learn his name until he had been there three days. Most of those days he slept between listlessness or bouts of weeping.

Then he began to speak, haltingly at first, but enough for the widow to find out what had happened. He said he had lost his daughter, but when she asked how, he only said, "The Lord took her." She also learned where he was needing to go. And so she went to the station and bought him a ticket to Kentucky, identified his luggage in the lost-and-found office, and made sure he got safely on his way. By that time Will was beginning to look considerably more alive, but still no suggestion of a smile traced its way across his face. Will still had some money—enough to survive the rest of the journey and a bit extra that the widow had generously given him. Evangeline's address was still in his breast pocket as well as his mind, for Cristina had made him memorize it just to be safe. All the while he clutched a small bundle of Cristina's writings that he would not part with for the world. There were still blank pages in her "Meadow Journal", and he found himself needing to write.

> Who is this God who has done this—whom I thought I knew? Who is this God who is bidding me crawl through dark fire just for the joy of His presence? Temptations to doubt encompass me on every side. Never has it been so hard to rest in Your sovereignty. For I know the truth that You form light and create darkness, but now I waver. I am ashamed of myself, and then I look around and see that my only comrade has become the night, and I despair. Why do I not die in the shadow of death? Death seems sweeter than life. And then I hear the rebuke of truth and sink down deeper into the pit.

The tiny butterfly of his faith in the midst of the storm was close to having its wings torn off. The beautiful hues were being pummeled by rain and by hail. But where else is such a creature to turn except to the one who creates tempests and commands them with his voice? The wind obeys him. He creates calamity, but He also creates Cristinas. With languishing heart, Will often recalled his own words, "Beware, Cristy. God is often kind in ways that will offend your mind." Just as Cristina had birthed psalms of praise in him, she now taught him the art of lament.

One particular evening while awaiting his next train, he crept into an abandoned shed. With fog blanketing around he poured out his tears until they ran dry, yelling until his voice grew hoarse, sometimes to God, sometimes to no one in particular, wiping his nose on his shirt. The dark shed was as empty and silent and cold as the smarting void that had been left within him. There was no escaping the finality of it. When one has tasted the bitterness of such finality one knows how the heart gags and chokes. It would be nice to say that every time these bouts of desperation overtook Will he came away with renewed faith and comfort. But that would not be the truth. He was often angry. He busied his thoughts with other things, pushing snarling, knotted roots of bitterness down as far away as possible. He neglected his Bible for a time. The storm looked as though it would triumph and destroy. The floodwaters rose over the highest peaks. And the dwelling place of the light was nowhere to be found.

But through the hurricane a strong hand sheltered that little frantic butterfly from being torn asunder. One has to feel the frailty of one of those flecks of art to understand—to see them powerless in the net, their flimsy, vulnerable life, the dusty wings more fine and delicate than a woman's eyelid.

What is more glorious, one must ask: a god who keeps the world storm-free, or the God who rumbles and lights up the world with flashing fire, but preserves a fragile creature in the face of raining fury? A butterfly has already been reborn once, but when it is brought into calm splendor after the walls of black wind have thrown and howled and blasted the world, it must feel like regeneration.

Slowly hope began sneaking into Will's broken universe. His heart and flesh had been failing, but he was being borne up—that much he knew. When he reached Louisville, Kentucky he almost felt sane again. A little golden haired girl on the train had smiled at him just hours ago, and he had felt himself smiling back.

He hired a driver to take him to 526 East Oak Street, not knowing what on earth he would say to Evangeline. Looking out the window, he admired the evidences of Spring's passionate blush beginning to stain the world with the hues of praise. The trees seemed glad to be living again. All along the road beautiful Victorian houses sat, looking contented and satisfied with the place.

The driver stopped and announced, "This is 526 East Oak Street on the left." Will looked out the car window. The house looked very much like he imagined that 125 Sunshine Lane had looked in its glory days, with white pillars, a lush, well-kept garden, and a spacious front porch. Just as he was about to get out, a man emerged from the front door holding Evangeline by the hand. He was tall and dazzlingly well-dressed, with a face that rivaled many a Grecian sculpture. In short, Will had to admit that his looks were altogether impeccable—something no one would think of him, William Millhouse, in their wildest fancies.

He began to feel small and tattered, homely and painfully ordinary. Evangeline and the man sat down and began to talk amiably, the man never letting go of her hand. An outburst of laughter soon followed from both of them. They never knew they were being watched, for the walkway to the house set it far back enough for Will to remain unnoticed in the shadow of the vehicle.

"Wait," he said to the driver. "I'm not sure if this is the right place after all."

Who was he fooling? Cristina was gone, and hadn't she been the main reason Evangeline had come to care for him? Certainty about what he was doing fled from him and doubts crowded in.

"I was mistaken," said Will to the driver. "It's the wrong address. Please take me back to the station."

Back at the station, Will stepped up to the ticket office with stooped shoulders. No one would have recognized him as the Will Millhouse who had preached at the mission in Kenai only a couple months ago. His gait was deflated. His money was running low. There was only one place left for him to go.

"To Dallas, please," he muttered to the attendant.

Once he had his ticket in hand, he wandered over to an empty bench to wait. A few yards down the way from him he noticed a man curled up on a bench who looked homeless. Every now and then he heard the man groan, and he recalled how he had once been in a similar plight himself. Approaching the man cautiously, he asked him if he might be of any help.

"Are you hurt or sick?"

"Yes," said the man.

"So you're sick? What is it? Do you know what you've got?"

The man said he didn't know, but he had one hellish fever and not a dime for medicine or a doctor.

Will reached into his coat pocket and drew out a blue vial.

"I don't have medicine or money to give you, but I can offer you something that's better than medicine."

The man looked up at him and the bottle. "What is it?"

"It's a mixture of love and sorrow and beauty—the three most powerful things in the world."

The man looked at him with not a little suspicion. Then he shrugged and said, "As long as you can swear there's no harm in tryin'."

"I can swear that...on the Holy Bible if you like."

"No, you look trustworthy enough, lad. And I'm desperate enough to try anythin'." And the man drank down every last drop without another word. He thanked Will gruffly, laid back down, and fell asleep.

An hour later Will boarded his train and took his seat. Gazing absently out the window, he noticed the old man up and about, and he appeared to be searching for someone. As the train began to pull away the man recognized Will in the window and trotted along beside. He grinned from ear to ear as he motioned with his hands that the elixir had worked and the fever was gone. Will smiled weakly back at him, and the train sped ahead southward.

Chapter 42

"I feel as though I have awakened from a dream and realized that reality is a nightmare," wrote Will.

Am I insane? Did I imagine the last year? All the clamoring voices of the commonplace tell me it is so, that no one can experience such unalloyed happiness. Surely I am the victim of a grand hoax, yet the vivid memories haunt me. Perhaps I am to marry someday, perhaps not. Nothing is certain anymore. Does a Meadow exist somewhere in this world? I have never known one, never heard talk of one. Did I think Evangeline would forever ignore any other suitors while her death loomed only a breath away? Surely I was a meathead to expect anything more or less than what I witnessed. God has given her a consoling joy for her last days in this torn world.

And so it was Will arrived in Dallas: with a mind full of doubts and a heart full of pain. His parents were surprised, having received no notice that he was coming. They hadn't heard from him in months and had been worried. More excitement and glad welcome glowed in their faces than Will ever would have expected. Yet in many ways they were the same. For months thereafter there would always be a tinge of sarcasm or tone of I-told-you-so when they referred to his time away.

Dallas had not changed. Its big busy world had kept on being busy, kept on chasing the wind with ever fresh vigor, kept on building monuments to itself, celebrating the temporal and ignoring the eternal. The rush, the noise, the bustling pride of the city were more alive and well than ever.

When Will first arrived he collapsed in his bed and slept for nearly three days. Then he fell ill and spent another week in bed. Although he had secretly hoped that the sickness would be fatal, it turned out to be nothing much worse than a bad cold.

Mother petted and indulged him during that time, and Will tried to drown out his heart's throbbing loss with sleep. It was an easy escape.

When he was better Mother took him to see the shiny new apartment building that had sprouted up where 125 Sunshine Lane had once stood. Then he went to Dallas Bible Church and saw many old friends. Not much had changed there either. One family had moved away, but otherwise the same people were sitting in their same places.

And what did Will tell them when they asked about Cristina? He followed his first impulse and told them that she had died. At the time it seemed the only way to explain it. He told the lie with the same sorrow that the truth had caused him. It had been the harsh Alaskan winter, he said. The sickness she had survived was now the sickness that he told them had killed her. Many bestowed their sympathies, but there were some, as Will expected, who cast glances of blame at him. He knew what the whispering lips were saying and the shaking heads were thinking: "What had he expected? Taking a poor young thing like that into such a savage wilderness!" This added to the sting of what he suffered. To be blamed for harm coming to his precious Cristina struck a hard blow. Yet who would believe the truth? Not until it was too late did he realize that he should have said that a family had adopted her in Alaska, and that he had nobly given her up to them for her own good. He had spoken out of acrid anguish, and now he had to abide the consequences.

Blaze came to visit. His time in Hollywood had been short lived, and now he was back home. He was still loitering around town, spending his money on fancy restaurants, avoiding responsibility, and waiting for an invitation back to L.A.

Sonny and his family had Will over for a meal, and afterwards Sonny's wife remarked, "If I didn't know any better I'd say that the man we entertained tonight was a sad, complete stranger. It's a miracle his own mother recognizes him."

And it was true. Will had lost much more weight than he could afford. He rarely took the time to groom himself with care as he once had. Dark shadows lurked under his eyes, the light had gone out of his face, and the life from his voice.

Months went by and he retreated into books. Then his parents told him he needed to move on and find a job and a place of his own. Work would do him good, they said. So he tried. He applied at many places, but the interviews went all wrong. No one wanted to hire someone who seemed so depressed. And the construction companies didn't want to hire someone who looked so frail. Therefore, back he went to the maintenance shop.

His parents who had been dreading this all along, threw up their hands in bewildered defeat. And they secretly wished he had stayed in Alaska. If he was there they would not have to make excuses for their son's failure to find a "successful career." Back at the shop Will saw that nothing had changed, except that Mr. G had retired. Bill, Mark, and Laura still wandered about, working half-heartedly. Without having to work under Mr. G Will actually managed to enjoy his job most of the time. There were things to be done that he knew how to do, and he was freer than ever to help in areas Mr. G had always prevented. His previous experience with the shop, combined with all the knowledge and skill he had gained from building his own house in Alaska fitted him to be one of the shop's best workers. Laura's father noticed, and gave him more responsibility along with a raise.

Soon after beginning to work, Will found an affordable apartment nearby his dream meadow. He laughed at the name now, always with a tincture of gall in that laugh. Yet he still visited it often, sitting on the same park bench, thinking, remembering, sometimes murmuring a prayer or two, watching the moon. And so the days went by. He kept the same routine: work from eight to noon, a simple sandwich during lunch hour, another four hours of work, and he was usually home by 5:30. He ate supper alone while reading a book, and then went to his dream meadow. Then he would come home and read for a while and go to sleep. But since Cristina had gone he had stopped eating breakfast. That had always been their favorite meal together.

Several times he had the impulse to write Evangeline, but he never followed through with it. Once he even got as far as writing a letter, but he decided not to mail it. This is what that letter said:

Dear Evangeline,

Can you forgive me? I came to see you at your home, but saw you with a suitor and left. I lost Cristina. She disappeared suddenly while in my arms. God must have taken her—whither I do not know. I am a broken man because of it. I hope you are well and that there is good news regarding your health. My apologies for not writing to you sooner. I hesitated to interrupt what seem to be happy days for you. After you left, Cristina and I were convinced that you were the missing part of our family because of your middle name, which means 'of the green meadow.' Weren't we silly? I don't know anything anymore for certain. I'm sorry to say I don't have better news, but I wish you all the happiness in the world.

Then a fat letter came in the mail, forwarded to him from Alaska. It was from *Poet's Corner* magazine in New York. Months ago Cristina had badgered him to send his poem, *Spendthrift Splendor,* to a magazine or two and get it published. It was the third poem he had written her for Christmas. He had finally acquiesced to his daughter, and here was the editor's reply. He opened it to find his manuscript returned, with a slip of paper that said:

We have read your poem with interest, and regret to say that we cannot accept it for publication at the present time. If you have other less flowery selections, please send them for our consideration.

Will smiled. He was not surprised. He had tried to warn Cristina that submitting such a poem was useless. He knew better than anyone that it was too "flowery." Even worse, the rhyme was too conventional. But she had been adamant and immoveable. Nothing would do but to yield to her demand. And he had done so with pleasure. All that had mattered was that she loved the poem. He remembered the evening he borrowed Aunt Kay's typewriter to make ready the manuscript for submission. The pages still held a faint scent of burning pine logs.

Spendthrift Splendor
A matchless dance of dusk and dawn,
Of music gay her features drawn.
Her face and form by light defined,
By Light Himself her heart designed.
With vivid hue of blushing skies
Her countenance His honor cries,
And every word upon her tongue
As if by Wisdom had been sung.
The tone of love's awak'ning sighs
Resounds within her splashing eyes,
Wherein meet truth and purity;
Where mingle peace and dignity.
Extravagance has made her hair
Wherein lies wild glory's lair.
This soft and silken radiance
Declares the grace of Providence.
These glossy strands of His concern
Can cause one's heart from sin to turn
And think upon whatever's true,
What's noble and makes all things new;
What's worthy of our praise, and chaste;
What's innocent and makes us taste
The fruit of righteousness and see
The goodness of His majesty.

For it is He who fashioned her
As heav'n's unlikely overture—
A child made of rain and rose,
Of sunrise and ebullient prose,
Of sparkling seas and silver streams,
Of bridal flush and youthful dreams,
Of Mystery's magic silences,
Of twilight's fleeting fragrances,
Of pensive meadows golden-green,
Of misty rainbows opaline,
Of moonlight-dappled virgin snow,
Of floating laughter's afterglow,
Of crystal fountains kissed by life,
Of realms untouched by sin and strife,
Of deathless, blooming asphodel,

Of rushing beauty nonpareil,
Of sweet perfume on summer breeze,
Of winter's crisp, delightful freeze.

How does one begin to explain
The joy of her presence, the gain
Of knowing more fully the face
Of Jesus my Savior, and trace
After fair trace of Gospel lines?
For nowhere are their sweeter climes
Than Your soft, holy mountain air
Charged with her nearness and her stare.

With spendthrift splendor You imbued
This tiny fairy, and renewed
The magic in my somber heart
By this Your peerless work of art.
For He—the Truth, the Life, the Way—
Outblossoms freely in her play,
And glens of His forgotten grace
Lie in her delicate embrace.

All of the starshine of His Name,
And all the whispers of His fame
Rush reckless from her rippling voice,
Demanding of my soul, "Rejoice!
Rejoice in Him who is the source
Of all her worth, the wondrous force
Who gleam of galaxies compressed
Into her smile and called her 'blessed.'"

Oh blessed among maidens sing!
Sing to your Maker and your King!
Give to Him sure and glorious praise;
Angelic anthems to Him raise!
And magnify Him with the flame
Of aspect yours; boldly acclaim
The Spring and righteous Fountainhead,
From whom strong hills have turned and fled,
Who poured forth fluid melodies
And liquid, tingling harmonies;

Who with these shaped your cheeks and nose,
Your slender feet, your bonnie toes,
Your hands of ivory symphonies,
Harmonic hair in filigrees.
And when for you He crafted limbs,
He sculpted them of sacred hymns;
And mirthful medleys did comprise
The moulded fabric of your eyes.

So rich and resonant His words
When first He spoke the flying birds
And what preposterous, mighty sound—
His voice creating beasts of ground.
The singing waves of divine glee
Brought forth the primal land and sea.
But ne'er a sweeter whispered song
Than when He sang you, sure and strong.

O tiny fairy, hear me now:
O never to another bow.
And keep Christ as your only love;
Keep His supremacy above
All else the world considers gain,
Its empty promises so vain.
He is your life, your length of days;
Hold fast to Him in all your ways.
Exalt His Name with every cell
Of your fair form, and always tell
Of the unparalleled delight
Of savouring His truth and might.

Ascribe to Him, O tender girl,
Ascribe to Him all strength, and twirl
Within your heart for joy in Him,
For then this tawdry world will dim
Before the Light who made you see,
Who made you from the darkness flee,
And say, "World, I bid thee adieu.
Christ taught me to abandon you."

It was the first time Will had read anything he had written about Cristina since she disappeared. Memories came flooding back, and a warmth began to grow within him, like a tiny spark of coal beneath rubble and ashes catches a breath of wind and begins to glow.

Chapter 43

"I want to ask you a question," said Mother. She had surprised Will that Saturday with a visit. "What was it that made you finally become a Christian—finally...I don't know how to put it? What convinced you?"

"Why?" asked Will. This was the first time she had brought up something about God on her own without a derisive tone.

"I...well," she fumbled, "I've been thinking a lot about...things lately. I don't know why. I simply can't get some certain things off my mind."

"Like what?"

"I suppose you might say...death, and what comes after, and if what I'm doing with my life really matters for anything. Of course, I'm not saying I want to be a Christian—that would be impossible, being married to your father and all. He wouldn't be able to stand it. Plus I'm much too old for any radical changes like that...but I'm simply curious. That's all."

Oh what a glory of promise filled Will's heart! It was a seed he had never thought possible with his mother. Mother! Thinking about eternity! More life began to creep back into his soul.

Later that night Will and Sonny had a long talk. He spilled out the story of Evangeline for the first time since he had returned, and Sonny said, "You've already waited too long, Will."

"What do you mean? Too long for what?"

"To hightail it back up to Kentucky and give her a chance to say yes!"

"Say yes to what?"

"Why to marrying you, of course!"

Will shook his head. "She's almost certainly married by now. Her days are limited. She's not going to wait around for me or anyone else."

"Then she isn't the kind of girl you described," said Sonny.

Will went home downcast. He looked for a book to read, but nothing appealed to him. Finally he pulled out a dusty old box from under his bed. Inside he took out a notebook. Opening it at random, he read:

Dear mother,
    Dad can be terribly dense sometimes. You have to make allowances for him not listening and not understanding some things. Just be patient with him.

There are moments in life when no one can explain the movements of the heart. Just then Will experienced such a moment—a surging change of volition and desire. His heart leapt and light rained upon it. All at once he knew what he must do.

The next morning Will was on the first train headed north. He stuck his head out the window and felt the exhilaration of the wind against his face. Lost time lay before him, waiting to be found and recovered. Whether Evangeline was married already or not, he knew he had to see her. He owed it to her for Cristina's sake. Cristina would not have rested until he made every effort to win her. Although his hopes were low his heart was high because he could imagine his daughter's excitement, her enthralling company, her simplicity that had made a true grownup of him. Even though the loss of her had made him poorer in spirit than ever in his life, his was now the kingdom of heaven. In his mind the words, "And a child shall lead them" echoed over and over. He had learned such big things from her smallness. Her childlikeness had slain his childishness. The least he could do right now was to follow through with her last wish and hope.

Did he really know what he was doing? No. What did he know anymore? His small view of reality had already been yanked out of his hand too many times. Yet now he was able to embark on this venture with a face open to a world teeming with more unpredictable miracles and untamable tigers than ever before.

Will arrived in Louisville in the middle of the day. He still had the address in his mind—he had not been able to forget it. "526 East Oak Street," he told his driver, and he offered him a tip if he could get there fast. He had no idea what he was going to say, nor did he bother gathering his thoughts for what lay before him. The houses whizzed by and his mind whirled in a turmoil of anticipation. There was a feeling in his chest that he hadn't felt for ages. Was it nervousness? It was, but he could scarcely believe it.

Then he was there, walking down the pathway to the front door, knocking hurriedly, waiting, knocking again. An old woman came to the door, whom Will supposed to be her aunt.

"Good afternoon," said Will.

"How may I help you?"

"I've come to pay Evangeline a visit. Does she still live here?"

The woman said that she did and introduced herself. "My name is Grace Chadwick. Pleased to meet you. I'll bring her right down."

"Will?" Evangeline emerged from the doorway. "What on earth? I...you were the last person I expected to see today."

The old woman left them to sit and talk on the front porch. Evangeline was looking anything but beautiful that day. She had had a difficult time sleeping the night before, her face was pale with dark circles under her eyes, and she wore an ugly brown and yellow gingham house dress, having expected no company. Her dark hair was not arranged as she had taken pains to style it in Alaska, and now it was in a careless, long ponytail.

"Where is Cristina?" asked Evangeline.

"That's one of the reasons I haven't come to see you. She's gone."

"Gone? What ever do you mean?!" Panic struck Evangeline's face.

Will explained all that had happened, how he had limped along in the aftermath for so long, how he was only barely beginning to pull out of the dark valley in which he had been sinking.

Evangeline was silent for a long time. Tears filled her eyes and she wept quietly. Will took her hand and held it. It was slender, cold, and colorless, but its touch burned. When she could speak again she whispered, "I'm so sorry."

"She thought much more of you than she let on, you know," said Will. "She loved you in the end. She wanted to see you again."

After some more moments of silence Will asked, "How is your health?"

"It's been much better, thank you. The doctor was right about getting away from the extreme cold. God has given me enough strength to keep moving."

"Have you married?" asked Will abruptly.

Evangeline sputtered incredulously. "What would put such a silly notion into your head? Of course not!"

"Will you marry me?"

The words hung in the air and seemed to sting Evangeline bitterly.

"Have you come all this way to mock me?" she finally said. "You know good and well I haven't got the right name for you."

"I'm not here to mock you, Evangeline. I'm here because Cristina and I found out that your middle name means 'of the green meadow.' Didn't you know that?"

"No," she admitted. "But I don't see how that proves anything. It's a weak piece of evidence."

"Perhaps it is, and perhaps I'm a fool, but everything else about you matches the little I know about Meadow."

"Like what?"

Will explained.

"You're crazy," she shook her head. "The last thing I want is someone marrying me because of my name, or a list of strange qualities—or out of pity."

"You darling little idiot! Pity? Pshaw! You can throw that lie to the dogs. If anyone would be showing pity it would be you upon me. Me! Who am I and what have I to do with beautiful heads?!"

But Evangeline remained unmoved and a stubborn line was about her lips. "I would be a fool to risk Cristina not being born," she said.

"But you've got it all wrong! Do you really think God is so small as all that? Do you think his plans so weak that he'd let a couple chumps like us ruin them?"

"But it's no use, Will. I don't want to cause you more grief than you've already suffered. I'm *dying*. Don't you see?"

"Well that didn't seem to matter with that other bloke I saw with you a few months ago."

"You were here?"

"I came here on the way back from Alaska. I saw you with a...man on the porch. He was obviously a suitor. He was handsome and charming, and I thought you might have married him by now."

"And you didn't come in to say hello? Whatever was the matter with you?"

"I didn't want to interrupt, I suppose. I was mourning. I didn't have the constitution for it at the time," said Will.

Evangeline shook her head. "I didn't know how to tell him no at first. He's a fine man, but not for me. He doesn't come around anymore. He didn't know about my...my condition at first, and when I told him he took it like a gentleman, saying it didn't matter and such. I knew it did though."

"You seem to be in the habit of not believing men who love you."

"Love? Ha!" she scoffed. "I used to think I loved or knew what love was. Wes taught me that I didn't."

"Who cares about Wes Carter. What does *God* have to say about it? Love's staring you in the face and you want to call it pity. Do you prefer the lie to the truth?"

"Please don't make this harder on yourself," she pleaded. "Just forget about me and find the real Meadow. She's bound to show up any day now. I'm not the kind of girl you need. I'm not worthy of any of this—I know that now."

"Woman!" but there was the chime of bells in Will's voice too. "I'll not have you casting slurs at the girl I want to marry! And what do I care about your name now? Even if your middle name was Hezekiah I could call you Meadow any time if I took the notion to, and who would stop me?"

"Please don't torture me," she said quietly. "There's no use. I won't let you make a mistake, especially in the aftermath of such grief."

"Will you not listen to reason? Girl, I'm not going anywhere until you realize I'm in earnest. What am I to do with the wild current of you running through my blood like lightning? What am I to do with every cell of my being thrilling to the sweetness of you? Oh no, I'm not leaving yet," he said with sneering lips.

"You act like that now, but you'll regret it someday. Don't make this more difficult than it already is."

Will stood and grabbed her by the shoulders, scowling, a flush of color in his face as he looked at her desperately in the eye. "Don't you know? Don't you know how I could scarcely help myself from loving you since the night under the glory shadows? Cristina could tell and she gave me a lot of trouble for it. Don't you know how I spied on you while you taught? How I listened with delight through cracks in the walls and the keyhole and wondered at how you did it? Don't you know how you fascinated me from the first moment in Anchorage? How I couldn't wait for you to show up in Kenai? How much I wanted to be your friend when you arrived? Didn't you feel my prayers for you? Don't you realize that everything within me was drawn to you all along, even though I knew you didn't have the magic name? Don't you know how I wanted to kiss you after you swore at the table? Or when you threw off your scarf after coming in from the cold? I wanted to kiss you when the wind played with your loose hair. I wanted to kiss you every time you wore the blue dress Aunt Kay made for you. Oh, you drove me mad and befuddled most days. Don't you know how jealous I was of Cristina getting to comfort you through the night? Or how my heart thrilled within me when you gave me a chance to serve you in some small way?"

Evangeline didn't know, but she wanted the hands that held her shoulders to stay holding longer. She wanted to throw herself into his arms, but she held back and stood firm with a wan smile.

"Don't you believe me now?" he asked.

"I…can't."

Will let go of her. A thought struck his heart and he said, "The problem is that you *can't* love me, can you? What you told Cristina was a lie. You only loved me because of her all along. And now that she's gone I'm useless. Oh, I understand now."

Evangeline was silent. He kept waiting for her to say something, to try to deny it—anything. But it didn't come. Who could have expected this? He was a sucker for having wasted so much time and money to come.

"I don't care if you don't believe me, but this belongs to you." He handed her Cristina's notebook. "Good bye, Evangeline."

She looked up at him with tears streaming down her face and said, "Good bye, Will."

Then he was gone.

Evangeline ran her fingers over the worn cover of the notebook. Then she opened it.

When Will reached the train station he could hardly think straight. He managed to find a ticket that would take him to Dallas, leaving in two hours. Nearly swearing under his breath, he took to pacing back and forth on the platform, wishing the clamor of the trains would drown out his thoughts. Soon his frustration died down and yielded to a deep sadness. In his heart he cried out into the noise of the machines, "Oh Lord, my God, help me."

After a while he sat down, feeling tired and worn in soul and body. It was all he could do to keep the icy hand of cynicism from closing entirely around his heart. He stared blankly for some time at the floor, much like he had after Cristina had disappeared. What had he done wrong?

The boarding of his train was called and he stood mechanically, ready to escape from this place that had opened old wounds. If he had only…

"Will!"

Only one word, but he knew that voice anywhere. It was just as Cristina had described once: mist and magic. He turned just in time to see Evangeline running toward him. Her face had changed and all the defiance had gone out of it. Now every hue and line held a tenderness and—was it true?—longing. Before he could blink twice she had rushed into his arms.

"Oh Will, please forgive me. Please don't go." There was the sound of tears in her voice and the sound of joy. And for the moments they held each other the world became innocent again.

"I read Cristina's journal," she said. "I read what she wrote about you—her advice. And I believe you now. I've been a little fool. Will you forgive me?"

"There's nothing to forgive. *I* was the fool. I waited too long. *I* broke your heart and made you leave Alaska by opening my big mouth."

"Nonsense, but don't let's quarrel again. I'm so glad you were still here when I came."

"So am I."

"Did you ever use my tears when Cristina disappeared? Did you get sick?"

"I'm afraid not. There was an old man who was a lot sicker and poorer than I was. So I let him drink them."

"You would," smiled Evangeline. But she was crying now. Will kissed a tear off her cheek and tasted it.

"It tastes like joy," he said.

"You're right." And she said it softly—oh, so softly.

There was nothing else around them now because they were looking into each other's faces.

"May I call you Meadow?" asked Will.

And her answer was quiet and near and eloquent—the kind of answer only a woman can make with her eyes and the curve of her lips. And when the two of them finally realized that they were still on earth, they walked down the platform and away from the station, hand in hand, lost in gratitude.

THE END

Maidenhood
by Henry W. Longfellow

Maiden! with the meek, brown eyes,
In whose orbs a shadow lies
Like the dusk in evening skies!

Thou whose locks outshine the sun,
Golden tresses, wreathed in one,
As the braided streamlets run!

Standing, with reluctant feet,
Where the brook and river meet,
Womanhood and childhood fleet!

Gazing, with a timid glance,
On the brooklet's swift advance,
On the river's broad expanse!

Deep and still, that gliding stream
Beautiful to thee must seem,
As the river of a dream.

Then why pause with indecision,
When bright angels in thy vision
Beckon thee to fields Elysian?

Seest thou shadows sailing by,
As the dove, with startled eye,
Sees the falcon's shadow fly?

Hearest thou voices on the shore,
That our ears perceive no more,
Deafened by the cataract's roar?

Oh, thou child of many prayers!
Life hath quicksands,—Life hath snares
Care and age come unawares!

Like the swell of some sweet tune,
Morning rises into noon,
May glides onward into June.

Childhood is the bough, where slumbered
Birds and blossoms many-numbered; —
Age, that bough with snows encumbered.

Gather, then, each flower that grows,
When the young heart overflows,
To embalm that tent of snows.

Bear a lily in thy hand;
Gates of brass cannot withstand
One touch of that magic wand.

Bear through sorrow, wrong, and ruth,
In thy heart the dew of youth,
On thy lips the smile of truth.

Oh, that dew, like balm, shall steal
Into wounds that cannot heal,
Even as sleep our eyes doth seal;

And that smile, like sunshine, dart
Into many a sunless heart,
For a smile of God thou art.

The treasures of the deep are not so precious,
As are the concealed comforts of a man
Locked up in woman's love. I scent the air
Of blessings when I come but near the house.
What a delicious breath marriage sends forth!
The violet bed's not sweeter. Honest wedlock
Is like a banqueting-house built in a garden,
On which the spring's chaste flowers take delight
To cast their modest odors; when base lust,
With all her powders, paintings, and best pride,
Is but a fair house built by a ditch-side.
                                    –Thomas Middleton

ABOUT THE AUTHOR

Andrew Case grew up on the mission field in Oaxaca, Mexico, and is a graduate of The Southern Baptist Theological Seminary and the Canada Institute of Linguistics. Currently he serves the ongoing Bible translation efforts in Equatorial Guinea, Africa as a member of Wycliffe/SIL. His joys include teaching, preaching, leading worship, dinosaurs, Hebrew, L.M. Montgomery, and song-writing. He is the author of several prayer books, which can be downloaded for free at www.HisMagnificence.com. The music he writes and records is also available there at no charge. To partner with him in Bible Translation through prayer or financially, please visit his website, click on "Bio", and follow the link on that page. You can follow him at www.facebook.com/andrewcasebooks.

ALSO AVAILABLE FROM ANDREW CASE:

Setting Their Hope in GOD: Biblical Intercession for Your Children

Prayers of an Excellent Wife

Water of the Word: Intercession for Her

Made in the USA
Charleston, SC
13 April 2015